D1642243

Napoleon is Dead in Russia

Napoleon is Dead in Russia

by

GUIDO ARTOM

Translated by Muriel Grindrod

London
GEORGE ALLEN AND UNWIN LTD
RUSKIN HOUSE · MUSEUM STREET

FIRST PUBLISHED IN 1970

SBN 04 808008 X

Translated from
NAPOLEONE E MORTO IN RUSSIA

PRINTED IN GREAT BRITAIN
in 11 on 13 Baskerville
BY CLARKE DOBLE AND BRENDON LIMITED
PLYMOUTH

To Tini

The facts, circumstances, and names of people and places in this book correspond to the truth in so far as it has been possible to establish it from documents, memoirs, records and historical works.

Contents

Chapter 1

Popincourt Barracks

Rain was falling on Paris as it lay asleep on that night of October 22-23, 1812. The rich slept in their family mansions, the poor in their garrets under the slate roofs; the ministers and dignitaries in their fine houses dreamt of fresh honours, with some peace at last to enjoy them; the prisoners in their gaols imagined in their sleep an unhoped-for freedom. No one slept at the Tuileries, in the imperial bed with the N and the golden bees on the canopy: the bed of the first Emperor of the French was empty, its owner the Emperor thousands of miles away in Russia waging war against the Tsar Alexander, once his friend. The Emperor Napoleon was far away under a tent or perhaps in a gilded chamber of the Kremlin, far from the palace of Saint Cloud where the Empress Regent slept beside her child, the heir to the throne who had borne the title of King from the moment of his birth.

Rain fell on Paris, and everyone slept, forgetful of all the political intrigues and ambitions, the anxieties about absurd far-off wars that no one wanted except that Emperor, unable to stay quiet and enjoy his conquests and let his associates enjoy them.

The streets were deserted under the persistent rain. There was no one about. Only the sentinels stood outside the barracks.

In the sentry-box at the gates of the Popincourt Barracks a soldier, Hippolyte Boudin, stamped his feet on the wooden floor to keep out the cold and damp. His companions used to tease him about those flat feet of his, calling him Polyte

Flatfoot, but it was because of his feet that he had managed to get put into the 10th Cohort of the National Guard, which consisted of men exempt from active service because they were unfit or specially favoured – instead of being pitchforked into a regiment of the line, in Russia or Spain.

In Russia it must be very different from the October chill and damp of Paris; the snow must already have begun. Not much news came from there, and it took three weeks to arrive. They had heard about the battle of Borodino, a great victory that opened the gates of Moscow, so the bulletin said, but people talked most about the dead, the greatest number of dead in all Napoleon's fifteen years of battles and victories.

If they went on conquering and dying like that, in that accursed Russia and in no less accursed Spain, would his feet suffice to keep him out of trouble, or would even the National Guard, in spite of solemn promises, be taken off garrison duties at home and sent off to fight far away, where men died like flies?

Such were the thoughts that Private Boudin chewed over in his mind between three and four in the morning on sentinel duty at the Popincourt Barracks, a few hundred yards from his house at the Barrière de Menilmontant; and such were the thoughts exchanged every day among the unfit, exempt, or specially favoured men who formed the 10th Cohort when they met to drink in Madame Michelet's canteen. They talked about revision inspections, requests for more men for the mobilized regiments, dangers ahead on every side.

What was wanted was peace, a good general peace, and that Napoleon and the rest should calm down and stop giving themselves indigestion with kingdoms and pricipalities, and the marshals stop gorging themselves with appanages and ducal crowns. A general peace, for the troops sent on leave to return home and start working again instead of dragging their feet across Europe and filling their mouths with foreign names, good only for embroidering on banners and providing a title for some Marshal of France, once sergeant in the Dragoons and now a duke or even a prince. Now the marshals had gorged themselves enough; they had crowns, castles, and enough golden napoleons to be able to forget their plebeian origins. Now it was time to think about the troops, and the only way to think about the troops was to say to them: 'Go home and start being civilians'.

It was just before the changing of the guard, at four in the morning, when a sound of rhythmical steps at the end of rue Popincourt startled Private Boudin and made him grasp his rifle. In the dark three people were advancing rapidly through the rain. They could not be night-birds or early workmen. It must be the usual patrol from Garrison Command that went out every three or four nights on the lookout for sleepy sentinels: so he had better look alive. Polyte came out of his sentry-box, unslung his rifle, and in a firm voice called on them to halt. The three men stopped, and the sentinel went on to the statutory 'Who goes there?'

One of the three answered at once: 'Headquarters patrol'.

Immediately afterwards he gave the password chosen for that night, a rather odd password for an authoritarian régime like Napoleon's: 'Conspiracy!'

The sentinel turned hurriedly to pull the cord of the bell that connected him with the guard post and shouted: 'Sergeant, come out and recognize!'

Inside they must all have been asleep, for minutes went by before someone peered out from the gate. Then a lantern appeared and the sergeant's voice was heard, grumpy at being wakened: 'What's happened? What do you want?'

The answer came from the one who seemed the most important of the three, the leader of the patrol, doubtless a general, with a plumed cocked hat on his head and a cloak down to his feet.

'Headquarters patrol! Hurry up, guard, open the door: there's no time to lose.'

The sergeant was now standing stiffly to attention with his hand at the salute, and a second later he hurried to open the gate and let the patrol into the entrance hall of the barracks.

'Where is the N.C.O. on duty? Where does the Commandant live?'

The General seemed to be a man who would stand no nonsense. The N.C.O. on duty hurried forward.

"Sergeant-Major Rabutel, N.C.O. on duty this week. At your service, sir.'

'Your chief is Commandant Soulier?'

'Yes, sir.'

'Take me to him at once.'

By now Polyte the sentinel had been relieved, but instead of going off to bed he had pushed forward to see what was going on: he didn't at all like this general turning up at the barracks in the middle of the night, it made him think of dangers that might threaten his own peace. It was better to know about trouble at once if one was to find a way round it. He therefore took a pace forward, seized the lantern from the hands of his companion holding it, and said: 'I know where the Commandant lives: it's just near by. I'll take you there, sir.'

Of course the N.C.O. on duty, Sergeant-Major Rabutel, knew this too, but he made no objection to Private Boudin's offer: Boudin was a clever chap, a Parisian who could cope with anything. They went off through the rain along the slippery cobblestones, Polyte in the lead with the lantern, then Sergeant-Major Rabutel, with the General beside him, frowning and taciturn, and his two companions, a young lieutenant and a civilian, both of them wrapped up to the eyes in their cloaks to keep off the rain.

The Commandant of the 10th Cohort did in fact live close by, and once under his windows Rabutel called out and managed to wake him and have the keys thrown down. A minute later the five men were mounting the dark steps leading to Commandant Soulier's house.

Soulier was in bed, but he had slept badly, troubled by the fever and pains in his bones that had dogged him for months. It was because of that fever and those pains that an old soldier like him, with twenty-five years of military service and fourteen years of campaigns under Napoleon, was not with the army fighting in Spain but had been sent to command this collection of pseudo-soldiers that formed the 10th Cohort of the National Guard in Paris. A seemingly peaceful post, but in reality one which, besides the humiliation of commanding a troop of weaklings and shirkers, exposed him to the vexation of a pedantic and extremely strict Garrison Command: circulars, inspections, daily and nightly patrols. For a man who had fought at Arcola, Marengo, Austerlitz, and Saragossa it was the worst that could happen. But perhaps it would have been even worse for him, at forty-five, with those fevers and pains he'd caught bivouacking in the open on the Spanish plateaux, to march with the Grande Armée through the snows of Russia in search of fresh glory and more rheumatism.

He sat on the edge of the bed which his wife had left hurriedly at the arrival of these unexpected visitors, and awaited the patrol that Sergeant Rabutel had announced at the top of his voice from the street.

In a minute all five were standing round his bed. Private Boudin held the lantern to light up their faces, and Commandant Soulier could discern a general of about fifty, with the gold on his uniform sparkling beneath his rain-soaked cloak, a young lieutenant standing beside the general like an aide-de-camp, and, a pace behind, a civilian dressed in a dark suit with a tricolour sash at his waist, like a magistrate or a police inspector.

The General was tall and thin, with grey side-whiskers emerging from beneath his hat and two piercing eyes, the eyes of a man accustomed to be obeyed and go straight ahead. He left neither Rabutel nor Soulier time to speak.

'Are you Commandant Soulier? I am General Lamotte.'

Soulier, leaning on the pillows, had hardly time to say 'At your service, General' when the latter went on to speak in a solemn voice, like someone in a hurry to execute a painful mission. 'Commandant, the Emperor died on October 7th beneath the walls of Moscow. I am the bearer of a despatch from the Senate addressed to you....'

'The Emperor . . . dead . . . but it's impossible. . . .' Commandant Soulier seemed ready to die himself at this incredible news. He went deathly pale and sweat covered his face and ran down on to the pillow. The Emperor cannot die. If he dies, it is the end of everything, of all of us.

But General Lamotte went on and plainly had no time to lose. 'Unhappily it is true. Thanks to special couriers the despatch was got to Paris in a fortnight. You will find all the details in these documents. You must now carry out at once the orders sent you by the Senate. Your cohort is charged to form the guard of the new Government. I would ask you, Commandant, to read the Senate's orders immediately.'

Polyte's face became suffused with joy: the Emperor was dead, no more war, everyone would go home: and he was the first to hear the news.

The aide-de-camp held out a packet of documents and opened it on the bed. Soulier tried to read those solemn papers with all their flowing initials and impressive stamps, but sweat and tears blurred his sight. Throughout his whole life, from recruit to commander of a cohort, Soulier had done nothing but obey: he had always found someone of higher rank to tell him what to do, and he had done it energetically and conscientiously. But now he could not read those papers as the General ordered him. He was ready to obey, but to read them was more than he could manage.

The General now became less stiff and prepared to

explain himself to the Commandant the orders he was to execute. Soulier was dripping with sweat and asked if he could change his shirt; perhaps that would help him to pull himself together in spite of his fever.

'Send for the Adjutant-Major,' suggested the General. 'You can hand over the command of the cohort to him so that he can prepare to carry out orders at once. You go, Sergeant-Major, but not a word to him or to anyone about what you've heard here.'

Rabutel hurried off, and the General, picking out a page from the sheaf of documents scattered on the bed, read out a decree appointing Soulier Brigadier-General. Soulier started: that this promotion, which had seemed like a remote and unattainable dream, should come about now in these extraordinary circumstances! Clearly, even though Napoleon was dead, they didn't forget tried old soldiers. Napoleon might be done for, but not so all the veterans – the country still had need of them. He forgot his fever and sweat: instead of a nightshirt he felt as if he was wearing his uniform on the parade-ground. The country still had need of him, old Soulier, and old Soulier, as always, was ready to obey and march: since he first put his uniform on he had never done anything else.

Just then General Lamotte showed him a 100,000 franc voucher issued by the Treasury for special extra pay for the officers and men of the cohort. Decidedly the Senate meant to console the army's grief for the death of the Emperor.

In less than a quarter of an hour Rabutel was back with Captain Piquerel, Adjutant-Major of the cohort. A glance sufficed to show that Commandant Soulier had chosen an adjutant-major after his own stamp: an old soldier like himself, like him accustomed to obey without bothering his head too much.

He clicked his heels before the General and stood stiffly to receive orders. Soulier gave him the orders himself: now that he was a general he felt energy and authority returning to him. He was a leader once again. The main order was to do everything commanded him by General Lamotte, envoy from the Senate bearing the news of Napoleon's death.

'The Emperor – dead – it's impossible. . . .'

Piquerel staggered. To him too it seemed impossible that the deity in whose name he had marched and fought for so many years should be dead. Piquerel too felt his senses reeling. Everything was finished if Napoleon was no more. But his arms were still held stiff along the seams of his trousers in the regulation posture, heels together. He summoned the strength to stammer, 'At your service, Commandant'.

As always, he was ready to obey. Never a glance at the documents scattered on the bed, the stamps, the flowing initials, the signatures. Documents were for superior officers, superior officers gave the orders, his job was to obey them.

General Lamotte gazed with satisfaction at this visible example of military discipline who in the country's grave hour restored confidence in France's future despite the disaster that had stricken her. But he did not seem surprised to find himself faced with such utter obedience. He too was a soldier like them, accustomed to regard the swift and precise execution of orders as an absolute rule. He glanced at his two companions, the young officer and the civilian, as if to say: 'See what stuff French soldiers are made of.'

Then he spoke again. 'Give yourself another hour's rest. I will leave you a company with which you will go to the Hôtel de Ville to prepare for the installation of the new Government there. You will make contact with the Prefect of the Seine. Our new Commander, General Malet, has already written to him about this. The details of the mission you are to carry out are all given in these orders—everything is arranged there. Your adjutant-major will follow me with the rest of the cohort whom he will assemble immediately. Till later then, General. In punctually carrying out the

Senate's orders you can be sure of serving the country usefully and meriting its gratitude.'

* * *

General Lamotte's visit to his new colleague Soulier had lasted about an hour, but Sergent-Major Rabutel had already been back in barracks about twenty minutes to awaken the troops and assemble them. The order was to make the least possible disturbance: therefore no reveille signals, instead the men were dragged out of bed one by one by the sergeants, while the orderlies ran off to waken the officers in their quarters. Thus there was no hubbub, but it took at least on hour to get the whole cohort up and dressed and on parade.

There had indeed already been some disturbance in the barracks two hours before when General Lamotte's patrol had arrived – enough to waken Widow Michelet, portress at the barracks and in charge of the canteen, who had not been able to get to sleep again. Better get up, she thought, and see what was going on.

Arriving in the courtyard, she found the troops under arms and the N.C.O.s busily getting them into their ranks. What could be happening? An N.C.O. came up to her and asked for the loan of a lamp, but he could tell her nothing. Madame Michelet hurried back to her quarters, picked up the lamp, and lit a new candle in it, but her curiosity only increased. Perhaps she might find someone in the canteen who could tell her what it was all about. Meanwhile she saw unknown people enter the barracks, a general accompanied by a young aide-de-camp and a civilian with a tricolour sash over his dark coat. Perhaps a police inspector. With them was Major Piquerel, who had the preoccupied look of someone in a hurry to carry out orders. Something important seemed to be afoot.

Madame Michelet had hardly entered the canteen, the

normal centre of all the barracks' news and gossip, when the General's young aide appeared. Evidently he was thirsty, and Madame Michelet was ready with a glass of the canteen's best brandy. He drank it straight off and readily accepted another. The officer was young, with a face that did not frighten Madame Michelet, indeed she seemed to have seen him before. She tried to get him to talk, but the attention of the young officer, a friendly fellow not above coming to drink in the troops' canteen, seemed to be drawn to the bust of the Emperor in the place of honour in the centre of the wall. His face darkened.

'That bust must go. Now that the Emperor's dead, there's no Imperial Government either, and no reason to have the bust there. The head of the Government now is General Moreau.'

So that was it. Madame Michelet took it in at once. The Emperor was dead. France was upside down. The whole business of changing governments would begin again like before the 18th Brumaire. For the moment, the thing was to answer the officer politely without comitting herself.

'Yes, sir, of course. I'll take it away. But first I've got to have my superiors' orders. I'm just like a soldier too, I have to obey, but if it's really true that he's dead, the Little Corporal, then. . . .'

'It's the absolute truth, in the face of a bullet all Frenchmen are equal. . . .'

'It was a bullet, then?'

'Actually it was a fragment of shot from a cannon. It went into his right eye and came out of his left ear. The Emperor had only time to cry out "Help", then he was dead. The Prince of Neuchâtel fainted from shock. And if you don't believe me, go and ask my General who got all the details by special courier. . . .'

Just at that moment a voice was heard, his General's voice calling him from the courtyard. 'Rateau!'

The officer turned with a satisfied air. Making no attempt

to pay, he put down the glass and went off into the courtyard where, thanks to the subdued efforts of the N.C.O.s, the cohort was already drawn up in two ranks. Facing the troops, beside Captain Piquerel who had presented the detachments to him, was General Lamotte who, despite the rain, had taken off his cloak and now appeared in all the splendour of his uniform. Near him was the civilian, he too without his cloak, but the tricolour sash, symbol of his civil authority, well in evidence.

The scene was illuminated by the lantern that Polyte Flatfoot had held on to for the past two hours and by Madame Michelet's borrowed lamp held high by a soldier. Madame Michelet herself had come out of the canteen hoping to hear what the General had to say. She slipped along the deserted corridors and came thus to a lavatory whose window opened on the courtyard just behind the General and his companions. From there she could hear every word.

As long as it was the General who spoke it was easy to understand, for he had the voice of one accustomed to command. He confined himself to a few words, spoken in a tone to rivet his hearers' attention: 'Soldiers! The magistrate with me will communicate the Senate's orders to you!'

There was a great silence. The civilian took a pace forward, stood under the lantern, and began to read a long document that he drew from his pocket. His first words were easy to understand: 'Senate meeting of October 22, 1812'; but after that less and less of his recital could be understood, and it lasted a good quarter of an hour. They all listened hard, Widow Michelet in the lavatory and the soldiers and officers in their ranks. Those furthest off in the rear, like Second-Lieutenant Gomont Saint-Charles, grasped no more than the first words, and the others had to have it all explained to them as best they could later on by their companions.

Nevertheless it was clear to all that the Senate had met under the chairmanship of Senator Sieyès in special session to be told of a message announcing the death of the Emperor on October 7th beneath the walls of Moscow. (At these words, received with a stifled gasp of astonishment, one officer left the ranks and made tottering for the lavatory. Madame Michelet saw him come in pale as death clutching his stomach. It was Second-Lieutenant Beaujean who felt his bowels revolt at such news, devoted as he was to the Emperor.)

The magistrate's voice went on quicker and less intelligible than ever to announce the Senate's decisions. They heard the words: 'The Imperial Government, having disappointed the hopes of those who believed it to be a source of peace and happiness for the French, is abolished. . . .'

Further on, they understood that the Legion of Honour was not abolished, but that pending reform, holders of it were asked to wear only the ribbon and not the cross.

Then came the appointment of a provisional government consisting of fifteen members. They heard the names of generals more or less known as enemies of Napoleon: Moreau, Prime Minister of the Provisional Government; Carnot, Deputy Prime Minister; Augereau. Names of senators such as Destutt-Tracy, Lambrecht, Volney, Garat. They heard the name of the Prefect of the Seine, Frochot, which everyone knew because he had been in office for ages. Names of aristocratic enemies of the imperial regime, like Mathieu de Montmorency and Alexis de Noailles. Names of left-wing opponents, former members of the Legislative Assembly: Bigonnet, Florent-Guyot, Jacquemont. There was an admiral, Truguet; and there was also a general whom none of those soldiers had ever heard of, a certain General Malet.

The next article seemed more interesting to those who were still managing to follow the recital: it announced the decision to start immediate peace negotiations with all the belligerent Powers and to withdraw from Spain, Italy, and Holland.

Next it was announced that His Holiness Pope Pius VII, then in exile at Fontainebleau, would be free to return to Rome, that the French people begged him to forget the ills he had suffered, and invited him to come to Paris before returning to Italy.

There followed resolutions governing the removal of ministers from office and the reorganisation of the Army and the National Guard, discharging all soldiers who requested it. There was also an amnesty for political crimes, and freedom for *émigrés* to return to France. Freedom of the press was announced. Then followed the appointment of that same General Malet, already appointed a member of the Provisional Government, to be Commander of the Paris garrison and of the first military division, with extensive powers both to punish rebels and reward the obedient. Four million francs from the amortisation fund were to be placed at his disposal to distribute among troops who distinguished themselves by their discipline and loyalty. The same General Malet was charged to proclaim the Senate's decisions in Paris and the departments, and make them known to all sections of the army.

The magistrate cleared his voice and intoned the signatures and final formulae which gave this communication all the charisma of officialdom :

. . . signed, Sieyès, *President*
Lanjuinais, Grégoire, *Secretaries*

Certified as being a copy of the Minute held by me.
Divisional General, Commander-in-Chief of the Armed Forces in Paris and the troops of the first military division.

True copy *MALET*

Minister of War
DUKE OF FELTRE

The troops were by now soaked through and would have liked to move about a bit to stretch their legs. Out of all that long recital they had grasped three things: that Napoleon was dead, that peace was at hand, and that they were soon going home. Consequently they were all ready to put up with the rain and the service orders they had got from that powerful and unknown General, provided they hastened the final conclusion: goodbye to the army, back to civilian life.

General Lamotte spoke again in his fine resonant voice: 'Commissioner, will you now please inform the troops of the proclamation of the General commanding the First Military Division.'

This time the Commissioner too strove to find the right tone of voice to read the words of the proclamation, much more high-sounding than the chilly accents of the Senate's resolutions.

'Citizens and soldiers, Bonaparte is no more. Tyranny has fallen under the blows of humanity's conquerors. Thanks be to them. They have deserved well of the Fatherland and of humankind. . . . If we must blush with shame at having for so longe borne as our leader a foreigner, a Corsican, we are too proud to accept a bastard child. . . . It is therefore our most sacred duty to support the Senate in its generous decision to free us from all tyrannies. . . .'

The proclamation went on for some time in this style which the older men present knew well, for it had been the fashion when they were young, before the days when Napoleon Bonaparte became First Consul and then abandoned Bonaparte to become just Napoleon. Faithful to that style, it spoke of liberty, equality among citizens, public regeneration, and the infamies committed by the tyrant. It concluded: 'Seize this glorious opportunity to show yourselves worthy of the name of Frenchmen. Let us die, if need be, for the Fatherland and for freedom; and let us always unite together at the cry of "*Vive la nation*".'

The signature was the same, 'Malet', followed by the words 'True copy: *Minister of War,* Duke of Feltre'.

The officers and soldiers had hardly had time to recover from the feeling of boredom induced by the reading of the proclamation, pronounced with all the emphasis of which he was capable by the 'commissioner', as they now styled him to themselves, before General Lamotte started speaking again. And it was like the roll of drums.

'Soldiers! The Emperor has died beneath the walls of Moscow. Measures have been taken to save the relics of the Grande Armée. The Government, provisionally installed by decree of the Senate, has appointed General Malet as Commander of the First Military Division. General peace is proclaimed. Conscription is abolished. The Legion of Honour is retained and its grant doubled. Within a week the soldiers of the Paris garrison who wish to return home will receive their travel permits; the others will form the Corps of Guards of the Government, with the same benefits and prerogatives as the former Imperial Guard. Extra pay of one franc and ten centimes a day for the troops, three francs for N.C.O.s, double pay for officers. Every captain with fifteen years' service is by right promoted to battalion commander. Within twenty-four hours, a month's pay will be distributed to soldiers of all ranks as a gratuity. Long live the Provisional Government! Long live the Nation!'

After a speech like that they all felt moved and ready to march, especially the old captains, like Piquerel, who found themselves suddenly promoted after years of waiting. The officers checked the ranks. The soldiers tightened the straps of their cartridge pouches so that they wouldn't swing when they marched. The pouches were in fact empty, for no munitions had been distributed, though there were ten thousand cartridges in the barracks armoury. In the guns there was the usual imitation flint, made of wood, that they used in practices on the parade-ground.

Meanwhile the General had asked Captain Piquerel to

put two men at the disposal of his aide, Rateau, who was to go and fetch other documents. Rateau therefore went off, followed by two soldiers from the 6th Company, Pillau and Gillet, with orders to rejoin his chief at the point to which he was preparing to go, at the head of the first five companies of the 10th Cohort, in other words at La Force prison. The 6th Company, Captain Verdet's, was to await Commandant, or rather General, Soulier, and then go under his orders to Place de Grève, to the Hôtel de Ville.

It was already six o'clock when General Lamotte, followed by the five companies – with Captain Picquerel in the lead and of course Private Boudin, who felt himself indispensible with his lantern since it was barely daylight and you could hardly see in the narrow rain-lashed streets—left the Popincourt Barracks and made for La Force prison.

Just at first many of the soldiers found themselves thinking how strange it was to be marching like this in serried ranks with their rifles and their cartridge-pouches and to know that Napoleon was no more. Then they reflected that really nothing had changed and everything was going on just the same; they stopped thinking about the dead Napoleon and bothered only about keeping in step and giving a martial appearance to this early-morning march through the streets of Paris – perhaps their last march before becoming civilians again.

Chapter 2

La Force Prison

From Popincourt Barracks to La Force Prison was something over a mile, well under half an hour at a good rhythmic pace through the streets and the rough cobbled alleyways. The streets all had saints' names: rue Saint-Sébastien, rue Saint-Claude, rue Saint-Louis, and lastly rue Saint Antoine which led to the rue Roi de Sicile where rose the old walls, low, blackened, and sordid, of what was known as the Grande-Force, the men's prison, to distinguish it from the Petite-Force, the prison for women. The name had stuck to the building ever since, seventy years before, the Duke de la Force had sold it to the State, which had made it into a prison.

A sinister reputation still clung to the old building from the September massacres under the Terror, and by night people tried to avoid passing beneath its walls and by day edged away from the kerb at the corner of rue des Balets, just in front of the entrance, where the Princess de Lamballe had been slaughtered: it seemed still to be dripping blood, and women crossed themselves and murmured a 'requiem' as if in a cemetery.

At the crossing between rue Saint-Antoine and rue Roi de Sicile, the General gave the sign to halt and ordered Captain Steenhower, in command of the 1st Company, to go ahead with his detachment alone. In the meantime the General's aide, the young officer Rateau, had arrived with the two men sent to fetch the other documents. They had two bags of them under their arms, while a soldier held in his hand a big package, roughly tied up: through a split in the wrapping could be seen the glitter of epaulets and stripes and the plumes of a cocked hat.

The General extracted some papers from it, looked them over, divided them under two covers, and then called Polyte, who was standing near by with his lantern, and another soldier, Maillard by name, and handed one packet to each of them with the order to take them to the respective commands of the two battalions of the Paris Guard, at the Minimes and the Courtille barracks. 'Give them to the officer in charge for the week with orders to carry out at once the instructions given in those papers. The commander of the regiment is out of Paris today, so the battalion commanders will have to see to it. Hurry, be off with you.'

Polyte made off as fast as he could with his flat feet that would soon cease to be needed as an excuse to keep him far from the dangers of war. The other soldier was even quicker.

With the rest of his party and the men of the 1st Company, General Lamotte went on along the rue Roi de Sicile and stopped before the closed gates of the prison. At a sign from him the official (whom the General sometimes addressed as 'Mr Commissioner', sometimes more familiarly as 'Boutreux') knocked loudly on the door. For a while no one answered. Then one leaf of the doors opened halfway and a warder's head peered crossly out. A couple of warders slept each night in the entrance hall of the prison and one of them had moved his bed up against the door, so that he hadn't even got up to answer the call.

It seemed to him at first that it must be the change of guard arrived a little earlier than usual. There was a guard post in the prison, and there should have been a sentry at the entrance, but at that hour everyone was fast asleep. The warder realized when he looked more closely, however, that this was something unusual: a civilian urgently calling 'Open!' and adding, queerly enough at the gates of a prison, 'in the name of the law.'

The warder, who figured on the personnel roll as 'under-gaoler Gaullier' (whether written Gaullier or Gaullié he didn't know himself, for he was illiterate), called his colleague, under-gaoler Petit, who got himself out of bed and together they opened the doors.

The first to enter was the General's aide who ordered one of the gaolers to call the prison head warder at once. The gaoler, thankful to be rid of the responsibility, didn't wait to be told twice but made off at a run.

Meanwhile, the General had brought a score of soldiers into the first courtyard of the prison, and himself stayed in the vestibule with the Police Commissioner and the officers of the company, Captain Steenhower and his subalterns, Prévost and Gomont Saint-Charles.

The head warder was called Bault, and he was an old official who would have merited the title of governor, but at that time prison governors still went by that humble title, indeed in official documents they were simply called *concierge*.

But whether concierge or governor, Bault knew his job, and in his many years of experience – and what years, too – he had seen all kinds of people, high-ups or simple criminals, pass through the prison gates. His memory was a filing-cabinet of faces, each one with a card beneath it on which the name was clearly written.

At the first glance he seemed to recognize the General and he went up to him in surprise:

'You here, General? But what....'

'Be quiet and listen to the orders I bring you. The Senate has charged me with a delicate mission.'

'But you, General, weren't you....'

'Be quiet, I tell you, and answer me. Are Generals Lahorie and Guidal still in your prison?'

'Yes, but....'

'That's enough. Mr Commissioner of Police, will you read....'

The Commissioner must by now have known the Senate's decisions practically by heart and proceeded to read the document without faltering. The vault of the entrance hall made the voice of the young man with the tricolour sash reverberate. It was daylight by now and even without Polyte and his lantern he could see to read quite clearly.

The head warder seemed to reel at every word of that reading. At the news of Napoleon's death he gave a grunt which for him might have been a sigh. The General left him no time to comment or ask questions. He took a paper from one of the bags of documents.

'And now, this is an order that directly concerns you.' He handed him the paper and Bault began to read with mounting attention:

> The concierge of La Force prison will at once set at liberty MM. Generals Lahorie and Guidal, together with the officers they will name, and with them M. Boccheciampe.
>
> The present order, given in virtue of Article 13 of the Senate's decisions of yesterday's date, shall be carried out in the presence of the Armed Forces and the concierge shall be responsible on pain of death for any delay, and the others warders with him.
>
> General in command of the Armed Forces and the troops of the First Military Division
>
> signed: MALET
>
> General Headquarters, Place Vendôme,
> October 23rd, 1812
> 3 a.m.

Bault read and re-read the paper twice over, bringing it close up to his nose as if to smell whether it had the odour of officialdom to which he was accustomed. The stamp was there, it all seemed quite regular. But it was the first time that he had received an order for release signed by a military commander. He made the objection that the order lacked the signature of the Minister of Police, or, at least an order from the Prefect of Police, especially seeing that the prisoners mentioned were detained by disposition of His Excellency the Minister of Police himself. If they would give him half an hour, he would get the Minister's signature himself and everything would be in order.

'So you refuse?' interrupted the General, his brow darkening.

'I do not refuse. But I repeat that I need only half an hour, which will in any case be necessary for the formalities of release, to send a man to the Duke of Rovigo for his signature.'

'The Duke of Rovigo is no longer Minister of Police. There is a general amnesty for all soldiers and political prisoners. Hurry up, and remember that you answer with your head for the execution of the Senate's orders.'

And when Bault still seemed to hesitate, the General turned to the soldiers around him and said in his biting voice:

'Soldiers! Get ready, you are armed, take action! If this man and his companions resist, they put themselves outside the law!'

Bault threw up his hands, gave a glance at his two assistant-gaolers as if to call them to witness his attempt to respect the rules, and taking the bunch of keys from one of them made off for the cells.

* * *

In sleep General Victor Fanneau de Lahorie managed every night to find complete abandonment, the nullification of every trace of his adventurous existence. Floating in his memory were only pleasant, almost happy, recollections which towards dawn invariably coalesced into a delightful dream that filled him with tenderness even in the unconsciousness of sleep. He was at the bottom of a big garden, almost a park. He well remembered the address: 12, passage des Feuillantines. And he remembered the smiling face of the lady beside him with her three children. 'Come and greet your relative.' The relative was he, and he had awakened, as he had done each morning for several months, in the old chapel at the bottom of the garden that the beautiful lady had given him as a refuge from Fouché's police. Often she would come herself to wake him, and then he blessed his persecuted existence which allowed him at last to live beside the woman he had loved for so many years, free now from every scruple in relation to her husband, his old friend and colleague, like himself a General, General Hugo, who had gone to the wars in Spain in the train of King Joseph. How long had their love lasted – nine years, or was it ten? He had been born in garrison surroundings, among uniforms and career gossip, and he had ended in a blaze in Paris in an ardent and secret atmosphere of military conspiracy: the Jacobin General Moreau had striven to oppose the lightning rise of the young Bonaparte at the cost of allying himself with the monarchists, and his chief of staff, the brilliant Lahorie, with his aristocratic ways, had been pushed into conspiracy, rather than held back, by his love for the impetuous Sophie Hugo, a woman who had in her veins the blood of fighters from the Vendée and a taste for dangerous action. She had come to him leaving her three children in her husband's care, and they had known brief days of happiness in the Castle of Saint-Just; then Sophie had had to rejoin her husband in Corsica.

On his return to Paris Lahorie was a proscribed man with the police after him: at each of their meetings the delight of their new-found love was made more acute and disturbing by the ever-present risks. They had little to fear from discovery by a husband occupied in far-away military campaigns, but a spy might always be put on their tracks by some indiscreet person.

Later, however, Sophie had had to leave her adored lover, the 'man with the diamond eyes', to his clandestine life and rejoin her husband in Italy. Colonel Hugo had covered himself with glory, capturing the bandit Michele Pezza, the legendary Fra Diavolo, and as a reward had been appointed Governor of Avellino. A governor must have a wife beside him to do the honours of his house, and Sophie had decided to go.

In the mists of his dreams, the years and memories, the secret meetings and the miseries of his life as an exile in his own country, mingled together. But always there came back to him like a shining light the figure in the garden, the long months of secret life in that refuge which, in the heart of Paris, seemed to be in another world.

Beside the face of the lady there were always too the faces of the three boys, especially the youngest, Victor, who was seven years old. He called him 'relative', that little boy, and he did not know that the guest who lived in the chapel at the bottom of the garden and ate at their table was his godfather and had given him his name, indeed, according to certain ill-natured gossip in military circles when he was born, was something more than godfather.

Little Victor Hugo, who had taught himself to read and had translated Virgil, would lead his great friend, his 'relative', by the hand to discover the mysteries of the garden: the dried-up well at the bottom of which lurked an imaginary monster, black and hairy, 'the Deaf One', or the thicket of trees that reminded him of the Black Forest as he'd seen it in a picture over his bed. Sometimes he would even recite to him in a shy voice the poems that he tried to write in his exercise books. Lahorie, who was steeped in the classics, brought back their conversations from such fantasies to more serious matters, to the truths that he would have wished to teach his own children had he had any: 'Remember, my boy, that liberty is the highest good'. He taught him to hate tyrants, to help those who suffer for love of justice.

Lahorie's dream was full of these conversations and the games with Victor and his little brothers, interminable games that had lasted a year and a half, the whole period of his life in that refuge. Then a hope had appeared, the hope that Napoleon might forget the part he had played so many years ago in Moreau's conspiracy. That hope was Savary, his old comrade-in-arms, who had become Duke of Rovigo and Minister of Police in place of the hated Fouché.

This was the point at which his happy nightly dream darkened and turned into a nightmare. The picture of Madame Hugo and little Victor was blotted out by that of Savary in his minister's office, a Savary who had received the wanted man with smiles, overwhelming him with promises – and then the agonising blow when police spies sent by that same Savary arrived to arrest him in his retreat, the Hugo family's tears, the fortress of Vincennes, the cell in La Force.

It was at this point that he usually woke, and on waking he eventually calmed down because he remembered that Savary was really at bottom a good fellow, for he had let himself be softened by an intervention from Sophie Hugo and had signed a decree exiling him to the United States, as Napoleon, when he was still First Consul, had done years before, with General Moreau. He was due to leave in a few days. Before leaving, would he be able to see his saviour, the woman who loved him enough to compromise herself, wife of a general, under the eyes of another general who was Minister of Police to boot?

* * *

He was wide awake by now, thinking about when the necessary documents for his departure would arrive, when the cell door opened and the head warder in person appeared, looking very agitated but with a smile on his lips.

'I congratulate you, General – you are free.'

'Have the documents for my departure arrived at last?'

'No, no. You are free. The Emperor is dead and political prisoners are to be set at liberty. People are waiting for you in the entrance hall. Hurry up.'

Bault went off to give the same news to the other captive general.

* * *

General Guidal was not the sort of man to indulge in romantic dreams, and perhaps he did not even have the kind of memories that would nourish them. In his memory there was only turbulence, intrigues, punishments, and further intrigues to avoid them. Sometimes there rose up in his mind the face of Barras, so sensible of the charms of Marie Guidal that he had been induced not only to reinstate her undisciplined and complacent husband in the army but even to promote him to be a general. And he also saw again the face of the royalist leader Frotté who had trusted him and whom he had captured by means of a trap on the orders of the First Consul.

The nightmare that often assailed him and made him wake in a cold sweat came from the thought of the council of war at Aix, where they were to bring him any day now. Before a tribunal like that, with witnesses and close questioning, the vague accusations of 'suspect manoeuvres' on which he had been arrested at Marseilles and conveyed to La Force would become definite, and it would emerge clearly that he, General Maximilien-Joseph Guidal, was none other than a traitor and a spy in the pay of the English, to whom for years he had been supplying information and had promised to convey military secrets which would enable them to capture the port of Toulon.

Every morning he woke in fear of hearing that he was

to leave for Aix, for the journey that would end before a firing squad.

The door opened. The day had come.

'General,' said Bault on the threshold, 'you are free! The Emperor is dead and there are no more prisoners.'

Was he still dreaming, or did miracles happen even for people like him? Like an automaton Guidal got up and began to dress.

* * *

The other prisoner whose liberation had been ordained by the Senate, the Corsican Boccheciampe, had by now been accustomed to prisons for so many years that he had transformed resignation into a punctilious method that made him less aware of the emptiness of those interminable days.

He had first encountered political troubles as a young man in Corsica in the days of Paoli, whom he had opposed. Exiled to Tuscany, he had gone on conspiring. Suspect both to the Corsicans and the French, he had ended up in prison in Florence nine years before, in 1803, at the request of the French Ambassador who had accused him of espionage. No tribunal had ever managed to condemn him, but as soon as he was set free the police resumed their watch on him, and police surveillance always ends by putting a man in prison. So, dogged by surveillance and suspicions, the Emperor's unfortunate compatriot, after filling the registers of the Napoleonic police of Italy and France with his name, had been sent to Paris and shut up in La Force, at the disposal of Monsignor the Duke of Rovigo, Minister of Police.

The papers that Boccheciampe had been allowed to take to prison with him were not political but literary: they were part of a work to which the prisoner methodically devoted his day and which allowed him to forget the miseries of his cell. It was a very serious and laborious work, as could be seen from the title, and it is still preserved in the National Archives in Paris under the number F7–6500: *Synonyms used by the Italian Poets to express the names of the Gods and Goddesses of Heaven, Earth, and the Lower Region, in alphabetical order.*

Every morning, at dawn, as soon as it was light enough, Boccheciampe got up, opened his folder of papers and set to work. The fetid walls of his cell vanished and around him as he bent covering the paper with his penny pen there crowded all the gods from Olympus and Hades. The sky that showed through the iron bars was not the murky sky of Paris but blue and luminous like the skies of Greece and Corsica.

Immersed as he was in the world of myths, the perpetual prisoner accepted quite naturally the miraculous announcement brought him by the head warder and rose almost unwillingly from his work to follow him.

* * *

In the entrance hall, General Lamotte impatiently awaited the return of the head warder with the three prisoners. The officers and soldiers who had come into the prison with him seemed to share his impatience and his desire not to delay the execution of the Senate's orders.

Outside, the waiting troops between the rue Saint-Antoine and the rue Roi de Sicile had broken their ranks, and some of them had begun to gossip with the passers-by attracted to the entrance of the prison by all this military to-do at that early hour.

The soldiers gave themselves the air of important people: they knew it, the incredible news that till then was known only to the most important personages, and by hints they were revealing it to the sleepy citizens. Napoleon dead in Russia. General peace. Not one of them uttered a word of grief for the Little Corporal whom they had so often acclaimed through the streets of Paris: the idea of peace made everyone happy and they hastened home to bring the good news.

At last Bault reappeared, preceding the two liberated generals, Lahorie short, slender, and elegant beside the tall massive figure of Guidal with his unshaven cheeks and dishevelled hair.

General Lamotte hurried to meet Lahorie and embraced him.

'It's eighteen years since we've seen each other, my friend!'

'This is certainly a surprise', stammered Lahorie, staring at his colleague in full uniform at the head of a detachment.

Guidal had remained a couple of paces behind, cold and somewhat suspicious. He exchanged a brief handshake with Lamotte, introducing himself, and Lamotte then drew the two Generals into a corner and swiftly told them what had happened, about the mission with which he was charged, and the tasks he was going to entrust to them, in obedience to the Senate's orders.

He took some other documents from the bag, looked them over, and handed them to the two Generals.

'I am leaving you four companies. First of all you must go at top speed to the Prefecture of Police and then to the Ministry of General Police. You will carry out precisely the instructions contained in these pages. The Commissioner here will accompany you and replace the Prefect of Police in his duties. As for the Ministry of General Police, when the operation is completed it will be entrusted to General Lahorie. General Guidal, after leaving the necessary troops to guard the Prefecture and the Ministry of Police, will go with the rest of the soldiers to the War Ministry to carry out the particular instructions I have given him, which involve the replacement of the present Minister Clarke, the Duke of Feltre, by General Guidal himself. Other instructions concern the next operation to be carried out in relation to the Arch-Chancellor, Cambacérès. Remember that the Senate's orders must be executed without delay. You are to fire on anyone who attempts to resist. Whoever fails to obey the Senate's orders is outside the law. Do you understand? It's all clear: the 2nd, 3rd, 4th and 5th Companies are under your orders. The 1st Company will march with me to the military command in Place Vendôme. One more thing: are there any other anti-Bonapartist soldiers detained in this prison?'

There were two, Lahorie said, and Bault confirmed it with a nod: Colonels Madier de Lamartine and Faujas de Saint-Fond, suspected of having taken part in a plot.

'Set them free,' said Lamotte to Bault, 'and order them to present themselves to me at the Command in Place Vendôme.'

Up to that moment Boccheciampe had stayed in the shadow of the entrance-hall with his folder of papers under his arm, intimidated by all these military men and still uncertain of his own fate.

'And you, who are you?' asked Lamotte, suddenly noticing him.

'I? I am Boccheciampe . . .' replied the latter with his Corsican accent.

'I congratulate you. The Senate has appointed you Prefect of the Seine. Present yourself at the Hôtel de Ville to take over your post.'

Boccheciampe made no reply. He passed a hand over his eyes. The only thing he had really understood was that he was actually free and in a few minutes would be outside the gates of La Force.

The General gave a sign to his two colleagues and all together, followed by the other soldiers, they moved off towards the detachments waiting at the bottom of the street.

Lahorie did not like his colleague Guidal, but he had no one else to whom to confide his impressions of the moment.

'All this story began with the 18th Brumaire and it seems to me to be finishing with another 18th Brumaire in reverse.'

This said, it seemed to him quite natural that he, who up to a few minutes ago had been a prisoner in La Force, should be marching to the Prefecture and the Ministry of Police with a Senate decree in his pocket ordering him to arrest the heads and instal himself in their place.

Chapter 3

Rue de Jérusalem

The soldiers of the 10th Cohort, delighted at the hit they had made with the citizens of rue Saint-Antoine by their stunning revelation of the Emperor's death, were longing to spread the news in other parts of the city. So they were impatient to get on, and as soon as they saw the General at the head of the 1st company emerging from the rue Roi de Sicile they quickly re-formed ranks.

Before giving them the word to go, General Lamotte took out his watch and said to Lahorie, who was beside him, 'Half-past six. We're late.' There was a faint note of anxiety in his voice as he ordered: 'Forward, march!'

The troops moved off and Lamotte, who had the two liberated generals and Boccheciampe at his side, rapidly informed them of the situation and gave them the written orders:

> As soon as he is freed, General Lahorie is to go to the Ministry of Police and arrest the Minister.
>
> Before this, arrange to leave a detachment at the Prefecture of Police and arrest the Prefect.
>
> Arrest Desmarest, head of the security division.
>
> Send Guidal to arrest Arch-Chancellor Cambacérès and the War Minister, Clarke.
>
> Arrest Councillor Réal, 1 rue de Lille.
>
> Arrest Councillor Pelet de la Lozère, 17 rue de l'Université.
>
> On completion of the mission rejoin me at headquarters, Place Vendôme.
>
> signed: MALET

'Is that all clear? I will go with the first company to the headquarters of Garrison Command in Place Vendôme. You, Lahorie, will take command of the other companies and proceed according to the orders. Don't forget to guard the Palais de Justice too. You, Guidal, with the detachment assigned to you will carry out quickly and precisely the tasks entrusted to you. You will then be given further instructions.'

They had reached the Saint-Jean market-place and the General called a halt. It was time to separate so that each general could carry out the missions assigned to him by the new military commander of Paris.

Lamotte, with the 1st Company under Captain Steenhower, set off along the rue Saint-Honoré towards Place Vendôme. The other four companies, under Adjutant-Major Piquerel, with the three men liberated from La Force and the Police Commissioner, turned towards the Seine to cross the Pont-au-Change and reach the Ile de la Cité where lay the Prefecture of Police, near the Palais de Justice.

There were people in the streets by now, for it was nearly seven o'clock, but the passage of the troops did not seem to make much impression on them. It was Friday, and every Friday morning a review of the Paris garrison was held in Place Vendôme. So it seemed just like any other Friday, and no one dreamt of the tremendous news that each one of those soldiers was longing to shout out at the top of his voice but for the presence of the officers.

Once arrived at the Cité, Lahorie divided his forces: Guidal with Piquerel and most of the troops went off to take possession of the Palais de Justice, while a half-company under Second-Lieutenant Lefèvre followed him to the Prefecture of Police.

At Quai des Orfèvres, the police were already stationed along the Seine, but the entrance to this gloomy building, where during the Terror the dreaded Watch Committee had resided, gave on to a street running parallel, the rue de Jérusalem, which ended in another side-street, the rue de Nazareth – names rather too biblical for the address of that building of sinister repute.

On guard at the Prefecture was a detachment of the first reserve company of the Seine department.

The sentinel saw the detachment approaching and gave the alarm: 'Sergeant, come and recognize....'

For Sergeant Roycourt, who commanded the guard post, it was a severe shock to learn of the Emperor's death, but he too could only click his heels before Second-Lieutenant Lefèvre and allow the Commissioner to enter together with the civilian in the cloak with a big hat on his head (they all called him 'General') and some thirty soldiers. The sergeant accompanied them up the stairs that led to the private apartment of the Prefect of Police. Second-Lieutenant Lefèvre disposed some of his men along the staircase and took the rest with him.

Baron Etienne Pasquier, a baron of the old nobility whose rank had been further confirmed by the Emperor, was accustomed to begin early his busy day as Prefect of Police. He had not desired this post, although he was ambitious, and it had come as a surprise to him two years before, after the great crisis of Fouché's removal and the appointment of the Duke of Rovigo as Police Minister. But it was obvious that Prefect Dubois, though he had disagreed with Fouché, could not stay on there, especially as he was said to have feathered his nest unscrupulously. Councillor of State Pasquier had had ambitions towards the higher spheres of politics rather than of the police, and was not at ease in command of that mob of policemen, all of them Fouché's men, beginning with the Security Chief, Desmarest, who by dint of hunting criminals had come to assume their mentality and, worse still, their manners and speech.

He had two consolations, however. First, he could send a report direct to the Emperor every day; and secondly he had all the police archives at his disposal. These provided an inexhaustible mine of information for one who loved politics and regarded it as a gallery of human portraits composed of people known normally only by sight, but about whom the archives could reveal what lay behind each one, what he had done on such-and-such an occasion, his weaknesses, his hidden faults, his compromises, sometimes even his secret crimes. All this was valuable information for the future, and first-class raw material for a politician in those times.

Early every morning, still in his dressing-gown, before beginning his careful toilet, he would sit at his desk with a big folder before him, searching out and writing down in a notebook more facts than a priest would ever discover in the confessional about the life of every important man, whether minister, financier, general or courtier. This was the hour of his own personal enjoyment, before encountering the vulgarity of his colleagues and embarking on the banalities of administrative duties.

That day his enjoyment was short-lived. Suddenly, without even a knock the corridor door opened and armed soldiers burst in, with two civilians among them, one in a cloak with a big hat on his head, the other a young man with a tricolour sash at his waist. Loud wails reached him from his servant in the corridor, complaining that the soldiers had struck him in the leg with their bayonets, but from his tone of voice it sounded as if it was just pinpricks rather than a serious wound.

The Prefect rose hurriedly and took a step towards the exit on to the garden staircase, but at a sign from their officer in command the soldiers pointed their bayonets at him. He sank back into his chair drawing his dressing-gown round him.

The cloaked civilian then addressed him. Though he did not introduce himself, and kept on the hat that half-hid his face, he had the manner and speech of a gentleman. 'As you may perhaps have heard, the Emperor has been killed at Moscow. I am charged with a mission, in accordance with a decree of the Senate which has abolished the Empire and ordered the dismissal of its ministers and high officials. My mission, sir, is to declare you under arrest. Here is the document.'

He waved on high a paper that Baron Pasquier, crouched in his chair, made no attempt to grasp. 'This gentleman is charged to replace you as Prefect of Police.' And he indicated the slim young man with the tricolour sash, introducing him by a name which Pasquier understood only as beginning with B.

The cloaked civilian bent over the desk, took up a pen, and quickly scribbled a note. 'This is the order for your arrest. Lieutenant Lefèvre, take the gentleman to La Force as soon as he is dressed.'

Pasquier began to pull himself together. 'A decree of the Senate? But when did the Senate meet? I should have known about it. Only yesterday the Duke of Rovingo told me that the Emperor. . . .'

The other gave him no chance to finish.

'You'll be seeing the Duke of Rovigo sooner than you think, and he'll tell you the same. . . . Hurry up and get dressed, sir, and don't try to be clever. Lieutenant, keep your eyes on him while he dresses. Tell the guard post to let no one enter without a pass like this.' He held out a card.

Baron Pasquier had seen too much in his life to attempt any rash resistance. He rose and walked to his dressing-room, followed by Lefèvre and two soldiers.

Before leaving Lahorie again told the lieutenant: 'Lefèvre, see that he hurries up and take him at once to La Force.'

It was not the first time that Pasquier had found himself in such a situation. Under the Terror he had twice been arrested: the first time he had been in prison for a day and had got off through a cleverly-secured, kindly witness to his character, whereas his father, like him a magistrate but less fortunate or perhaps less astute, finished on the guillotine. The second time he himself had escaped the guillotine by a hair's-breadth. Arrested and brought to Saint-Lazare on the 8th Thermidor, he was to be executed the day after. But the day after was that 9th Thermidor on which Robespierre fell and the Terror ended, and so Pasquier got off free.

For the moment there was nothing to be done but to get dressed and not lose his head. As he began to put on his underclothes and hose without the habitual aid of his valet, he narrowly eyed the two soldiers watching him and the lieutenant fidgeting at the door. They were all young and had seen nothing of all that he had known in his forty-five years – this was certainly their first big 'day'. He had been at the taking of the Bastille, he remembered it well, arm-in-arm with a young actress, and he also remembered that there had been no question of a great battle, because the old soldiers defending the fortress merely wanted to surrender. He had been present at the execution of Louis XVI, pushed by the crowd to within a pace of the scaffold, a revolting scene of blood and rolling drums, and then he had seen the deputies escape through the windows, pursued by the grenadiers, on the 18th Brumaire. Now another 'day' had come to be added to his future memoirs: his belief in the fate that protects clever men who know their way about the world was so strong that his first terror had almost subsided and he was already beginning to think how to get out of it.

It was best to be quick, and for that day he renounced his usual careful shave and combing of his hair, which he wore in well-brushed waves at the forehead and temples, and the short dark whiskers that adorned the sides of his fat cheeks. He twisted the white tie round the collar from which his sharp chin stood out. Over his morning coat he put on a heavy cloak: colds are sometimes more dangerous than revolutionaries.

Now he was ready, and Lefèvre took him back into the study. 'Wait here. I will call a carriage.' He left the two soldiers at the door and went out.

At the desk, sitting rather shyly in his chair, was the young man who had been pointed out as his successor. Before him were the documents that the cloaked personage of a few minutes before had waved before his eyes without showing them to him.

Pasquier saw at a glance that the individual before him was not too dangerous. Perhaps it was just a question of handling him the right way, and knowing how to handle men was an art in which Pasquire excelled.

'So, here you are in your new job. You're very young for a Prefect of Police. You'll find it's not all a bed of roses. . . . Allow me, as an older colleague, to give you my best wishes. Where do you come from? What were you doing before? May I ask your name?'

'My name is Balancié and I come from Angers,' answered the young man rather hesitantly and pointing to the tricolour sash. 'I'm a police official, of course, sir.'

'I see, I see. You've certainly got on quickly. And you owe it to the Senate decree before you—that's why you're still reading it. . . .'

Moving quickly round the desk, Pasquier stood behind the commissioner and cast an eye over the papers in front of him: a glance was enough for an old hand in bureaucratic matters like himself to see that those documents, regular enough to all appearances, had something odd about them. The stamp, that was it, the inked stamp bearing, for some reason, a handwritten letter 'L' instead of the usual eagle.

'But these documents aren't regular. There's no stamp with the eagle. This is just an imaginary stamp!'

'You're forgetting, sir, there is no Empire now. No empire, so no eagle. They used another stamp in the Senate. As to the authenticity of the documents, there's no doubt about that. They were handed to me by the Garrison Commander himself, General Malet!'

'General Malet! But my good man . . . General Malet is an agitator, a dangerous subversive! I haven't heard anything about him lately, but I believe he must be in. . . . Anyway, the whole business is far from clear. Mind what you're doing. You might be risking your head!'

The young man, Boutreux or Balancié or whatever his name, had risen to his feet very pale, trying to answer that General Malet had been chosen by the Senate just because he was a notorious enemy of Napoleon. But he knew that at times like this he was liable to stammer and get flustered, and he was afraid of seeming to Pasquier a timid and incapable person.

'The carriage is there. Hurry up, Monsieur Pasquier', said Lefèvre coming in.

Pasquier gave his successor another look as if to say, 'Be careful of what you're doing, young man', and went out shaking his head.

At the end of the corridor Baroness Pasquier had appeared, brought from her bed by the noise made by the soldiers. Her husband, as he followed Lefèvre, stopped her with a gesture and a meaning look that signified: 'I've known worse things than this. I'll be back soon!', and went down the stairs to the waiting carriage.

* * *

The head of the Security division, Napoleon's secret police, the most notorious policeman in the Empire, was Desmarest, who lived not far from the Prefecture, in rue de la Planche. His arrest had been entrusted to Lieutenant Régnier, of the 4th Company.

Desmarest, not such an early riser as his chief, was still in bed. The officer seemed somewhat embarrassed at the idea of taking so famous a police officer to prison.

'My mission is anything but pleasant, and I'd gladly give fifty louis to be somewhere else. I have orders to arrest you.'

Desmarest gave no sign of reaction to the news of Napoleon's death, nor did he attempt to resist the order for his arrest. He was shocked, but he said not a word. In his youth he had been a priest, indeed a canon of Chartres, and had learnt that you open your mouth either to pray or to say something useful. Therefore he kept silent and hastened to dress himself and follow the officer into a carriage escorted by soldiers.

Only then did the officer tell him how, so far as he knew, the Emperor had died, and what was happening in Paris. 'The Emperor was killed by a pistol-shot under one of the bastions of Moscow, at two in the afternoon. The Minister of War and the Finance Minister are already shut up in the castle of Vincennes.'

Desmarest made no reply, no attempt to contradict him; he was trying to think. Napoleon had died on Ocotober 7th, sixteen days ago: what had happened at his death? The only man capable of taking the situation in hand was Bernadotte, Crown Prince of Sweden, who would certainly have become an intermediary between the Russians and the now leaderless French generals. Therefore it must certainly have been Bernadotte who had set up this Provisional Government that was being organized in Paris, and that naturally would begin by putting in prison Napoleon's ministers and high officials. Bernadotte? Yes, it could only be he. Desmarest's mind began to gallop, as if he were in the archives of the Prefecture looking through the secret files. Yes, there was certainly something about Bernadotte, something that he would not want the allies to know. And his old chief Fouché, what part had he had in all this? No use asking this stupid officer. Desmarest was already making his plan of action: from prison it would be easy for him to get into touch with Fouché, who was probably still free since he'd been in disgrace for the past two years: the new Government would certainly have need of him. Once in touch with Fouché he would find some way through him of reaching Bernadotte and showing him that the Russians, the Allies and the new Government needed the services of France's foremost police officer – who would naturally be happy to forget those unpleasant things he knew about Bernadotte.

Lieutenant Régnier was still talking, saying nothing of importance, largely to hide his embarrassment at this awkward mission, but Desmarest took no notice, absorbed as he was in the plan forming in his mind. They reached La Force and got out of the carriage.

The concierge, Bault, had still not recovered from the emotions of an hour ago when they came to tell him that in the guardroom there was a new prisoner to be admitted.

'But, sir, you, the Security chief, you a prisoner! This is the end of the world, it's the revolution all over again!'

'Be calm, my friend. Take me to a quiet cell and bring me writing materials.'

Bault meanwhile had opened the register and was beginning to sign in the new prisoner: the rules had to be respected however much one disapproved of what one had to do. In any case one never knew, and it was as well to keep up to the mark and have everything in order. At that moment another carriage was heard stopping at the prison gates.

After leaving the Prefecture, confined in the carriage between the lieutenant and a soldier, with another soldier on the box and four more walking at each side, bayonet in hand (people stopped and seemed to be saying: 'Who can that great criminal be that they've arrested!'), Pasquier felt less sure of himself. In situations like this, as he knew from his experiences during the Terror, the important thing was to get through the first twenty-four hours safely. Then, if you had saved your skin, some way out would be found – there was always some old friend in the new government, if there was a government, or someone who found he still had need of your services, and at the worst, if they couldn't let you go free, they would send you into exile somewhere in the country, far from Paris, and he would really be quite glad to go back to his estate at Coulans for a while. But who could help him to get over the first twenty-four hours without disaster? That lieutenant didn't seem to be such a bad lad, just a bit rough in manner and with a rather plebeian name. Lefèvre. Let's see what can be done with him.

'Are you perhaps a relation of the Duke of Danzig?'

'Goodness, no. My name is spelt Lefèvre and his Lefebvre, with a "b" in the middle. We might even be related, for we've both risen from the ranks. But he married a laundress, whereas I'm a bachelor.'

Nothing to be done by way of social relations. Let's try and make him see reason, make him understand that he's let himself become involved in an illegal enterprise.

'Excuse me, Lieutenant, but have you read those documents, that famous decree of the Senate? I have, and I can assure you that they are absolutely irregular. The whole business is irregular, and I'm afraid that you and the others who have got into it will be running great risks – do you realise that?'

'I don't know anything about documents and Senate decrees. I have received an order from my adjutant-major and I must carry it out. I'm a soldier and nothing more. It's no good your trying to get round me with all that talk of Dukes of Danzig and documents. All I know is that I've got to take you to La Force, and to La Force I shall take you. In fact, here we are.'

Bault was still busy registering Desmarest's arrival when he saw coming into the guardroom between two soldiers, preceded by an officer, no less a person than the Prefect of Police.

'You, your Excellency? You've come, I suppose, to clear up any misunderstanding.'

'No, my friend. I have come to be put in prison. So get on with your job.'

Desmarest was still sitting on a bench in a corner. He saw his chief come in, for whom he had little love, but who in their common plight seemed to be almost likeable.

Better be prudent and talk Latin.

'*Quid advenit*?'

'*Nescio*', replied the prefect. So not even he knew what had really happened.

Bault approached with his bunch of keys, and with signs of the deepest respect asked his two guests to follow him to the cells he had assigned to them in accordance with his orders for their 'complete segregation'.

'It won't be for long, gentlemen, let us hope, not for long.'

* * *

The new Prefect of Police, young André Boutreux *alias* Balancié, could not convince himself he was not dreaming. Now that he was left alone in that room with all its stuccos, eagles and gilt friezes, he had more than ever the feeling that he had landed in an unreal world. There he was sitting at that desk adorned with bronze fittings, its surface covered with green leather. The chair in which he sat was soft, with an imposing high back. On the desk were scattered papers and files which he hadn't the courage to look at: on the files was written: 'Secret. For the Prefect alone'.

On the right was a candlestick with sealing-wax and seals: the visible symbol of his new authority. He stretched out his hand to the seals. But it seemed to him that Napoleon was gazing at him from the bust in the middle of the opposite wall: the look in those marble eyes frightened him, and he drew back his hand.

There was a faint scratching at the door on to the corridor

and it opened. At last a familiar face. Boutreux went forward to greet the newcomer respectfully: 'Welcome, Monsieur l'Abbé.'

He was a man of about forty, wearing a dark coat, a closed collar, and a priest's three-cornered hat. Of middle stature and thin as a lathe, his every gesture seemed to spell both caution and decision. He took a couple of paces towards Boutreux, stopped as if at some sudden recollection, and then came on again. This time he limped, dragging his left leg a little. In one hand he grasped a card, the pass that had enabled him to get in.

'How is your leg, Abbé Lafon?'

'A bit better, but the left ankle is swollen. I must have twisted it. I'm certainly not much used to jumping off walls.'

He stopped again, just in front of the table, and fixed Boutreux, who had sat down again, with his steely blue eyes beneath bushy eyebrows.

'Do you know what time it is, my son? Do you realise we are an hour late? Where is *he*? How are things going?'

'Everything is going well, Monsieur l'Abbé. As you know, I have read the Senate decree at the Popincourt Barracks and at La Force, and there were no difficulties. The Paris Guard has been told. Our General is now marching to Place Vendôme and the others will by now have arrested Savary and the rest. Don't you think it's all going well?'

'Yes indeed. I will go now to see for myself. On days like this even a trifle can . . . One can never think of everything. That reminds me, you must sign me an order for the release of three or four political prisoners. They can be useful to us. Everything can be useful, and above all the prayers of the Holy Father, who will not be a prisoner much longer.' He drew a paper from his pocket and prepared to dictate. But Boutreux seemed uncertain.

'I am to sign orders for release? But really. . . .'

'Are you or are you not the Prefect of Police? I'll show you what to do, and the seal is there in front of you.'

'I really think it would be more regular. . . . I mean so that you shouldn't expose yourself to possible difficulties and loss of time . . . If I were to have the orders prepared by the secretary who should be here any minute now. There must be proper forms for it. Then I'll have them brought to you at Place Vendôme.'

Abbé Lafon gave another glance at his watch, a big onion-shaped silver watch that he drew from his pocket, and shook his head. His cheeks seemed more yellow than usual. Only his steely blue eyes with their rapid movements showed clearly that this peaceful priest was made more for action than for reading his breviary. He moved towards the door, dragging his leg.

'You had better bring them yourself to Place Vendôme, within an hour at latest. You'll find me in the General's office. And if you don't find me, take care of yourself and run off to you know where without a moment's loss. I give you my blessing, my son.'

Boutreux accompanied him to the door and shut it. He therefore did not see the Abbé make off in great haste down the stairs: his twisted ankle must suddenly have recovered, for he no longer limped.

Chapter 4

Quai Voltaire

They had crossed the other arm of the Seine and were now marching along Quai Voltaire, to the Ministry of Police. Lahorie was worried. The business might be more difficult here: the guard corps was bigger, there were police about, and he had been warned that there were several exits on to side-streets. It would be necessary to surround the place, make a plan of war in fact, taking care of every detail, and putting to good use his old experience as Chief of the General Staff and his great knowledge of Paris, where he had lived for years in hiding from the police.

He turned to Guidal and called him to his side. From the newly liberated General's mouth, hidden under his beard, there issued a wine-laden breath and a raucous 'Here I am at your command, colleague.' Guidal, after leaving a squad on guard at the Palais de Justice, must have spent the time, while Lahorie was arresting Pasquier, in some nearby hostelry. He smelt of wine, and showed an excitement that was evidently not solely due to the desire to act and carry out orders. By now they were near the imposing block which housed the Ministry of General Police: a long façade with two projecting wings and flanks that continued into a side-street, the rue des Saints-Pères.

Lahorie put his plan into action.

'You, Guidal, with a half-company will go to block the exit into rue des Saints-Pères. You, Piquerel, with the rest of the men will come with me.'

'And I?' said a voice that had not been heard for some time.

It was Boccheciampe, who up till then had marched bravely at the head of the troops with the commanding officers, but had confined himself to looking on. Now he wanted to do something too, to justify in some way his new office as Prefect of the Seine.

'You can rely on me, General. I fought in Corsica against the tyrant Paoli. . . ."

'All right, Boccheciampe, you take eight men and go to the rue des Petits-Augustins, behind the Ministry. You'll see a little building that they call the Museum, which looks on to the courtyard of the Ministry. Occupy it and take care that no one comes out that way.'

'No one will come out that way, I'll answer for it, General. I'll keep good watch.'

Museum : the objective he had been assigned to pleased him – might not the name perhaps derive from the Muses, his favourite divinities who occupied several pages of his catalogue of Olympus?

Piquerel meanwhile had halted his men before the sentinel and summoned the head of the guard-post. 'Have you received the orders?'

'No, sir, no particular order.'

'Never mind. You will help us to carry out the orders of the Senate, of which I am the bearer. Have your men drawn up in the courtyard and await instructions. Give the same order to the gendarmes on duty. I will enter the Ministry with my troop and the General who has been charged to carry out the Senate's mission.'

The guard-post head stood to attention and at a sign from the captain told the sentinel to withdraw; his place was taken by a man from the 10th Cohort.

'You will let no one enter unless he has this special pass'.

Piquerel and some fifty men were already mounting the stairs leading to the Minister's apartment.

General Savary, Duke of Rovigo, an old gendarme more accustomed to dangerous missions than to files and papers, was used to working better at night than by day.

In the silence of the night he could fancy himself under canvas rather than in that office of the Ministry with its heavy furniture, where he felt half-suffocated.

And then, too, it was always at night that serious things happened, things that demanded the immediate intervention of the supreme Chief of the Police of an Empire as big as Europe.

He had been at his desk up to five o'clock, reading reports, writing out orders and consigning them to the couriers who made off at once on horseback to the French provinces, to the army in Spain, to the garrisons in Germany or Poland, to that remote, unknown and terrible land called Russia where the Emperor was with the Grande Armée.

Behind the army, amid treacherous peoples and enemy spies, the police and the gendarmerie had to keep their eyes open, and at the head of all those police, whether in civilian dress or in uniform, was he, Savary, ready to act at any sign of unrest, any symptom of rebellion, any suspicion of intrigue. If the French slept quietly in their homes, if the Emperor rested among the soldiers in their bivouacs, Savary stayed awake: he knew everything, and intervened in time with an iron hand.

Right up to dawn messengers had been seen beneath the gateway mounting their horses and trotting off in the rain over the cobblestones towards the city gates and the main roads out.

At five he too had gone to rest, climbing into the great canopied bed beside his sleeping wife.

He had been asleep for little more than two hours, in the deep sleep of one accustomed to make the most of the short time available for rest. He had given orders not to be disturbed for any reason and had bolted the door of the study leading to his private apartment.

He was roused suddenly by a tremendous din: someone seemed to be not only knocking at the study door but trying to break it down.

'Fire,' he thought half-asleep, 'a fire must have broken out and they've come to wake me.'

He got out of bed in his nightshirt, his feet bare, while his wife continued to sleep peacefully, and felt his way in the dark towards the study. Gleams of light filtered through the splinters of the door, about to give way under the blows.

'I'm awake, I'm coming.'

He drew the bolt, flung open the two leaves of the door, already half off their hinges, and there rushed into the room a crowd of soldiers with fixed bayonets, shouting excitedly.

What could be happening? The General was wide awake now and well aware that he was in a nightshirt with bare feet, surrounded by a mob of soldiers who were not part of the Ministry garrison, but were wearing the uniform of the National Guard.

A captain was in command of them, but before Savary had time to speak to him he was calling to the men outside: 'The General! Call the General!'

He heard this command repeated along the corridors and down the stairs, like an echo.

The General? What General? Would someone come at last who could explain to him what was happening?

There entered a man of medium height, thin, in civilian dress, who on the threshold took off his hat and looked at him with a smile very different from the soldiers' threatening looks.

At the first glance Savary recognised him: it was Lahorie, his old companion-in-arms from the Rhine army, the man whom he himself had had arrested for treachery, but whose prison sentence he had later commuted to exile. Indeed, he should by now have embarked for the United States, or if the order had not yet arrived he should be in prison at La

Force. Instead, there he was before him, free, at the head of an armed troop which obviously awaited his orders and called him 'General'. What on earth could be happening?

Lahorie, very quiet and polite, was saying to him: 'You must be surprised to see me, aren't you?'

"Surprised – why, that's hardly the word.'

Now that there was someone there to whom he could speak and ask for explanations, Savary began to feel once more master of himself.

Lahorie took a step towards him, looking with a half-smile at the Minister's night attire, so little suited to his rank, so different from his glittering uniforms. He seemed anxious not to alarm him.

'You're under arrest. But be thankful you've fallen into my hands. I'll be responsible for you. They shan't hurt a hair of your head.'

Then, turning to the Adjutant-Major: 'Piquerel, arrest the gentleman. You will answer for his safety with your head.'

Piquerel took a step forward and grasped Savary by the arm. The other officers and the soldiers closed in around the man in the nightshirt: so this was the Duke of Rovigo, the minister that everyone hated, the man who hunted recalcitrant conscripts, shot deserters, enlisted by force the half-blind or crippled, the accursed gendarme who grew rich sending soldiers to be killed, who lived in luxury while they slept on straw in fetid barracks or on the ground in bivouacs, the man with the handcuffs, the man of the shootings, the one who had murdered the Duke of Enghien and then as a reward had become a duke himself. The hour of judgement had come, the hour to make him pay up for it. But for those orders of the General's they were ready to stick him in the stomach with their bayonets.

Lahorie sat at the desk to make out the order for arrest. He seemed perfectly calm, but in reality he must have been agitated and almost overwhelmed at this unexpected turn of fate which put him in the position of sending to prison the man who had betrayed and captured him in the very house of his beloved.

He wrote, and the pen seemed to be slipping from his fingers :

> M. Beau will receive in prison, and will hold in segregation until further orders, M. Savary, ex-Minister of General Police, and will keep him in segregation.
>
> Signed : V. F. Lahorie, Minister of Police.

In just three lines his agitation had been such as to make him spell Bault's name wrongly and repeat twice over the order for segregation. There was also a blot of ink, so nervous were the fingers that held the pen.

But Savary naturally wanted to know more.

'Can you explain to me what's happening?'

'There's not much to explain. You must have grasped how things are. You know better than I do that the Emperor was killed on October 7th beneath the walls of Moscow. There's a new Government. I am charged to arrest you. . . .'

The Emperor dead . . . Savary was struck dumb. Certainly, there had been no courier from Russia for at least a week, but if anyone should have known the news before it became public, it was he, with his gendarmes, police, and messengers on horseback. The Emperor dead, a new Government, and he, the Chief of Police, knew nothing of it. It must have been a coup of Fouché's, that confounded Fouché who had never forgiven him for getting him turned out. But he mustn't lose his head, he must think up something, put a bold face on it with this little Lahorie, who wasn't a bad fellow at bottom.

'These are wild stories that you're telling me. I have a letter from the Emperor of that very day, I can show it to you.'

'That's impossible,' said Lahorie curtly.

'But I tell you, if you'll just give me a minute to go and

look in my private file I can show you that letter dated October 7th.'

'No, I say.'

The soldiers had been listening to this dialogue and began to exchange glances. Even in the eyes of Piquerel, usually so expressionless, there were signs of dawning wonder or even doubt.

Lahorie turned to him: 'Where is the sergeant, that little man? Call the little sergeant to me.'

Who was this sergeant? Anguished fear seized Savary: could it be a cut-throat, an assassin?

'Do you want to murder me like a dog?'

'Murder you? Who's talking about murdering you?'

Savary pointed to the bared swords of the captain and the two lieutenants who had followed him, to the bayonets and the ferocious countenances of the soldiers.

'What does all this look like if it isn't a threat of death?'

From the corridor and the courtyard a great uproar could be heard, with indistinct cries of 'Napoleon finished', 'the empire done for', followed by cries, applause, and laughter from the soldiers.

At last the 'little sergeant' whom Lahorie had summoned appeared. Lahorie whispered an order in his ear and the sergeant saluted quickly and went out. But a second later Lahorie, as if he did not trust him, went after him, leaving the Minister's study.

Savary felt that perhaps the moment had come to try on something, especially as it had not escaped his experienced eye that the soldiers' rifles were not cocked.

He turned to Piquerel, who no longer held him by the arm but still stood close beside him.

'Do you know who I am?'

'Really, I. . . .'

'And you, who are you?'

'I am the Captain Adjutant-Major of the 10th Cohort.'

'Whether you know it or not, I am the Minister of the General Police. Are these men under your orders?'

He had assumed a tone of command. The soldiers were listening to him and had almost forgotten his long nightshirt and absurd bare feet.

Piquerel gave the only answer he could: 'I am here on the direct instructions of my cohort Commander, who placed me and my men under the orders of the General who brought us here.'

And as if to show that he was a man who obeyed orders, he grasped Savary once more by the arm. But the latter insisted with ever greater authority. 'But this General, do you know who he is? A traitor, a conspirator, the former aide-de-camp of that other traitor, Moreau! You must have heard of him. That's who your General is. If you follow him, you are his accomplices and you'll finish before a firing squad.'

Piquerel kept silence and continued to hold him firmly.

'You're a brave man. Don't stain your record with a crime. I can still save you, and your men too.'

When Piquerel still said nothing, Savary threw off his hold and made a move to grasp the sword that the officer held under his arm.

'Then at least let me try to save my life on my own. . . .'

Piquerel merely seized him again more firmly. 'No, sir, you are entrusted to my care and I am responsible for your life. . . . Don't move or I shall be forced to tie your hands.'

The Duke of Rovigo resigned himself. 'Very well, as you will. You are responsible for what will happen to you. So much the worse for you.'

Lahorie was returning with Guidal. He had felt incapable of overcoming alone the resistance of that old soldier and comrade. The role of gendarme did not suit him: it was better to call in Guidal's help – he was an energetic man with no scruples.

He had gone down into the street, and it took him a little time to find him until one of the men that Guidal had left on guard at the entrance to the rue des Saints-Pères showed him a wine-shop at the corner.

Now Guidal was returning with him, redder in the face and smelling more of wine but seething with hatred and determined to act. Guidal had never seen Savary, but he knew that it was he who was the cause of his misfortunes, who had had him arrested at Marseilles and was preparing to have him condemned to death. Fate had unexpectedly offered him the means of revenge.

Behind Guidal an officer of the 10th Cohort, Lieutenant Lebis, came running up shouting excitedly with his sword unsheathed.

'What are we waiting for? Men like those, you must skewer 'em like frogs on a spit!'

Guidal seized the sword from him and thus armed, his face distorted with hate, rushed into the Minister's study. Lahorie followed him prepared to intervene and calm down this madman.

Savary saw a furious being rush into the study, his face contorted with rage, brandishing a sword. He stiffened: it was not the first time he had faced death. He would show that a soldier knew how to die.

But Guidal's whirlwind violence collapsed in a moment: rushing in like a madman, he failed to notice a big gilt chair, stumbled against it, and sent it flying.

He must have knocked himself pretty hard. He picked himself up, limping and rubbing his shinbone. It gave Lahorie the time to enter and Savary to draw breath. A pause ensued.

Guidal approached the prisoner chafing his leg, rage and disappointment vying with his hatred. He pointed the sword at Savary's breast.

'Do you know me?'

'No,' answered the Duke of Rovigo, 'I do not know you'.

'I am General Guidal whom you had arrested at Marseilles.'

'Ah,' replied Savary, recovering himself, 'I know all about that. And now you have come to besmirch yourself with a murder?'

'No, but you are coming with me to the Senate.'

'To the Senate? Why the Senate?'

'I have no explanations to give you. Men, take him away.'

The soldiers were waiting for this and threw themselves upon Savary to seize him. But Lahorie stopped them with a curt command: 'Stop, the Minister must be given time to dress.'

Whether he spoke in irony or from good manners was not clear. But they all obeyed him, and at a sign from Savary someone pulled the heavy cord of the bell hanging behind the desk.

In a moment the frightened face of a servant appeared. Lahorie, in the tone of one accustomed to give orders to servants, said: 'Get the Minister's clothes, and be quick about it.'

The soldiers' anger seemed to have changed to good humour, indeed almost to amusement, as they watched the servant feverishly helping the Minister to put on his white silk stockings, his cashmir knee-breeches, his patent-leather shoes with silver buckles, his tie, and his tail-coat with its high lapels. They could not forget the man in the night-shirt, and ministerial attire seemed to inspire no respect in them.

Lahorie charged Guidal to take the prisoner himself to La Force and gave him the order for imprisonment which had been left on the desk. Guidal had no need to be told twice; he was only too delighted to return to La Force not as a prisoner but as the captor of such a prey.

The other orders they had received were all forgotten, but they were highly significant: to arrest Réal, Pelet de la Lozère, the Duke of Feltre, and Cambacérès. Now Lahorie and Guidal had but a single thought, to rid themselves of this obstinate, dangerous Savary.

In the corridor, standing among the soldiers lining its sides, Savary saw a friendly face, one of his secretaries, an old officer of the *chasseurs*, de Clouys; he made a sign to him and said under his breath, for what worse could happen to him now?: 'Calm the Duchess, tell her not to worry, and tell my neighbour what has happened.'

De Clouys made off quickly: he had grasped at once that the neighbour to be warned and saved from danger was Councillor Réal, who lived near by.

Guidal walked proudly down the stairs ahead of the Duke of Rovigo, escorted by an officer and eight men, and went to the carriage waiting at the gate.

* * *

In the carriage, sitting beside Guidal, with a soldier beside the coachman, Savary thought over what could be done, for he was not even sure where they were taking him. Lahorie had spoken of La Force, Guidal of the Senate: could they simply be going to take him to some lonely spot and have him killed by the soldiers who were marching as escort behind the carriage?

All along the Seine, from Quai Voltaire to Quai Conti, he tried to talk to Guidal and persuade him that he had got himself involved in a bad business, that there was no proof of the Emperor's death, indeed far otherwise, and therefore there was still time to retreat and trust in him, in the clemency of the Duke of Rovigo. But Guidal just looked sideways, digesting in silence the wine he had swallowed to give him Dutch courage for the affray.

They had reached Quai des Lunettes, by the Tour de

l'Horloge, and plenty of people were staring at the carriage with its escort. He took a sudden decision: perhaps these soldiers hadn't got their guns cocked either and so couldn't shoot at him, and all those people would help him.

With a swift movement he opened the door and jumped out. He had guessed his jump badly (though no longer a young man he was still strong and agile) and fell as he landed. Guidal had barely time to lean out and cry: 'Stop him!' before Savary had got up and run off at top speed towards the crowd in search of help. The officer and soldiers of the escort ran after him crying: 'Stop him! We're taking him to prison!'

At least ten or a dozen bystanders leapt on him and handed him over panting to the soldiers.

'Who is he? What's he done?'

'He is the Minister of Police. Or rather he *was* the Minister of Police, for Napoleon's dead and so is the Empire!'

They crowded round the carriage into which Savary had been dragged by force. Clamouring to know what it was all about, some were laughing at the idea of a Minister being arrested, others rejoicing at the prospect of peace, and some said, 'That's the way it had to end.' Not a single one said: 'The poor Emperor!' The news spread like wildfire through the *quartier*, and there was much laughter as each one added further details to the story.

* * *

At La Force Bault himself had taken up his stand at the gateway beside the sentinel to see who his next prisoner would be. But though by now he was prepared for anything he was amazed to see his ex-prisoner descend from the carriage dragging with him almost by force the Duke of Rovigo.

Guidal was plainly both happy and excited. 'Splendid,

Bault. I see you're awake and on your toes here, ready to receive guests. Not like some people who have to be arrested in their beds.'

Savary bore himself proudly, and Bault, while paying attention to Guidal's words, strove to let the Duke of Rovigo understand that he could rely on him, his humble servant, to do the best he could for him.

'Put him in complete segregation! You'll be answerable with your head! I shall come back soon, and if I don't find him in isolation, you've had it! He owes me his life, this gentleman, for I had orders to throw him in the Seine!'

Guidal was by now quite frankly drunk, and Bault quickly cut short the scene and brought Savary into the guardroom, while Guidal went off in the carriage followed by the escort.

'Follow me, sir, and don't be afraid.'

'All I want is a cell with a good strong lock of which you keep the keys yourself. Give me something to eat, and let no one enter the cell.'

'We've just had some other famous guests. Without betraying the rules I can let you see them for a minute through the spyhole.'

That minute sufficed to tell Savary, Pasquier, and Desmarets that some very odd things were happening in Paris that day.

Chapter 5

The Minimes Barracks

For Colonel Rabbe, Commander of the regiment of the Paris Guard, military life rested on two fundamental requisites: physical presence and obedience. His career was the perfect proof of the validity of that simple doctrine, and he felt so solidly sustained by the consciousness of living up to it in every way that he had known no doubts, hesitations, or crises throughout his service, which had been long and satisfactory alike in peace and in war.

Physical presence, his stature made to measure for a uniform, his shoulders fashioned to bear epaulets, his chest the natural place for decorations, had enabled him at a very early age to take the first step upwards, which at the time seemed to him both beyond his hopes and the furthest he would get: a simple drummer-boy, he had been promoted to be drum-major, the most decorative man in the regiment, the one who walked in front twirling his staff, eyed with admiration by every girl and the envy of all, soldiers and civilians alike. That this drummer-boy was a fine figure of a man had at once been apparent to his superiors, and they soon discovered that he could also obey with blind precision and with the mechanical aptitude of one of those automata recently made fashionable by Vaucanson. A fine fellow like that, who knew so perfectly how to obey and would therefore know how to exact the same obedience from his subordinates, seemed to his superiors the very man to assume the heavy and honourable responsibilities of the office of regimental drum-major. They never regretted their choice, for that office of which Rabbe was so proud fitted him like a glove.

So, young though he was, he seemed to have reached the apex of his career and to be destined to incorporate, for years to come, at the head of all the drums and fanfare, the virile splendour of one of the oldest regiments of the French Kingdom – when suddenly the Revolution broke out and the Kingdom collapsed. In revolutions everything is turned upside down, and while some crash down, others find themselves swept aloft, far above their own station, and it seems as if nothing can arrest their ascent.

Thus in 1792, three years after the assault on the Bastille, Drum-Major Rabbe found himself promoted an officer, second-lieutenant to begin with, a less decorative rank perhaps and less full of charm for the nursemaids in the Luxembourg Gardens, but a good deal more promising for the future, especially in times like those, when a mere artillery captain, and half a foreigner to boot, was to find himself within a few years General, then Commander-in-Chief, then actually First Consul, which meant head of the state and thus direct successor to that poor French king who had lost his head on the scaffold.

General Bonaparte appreciated more than anyone else those soldiers who knew how to obey, and it did not displease him, skimpy and sallow as he was in those days, to surround himsef with finely-built men: thus Lieutenant Rabbe, good-looking and obedient, was promoted captain of the First Consul's personal guard. Bonaparte, who knew so well how to command and how to choose men capable of obeying him, became his god, the being to whom from that day he offered all his spirit of devotion, his natural tendency to make himself an accurate and passive instrument.

Four years later he was a colonel and sat among the judges of the war tribunal at Vincennes to decide the fate of the Duke of Enghien, seized in foreign territory and imprisoned in that French fortress on the charge of plotting an armed action against the First Consul.

It was an obscure manoeuvre of high politics, probably plotted by Talleyrand in order to create a definite breach between Bonaparte and the old dynasties of Europe. The military judges had consequently received the order to condemn to death the young prince, whose only fault was to be a Bourbon. Rabbe naturally obeyed the order like his other colleagues on the tribunal, signed the death sentence, and young Enghien was shot in the moat of the fortress, through the agency of General Savary.

Since then Rabbe had always commanded the regiment of the Paris Guard, a corps which really had police rather than military duties, and which had been to the wars with Napoleon, though only in a couple of campaigns, in Prussia and Spain, and without achieving any particular distinction.

For the time being Rabbe's career had come to a halt, for he had not become a duke or a marshal like other colleagues who had begun at the bottom of the ladder. But to Rabbe himself it seemed that he had, all the same, reached an enviable goal, especially since, as he now realized, on parades the Colonel on his splendid horse, with his white and green uniform glittering with gold braid and the trumpeter following two paces behind, was even more impressive than the drum-major, and his admirers in the salons certainly gave him no cause to regret the nursemaids in the Luxembourg Gardens.

Now that Napoleon was far away in Russia with the Grand Armée, the safety of the capital, centre of the far-flung empire, was entrusted to stout leaders like this sturdy Colonel, on whose complete obedience full reliance could be placed, as also on his troops so well trained by him for the maintenance of public order, chosen trusted men ready to carry out every command.

* * *

Every morning punctually at eight o'clock the guard drew up before the entrance to the Minimes Barracks to await the arrival of the Colonel, officers and men anxiously looking over every detail of their uniform to make sure that everything was correct – for nothing could escape the Commander's eye, not a single badly-polished button or a belt that hadn't been pipeclayed – or punishments would rain down. But that day they knew the Colonel was not coming, and they anticipated a peaceful time.

In his lodging in Place des Vosges Colonel Rabbe was getting ready to go. It is one of the duties of a good soldier to attire himself in the way most suited to circumstances, and since that day Colonel Rabbe was to travel among civilians, in an ordinary vehicle, the Paris – Beauvais diligence, he had put on civilian dress. It would also be more comfortable for him without boots and spurs, since he would have to sit for hours closely confined among the other travellers.

His batman had carefully folded his uniform in his travelling bag, put his sword in its case of green cloth, and arranged everything properly so that as soon as he arrived at the inn at Beauvais the Colonel could quickly change out of civilian into military dress to go and preside at the conscription board. For he had some unpleasant jobs like this one, which involved examining naked civilians, short-sighted, with twisted legs or protruding knees, who tried to make themselves smaller than they were in hopes of being declared unfit. Well set-up men seemed to have disappeared from France, the armies in Russia and Spain had swallowed them all up, and those left at home were the last dregs among whom it was hard to find even passable men to fill the ever-increasing gaps in the forces.

Rabbe was ready to go when the bell rang. The batman, who was already hoisting the baggage on to his back, opened the door to the regimental adjutant on duty that week, who seemed to be out of breath and upset.

Behind him came a soldier in the uniform of the National Guard.

'What's the matter, Limozin?"

'Terrible news, Colonel! I've run all the way because I was afraid I shoudn't catch you in time. The Emperor is dead – killed at Moscow. . . .'

'The Emperor . . . His Majesty . . . dead? But it's impossible. . . .' Rabbe leaned against the mantelpiece to steady himself.

Adjutant Limozin was struggling to get his breath back. 'Quarter of an hour or twenty minutes ago this soldier of the 10th Cohort arrived at the barracks with an envelope containing orders from the divisional command. He was to hand it to the adjutant on duty and I opened it. . . .'

The guardsman intervened from the background: 'The General who ordered me to bring these papers told me to hand them to the adjutant on duty because he knew the Colonel Commandant would be out of Paris.'

'Yes, of course,' muttered Rabbe mechanically; 'the command was informed about my departure for Beauvais and so. . . .'

Limozin went on: 'A glance at the orders was enough to show that it was something exceptional. The Senate had met following the news of the Emperor's death, killed outside Moscow on October 7th, and a Senate decree appointed a provisional government, there were new generals in command, and orders for our regiment. The most incomprehensible stuff. I tried to reach you in time and I've brought the messenger with me, perhaps he can tell you more.'

Rabbe still could not regain command of himself. Being in civilian dress did not help him to recover the necessary strength to meet this terrible situation. He said: 'The Emperor dead! I can't believe it . . . Tell me everything you know about what's happened. You, my man, tell me word for word what you know, what orders they gave you to bring to my barracks. You spoke of a general. Tell me all you know. . . .'

'Yes sir, yes sir. Two hours ago a general came to our barracks at Popincourt, with a police commissioner. I didn't rightly hear his name. Something like Monte or Mothe, but it might have been something different. First he went to Commandant Soulier's house, and I went with him, then they called everyone together and the Police Commissioner read the documents, the same, I think, as those I brought here, which said that the Emperor had been killed on October 7th outside Moscow, that the Senate was making another government and gave orders to our cohort and the other military corps about what they were to do, and it said that the troops would be paid a bonus. Then this General came out at the head of five companies and went to La Force prison. And there he gave me these orders to bring at once to the Minimes, and another soldier was given orders for the Courtille barracks. I ran all the way and handed over the orders to the adjutant on duty.'

'Good, my man. What is your name?'

'Second-class soldier Boudin Hippolyte, at your service, sir.'

And Polyte stood to attention, trying to appear as soldierly as possible before this impressive being, who even in civilian clothes was obviously a great soldier.

* * *

Rabbe had tried to read attentively the papers that Adjutant Limozin had brought him. But he realized that only two things had struck him in all those pages full of solemn phrases and signed impressively with seals : Napoleon was dead, and the head of all the military forces in Paris was a certain General Malet whose name he remembered vaguely but of whom he knew nothing.

Two incontrovertible facts : Napoleon was dead and so

would give no more orders, and General Malet was appointed Commander of the First Division and the Paris Garrison and so he would be giving the orders now. Conclusion: it was the bounden duty of every well-disciplined soldier to obey General Malet.

He could not yet see how he could live without his god, Napoleon. But one thing was certain: even at a terrible moment like this he would be betraying his military duty if he yielded to his own personal feelings.

'Limozin, go back to barracks and assemble the I Battalion immediately. Send a man to the Courtille barracks to make sure that the adjutant on duty of the II Battalion has received the orders and carried them out. This soldier from the National Guard can stay with me to act as messenger if necessary. I will come to the barracks as soon as I'm ready. Let everything be done with the greatest speed. And say nothing to anyone about the news concerning His Majesty the Emperor.'

Limozin saluted and went off at a run.

Rabbe called his batman, 'Take my uniform out of the bag and help me to dress. I shan't go to Beauvais. I must be at the barracks in ten minutes to carry out the orders of the divisional Commander.'

The batman followed him into his bedroom with the travelling-bag and sword, while Polyte Flatfoot waited in silence in the hall. That day being a soldier seemed to him less boring and monotonous than usual.

The Colonel was ready in five minutes and went off with long strides and much rattling of sword and spurs, with Polyte bustling along and dragging his feet behind him, under the arcades of Place des Vosges to the nearby rue Saint-Gilles and the Minimes Barracks, where the I Battalion of the regiment of the Paris Guard was quartered.

It was just about half-past eight.

* * *

Adjutant Limozin had done everything he should and the six companies were drawn up in perfect order under the command of the most senior officer, Captain Borderieux. Polyte, anti-militarist though he was, could not help noticing with a certain admiration the difference between these impeccable troops and the ragtag soldiers who made up his cohort of the National Guard.

A glance sufficed to assure Rabbe that everything was in order. From left to right the six companies of the Guard were drawn up, one company of grenadiers, one of *voltigeurs*, and the rest fusiliers, all in their white and green uniforms, the grenadiers with their busbies, the *voltigeurs* with their tall shining shakos, the fusiliers with their cocked hats and white pompoms.

Rabbe was sombre and withdrawn, like someone stricken by grief trying to concentrate on the execution of the practical actions that the circumstances demand. He ordered Limozin to read the documents that the messenger had brought – the Senate decree and the proclamation to the army. Not a murmur was heard, not an arm moving or a hand raised to the eyes betrayed any sign of surprise. Those soldiers, so perfectly trained and disciplined, learnt the astounding news with the same immovable indifference with which they listened every evening to the orders of the day.

Rabbe bestirred himself and went on to carry out the instructions that the divisional commander had given to the Paris Guard. He called Captain Borderieux and the other company commanders to him, and the orders written out in such precise detail by General Malet were distributed:

'Captain Borderieux with the grenadier company: to go to the Senate. Captain Godard with the 1st Company, to the Treasury, rue Neuve-les-Petits-Champs. Lieutenant Beaumont with the 2nd Company, to the Prefecture of Police. Captain Lamarre with the 3rd, to the Ministry of Police. Captain Martin with the 4th to the Hôtel de Ville. Captain Lavarde with the *voltigeurs*, to Place Vendôme.'

'Carry out these orders at once', Rabbe concluded.

In less than twenty minutes the six companies had gone off and left the barracks courtyard deserted.

'I am going to my office to wait for news. You, Limozin, send a non-commissioned officer to the Courtille, to make sure the orders are being carried out there, and he must come back at once and report to me. In an hour I shall go on horseback to inspect the various companies in their positions.'

The Colonel moved off with the lightened conscience of one who has done his duty.

'Excuse me, sir – what am I to do? Should I stay here or go back to the Popincourt Barracks?'

'Oh, yes, you – I'd forgotten about you. What did you say your name was? Oh, yes, Boudin : I never forget a good soldier's name. Go back to your barracks, but first go to the canteen and have a glass of wine. Tell the woman in charge that I'll pay for it.'

'Thank you, sir.'

There are some days, you have to admit it, when a soldier's life isn't so bad.

* * *

At the Courtille Barracks they were behind time. Adjutant Valhavielle, having received the papers from the messenger, had sent them to the battalion Commander, Captain Rouff, who was still at home. The news had struck him as so serious that he did not feel like seeing to the execution of the orders himself. So he had to wait for Rouff, who arrived after half-an-hour out of breath from running.

'Assemble the companies immediately. And the officers and the adjutant on duty are to come to my office.'

There was no time to read the Senate decree and the proclamation. Rouff grasped that if he delayed any longer in sending his companies to the places indicated in the divisional Commander's instructions he would risk arrest or even imprisonment. But then, what need was there for soldiers to know the reasons for an order? Their duty was simply to carry out orders, not to know why they were given, whether it was a case of a parade, or the purchase of victuals, or an event like this.

'Gentlemen, according to the news I have from the divisional Commander, the Emperor is dead and there is a change of government. Here are the official documents. Adjutant Valhavielle, take these papers and lock them in the battalion chest without showing them to anyone. Here are the orders for each of you. I will take the 1st Company and go to the Prefecture of Police where there are already other troops. You, Viotty, with the grenadiers, go and occupy Porte Saint-Martin. You, Lemonier, with the infantry, go to the Porte de Vincennes. Station detachments at the intervening gateways so that each one is guarded. Bazoncourt, you will go with the 2nd Company to Quai Voltaire, while Moizy with the 3rd will go to Place de Grève and Labine with the 4th will draw up in the enclosure of the Palais Royal, putting sentinels at each exit both on the Louvre and on the other sides. Carry out these orders at once and quick march. We are late as it it.'

In fact it was already well after 9 o'clock.

* * *

At the Luxembourg Palace, the seat of the Senate, Captain Besse, in command of the permanent guard consisting of a battalion of veterans, was much amazed when one of his men came to tell him that a company of grenadiers of the Paris Guard had arrived.

The grenadier captain came up and introduced himself: 'Captain Borderieux: I am here to take over from you in accordance with the orders received.'

'Take over from me? But what orders are these?'

'The orders of the divisional Commander, given after the reading of the Senate decree.'

'A Senate decree? But has the Senate met? When?', asked the puzzled Captain Besse.

'It seems only natural,' answered Borderieux, 'seeing that the Emperor is dead and they had to form a new Government. . . .'

'What on earth are you talking about? I should be bound to know if the Senate had met, for I haven't left the Luxembourg for three days. It all seems most peculiar. Wait, I'll go and find out.'

He ran into the Palace. At that hour there was no one about except the cleaners. He went and knocked at the office of the Chief Justice of the Senate, Clément de Ris, but he was not there either.

The grenadiers, with their arms grounded, awaited orders; the veterans were still in the sentry-boxes and the guardroom.

Besse returned to Borderieux. 'Wait just a few minutes, Captain,' he said. 'It seems too strange to me. I'll saddle my horse and go and ask at the Hôtel de Ville. I'll be back in half-an-hour.'

Borderieux told his men to stand easy. The grenadiers lost no time in getting into conversation with the veterans, proud to be able to communicate the great news to those old men who had heard nothing of it.

Taken all in all, the grenadiers commented, it wasn't bad news if it meant peace and a return home for all those men in Russia, Spain, or goodness knows where.

But the veterans did not see it that way. Some among them had been through the Italian campaign, had stopped a bullet at Montenotte or Rivoli, there was a grey-whiskered sergeant who had had an empty left sleeve ever since Wagram, where he had lost an arm. For them the news had a different meaning. Peace signified nothing to men like them who had never known anything but war. For them the only thing that counted was that Napoleon was dead, and it seemed as if with his end their own lives were ended too.

Borderieux had been till then completely occupied in carrying out the orders he had received; but now, in this pause, as he listened to the broken phrases and stifled curses with which the veterans received the news of Napoleon's death, he too felt emotion. He too was an old soldier who had followed the eagles for many a year, and now he had to stand by at this finale, this liquidation, as if it was just ordinary duty. It was a rotten business being a soldier; but as he'd begun it there was nothing for it but to carry on to the end.

Besse was speaking to him: he had returned within the half-hour, sweating from his gallop and looking much disturbed.

'Unhappily it's true. At Place de Grève, in front of the Hôtel de Ville, there's a company of the National Guard. The commandant was talking to an official of the Seine Prefecture just when I came up, and they both confirmed the news. They were awaiting the arrival of the Prefect, who is in the new Government. But I still don't understand how the Senate can have met without my knowing about it. But anyway, Captain, go ahead and carry out the divisional Commander's orders.'

The veterans, still muttering among themselves, yielded up the guard post to the grenadiers. Borderieux followed Besse to take over from him. After which Besse, leaving the guard of the Luxembourg in other hands but still tormented by doubts about that incredible meeting of the Senate, decided to go off in search of further news and made for the command in Place Vendôme. He was an obstinate man, and, to convince him of the truth of things that to his simple logic seemed impossible, he needed solid proof.

Chapter 6

Place de Grève

As soon as she heard the General and the other soldiers leave the room, Madame Soulier hurried back to her husband. Through the half-shut door of the next room she had managed to hear everything. Not wanting those nocturnal visitors to find her in her nightdress and curling-pins, she had slipped out of bed a minute before they came in, but all the same she simply had to know what they wanted of her husband at that hour.

'Well, I'm the first to congratulate you on your promotion. After all these years of waiting it was high time. . . . But what's the matter? You ought to be delighted, but you seem sad and downcast.'

Soulier sighed, leaning back on the pillow: 'Didn't you hear? The Emperor is dead, Napoleon is done for. . . .'

'Hundreds of thousands have died for him in these last years. And sooner or later he had to die too. Now we shall have some peace. But hurry up, for I know you have orders to carry out and won't want to arrive late on a day like this and cut a poor figure with the new Government.'

Soulier was again perspiring so much that his wife had to help him with another change of linen before he laboriously got into his uniform and boots. He was on the point of going out, absorbed in the thought that next time he would be putting on the uniform of a general, when his wife stopped him:

'I suppose you examined those orders, the documents the general read you? Did you see if the signatures and seals were all correct?'

'Yes, of course, all correct. And anyway I've got authentic copies with me that I have to take to the Hôtel de Ville and hand to the Prefect of the Seine. Here they are. But don't keep me : I have a delicate and urgent mission.'

'And mind you make the most of it, now that for once you've got the chance to meet the high-ups. . . . Try to make them give you a really important command with something to show for it, since you'll be the first to meet the members of the new Government. Don't hang back as you generally do.'

His wife was still leaning over the banisters calling advice after him when Soulier reached the bottom of the stairs.

* * *

Only the 6th Company of his cohort had been left him, and on horseback at the head of that rather exiguous group of men the new-made General Soulier arrived at Place de Grève before the solemn edifice of the Hôtel de Ville soon after half-past-seven. He ordered the company Commander to line up the men in front of the building, stacking their rifles, and to put a sentinel at the entrance. With a firm step, conscious of the importance of his mission, Soulier went in to hand the Senate's orders to the Prefect of the Seine.

The doorkeeper hastened to tell him that His Excellency the Prefect, Count Frochot, was not there, since it was his custom to go every evening to his country house at Nogent-sur-Marne, returning to the Prefecture next morning. If the commandant would be so kind as to wait a moment, he would get the highest official present to speak to him.

This was the head of the first division in the Prefecture, the zealous and courteous M. Villemsens, who at once asked Commandant Soulier the reason for this early morning visit with an armed escort. Soulier held out the documents with a few words of explanation.

Villemsens was thunderstruck. 'I must inform His Excellency at once, he must have set out already. He must hurry here. I'll arrange to let him know. What a disaster, good heavens, what a disaster!'

He called a stable-boy, Francard by name, and ordered him to saddle a horse immediately and go off at top speed to meet the Prefect. Taking a piece of paper he wrote a few lines in pencil and gave it to Francard with the order to hand it to His Excellency and escort him back to the Hôtel de Ville.

In the interval he took Soulier into one of the rooms on the ground-floor and tried to learn from him further details about the Emperor's death and the Senate's decisions. Soulier told him what little he knew, at the same time stressing the delicacy and importance of the mission that had been entrusted to him.

Time passed slowly as the minutes grew into an hour. Suddenly the sound of a four-horse carriage was heard at the gate. Villemsens went to the window and thought he recognised the coach of the Minister of Police. The footman got down and ran up to the doorkeeper of the Prefecture. They exchanged a few words and the man in livery and wig went back to report to the personage sitting in shadow in the coach.

The order was evidently given to move off again, for the footman returned to his place beside the coachman and the four-in-hand, making an elegant semi-circle before the drawn-up troops, drove off. An usher entered and announced breathlessly to Villemsens that the Minister of Police had come to speak to the Prefect, but hearing that he had not yet arrived had gone off again without getting out of his carriage.

'What a terrible day,' murmured Villemsens. 'The Duke of Rovigo must be overwhelmed at the news. That will be why he came in person to confer with the Prefect.'

In the four-horse carriage General Lahorie, for the last

hour Minister of Police, having learnt that Count Frochot was not at the Hôtel de Ville, and having seen that the Prefecture was guarded according to plan by the 10th Cohort, was driven back to the Ministry at Quai Voltaire.

He would have liked to drive to the Passage des Feuillantines and show himself to Sophie Hugo in his Minister's carriage, but he must be patient and postpone for a few hours his triumphal return to the lady he loved, the lady who had not hesitated to compromise her reputation for him.

Up till then Lahorie had not had much to do. In the Ministry only those with special passes were being admitted, and consequently the officials and clerks were being sent home by the sentinels as they arrived to start the day's work. The only person who had managed to reach him, thanks to his pass, was Boccheciampe, but he had not been much help. According to the orders the Corsican should by now have gone to the Hôtel de Ville to take over the duties of Prefect of the Seine. He had in fact gone to Place de Grève after taking part, as we have seen, in the operations culminating in General Savary's arrest.

He had got as far as the Place, but when he raised his eyes and saw that magnificent edifice with its rich Renaissance architecture his courage failed him. How could he, in his wretched clothes worn out after his long sojourn in prison, with his Corsican accent that seemed a caricature of French, how could he stride in there and say: 'I am the new Prefect. You must obey me?'

He simply didn't feel equal to it. He had walked without a word past the troops and their stacked rifles. He had circled the whole building, almost as if he were seeking a side entrance that would be less intimidating, and had found himself once more on the Seine near the bridge he had crossed shortly before. Thus half-mechanically he had finished by returning to the Ministry of Police and after showing his pass to the sentinel had gone up to the Minister's study.

He had need of a friend to talk to and advise him, and the only real friend he had in Paris, apart from a girl he had not seen for some time, was a man named Muller whom he had left behind in prison at La Force. The first thing to do, then, was to set Muller free, making the most of the new situation and the highly-placed acquaintances he now had.

Lahorie, all on his own and with nothing to do in that silent deserted Ministry, was quite delighted to have found a way of occupying five minutes in drawing up the order to liberate Muller and stamping it with the ministerial seal.

Boccheciampe went off then and Lahorie, seeing that the Corsican had not yet managed to instal himself at the Hôtel de Ville as prefect *malgré lui*, decided to go there in person and confer with the present incumbent, Count Frochot. He had the Minister's carriage brought round. But, as we have already seen, that was a fruitless journey.

* * *

Every morning during the fine weather, as he crossed the city's confines and slowed down his horse to a walk, Count Nicolas Frochot, having passed the night in the peace of his villa at Nogent-sur-Marne, had the pleasant and reassuring feeling of a father who returns home to his family and finds everything in good order.

That order, those clean paved streets, those markets full of all kinds of goods, those shops becoming finer and more elegant as one moved in from the outskirts towards the centre, were, he could not but recognize, his own handiwork. He had become Prefect twelve years earlier, in a Paris still suffering from the ravages of the Revolution, with streets torn up, public services non-existent, disorder everywhere, and he had managed to restore order, clean up the streets, revive trade, start new building, open schools and orphanages, allay the fears of the bourgeoisie, pacify the working-classes in the suburbs, in a word to prepare the city, in accordance with the will of the First Consul, to be the capital of the new Empire.

He had even thought of the dead, the millions of skeletons which for the past ten centuries had been piling up in the interminable catacombs of Paris. He had brought order among their bones, even composing extraordinary macabre decorations with them and transforming the underground regions of Paris into a sort of solemn, silent capital of death. Frochot passionately loved his mission as restorer of the grandeur of Paris, as model administrator of the first city of the world, and to retain that office he had renounced a political career which had looked quite promising after the 18th Brumaire.

His summer luxury was to go off to spend every evening and night at the villa, and, with the Emperor at the war in Russia, the court at St Cloud, and the official life of Paris practically at a standstill, it had been possible to prolong that pleasurable practice far into the autumn. When it rained, as in those last days of October, it was to him a perfect form of repose to spend the night in the quiet of the countryside on the banks of the Marne, even if he had to leave early next morning to ride back to Paris.

It was shortly after eight o'clock and he was riding at a walk down the long rue du Faubourg Saint-Antoine when, just at the Orphans' Hospice, he saw approaching at a rapid trot Francard, the stable-boy from the Prefecture. He held a paper in his hand.

'Your Excellency, M. Villemsens has sent me with this note for you.'

It was scribbled hurriedly in pencil. Frochot, who at fifty-one years old declared he could still see perfectly and refused to wear spectacles, had no difficulty in reading the first line: 'M. le Préfet is urgently awaited.' Two words in Latin followed which seemed to him quite incomprehensible: '*Fecit Imperator*'. What could the blessed man mean? But anyway he would hasten his pace and find out.

Frochot scrunched up the note, threw it on the ground, and prepared to move off. A little boy who had been watching the scene bent down to pick up the paper, curious as to what it might be.

But Frochot was still uneasy.

'Boy, give me back that paper.'

That's it, he'd got it. Spreading out the paper on the palm of his hand, the Latin words now seemed to make some sort of sense: '*Fuit Imperator*.'

He broke out into a cold sweat. The Emperor was no more. The Emperor was dead! In this way, intelligible only to educated persons, the good Villemsens had meant to warn him. He thrust the note into his pocket.

'Quick, Francard. To the Hôtel de Ville, as fast as you can!'

Had he not been afraid of slipping on the damp cobbles he would have gone off at a gallop.

* * *

To find Place de Grève unusually full of troops so fully confirmed that fact laden with portent for France that when on dismounting he saw Villemsens coming to meet him he never even asked if the news were true but said at once: 'How did it happen? When? Where?'

'On October 7th, outside Moscow, Your Excellency. A fragment of cannon-shot hit him,' answered the official equally tersely. 'The news was brought to us by a superior officer sent by the military command with orders from the Senate for you and with a detachment from the public order service to guard the Place. Follow me, Your Excellency: the officer is waiting to see you. Oh, I was forgetting to tell you – more than half-an-hour ago the Minister of Police came to see you.'

'Poor Savary! A terrible blow for a faithful comrade of the Emperor. A terrible blow for us all, and for France. But we mustn't give way to our feelings. At a serious time like this we must act according to higher orders and do our duty. Where is that officer you speak of? Bring him to my office.'

Frochot had not yet sat down at his desk when Soulier was announced and introduced himself. It was hard to say which of the two men was most anxious to open the conversation: Frochot, impatient to hear the news that could spell catastrophe not only for France but for his own personal position; or Soulier, who after years of obscure, monotonous life as a soldier had for the first time found himself entrusted with an important mission that might have considerable consequences for his whole career.

While awaiting the Prefect's arrival for the past hour, he had asked himself how he would open the conversation, and naturally he had finished by doing as he always did, sheltering behind his superior officers.

'M. le Préfet, you will no doubt have received a letter from the General Commandant. . . .'

'No, I've had no letter. I'll find out if it came while I was away. But who is this General?'

'General Lamotte, who came to the barracks to transmit the Senate's orders to me, assured me that General Malet had written to you telling you officially of the Senate's decisions. But anyway here is an authentic copy for you.'

Lamotte, Malet? These names of generals meant nothing to a high official and consummate politician like Frochot. He read the papers quickly, skipping to the signature and seal.

'But who is General Malet?'

'I don't know him personally. It seems he is now in command of the division, or perhaps he will be one of the new heads of the General Staff.'

'I've no idea, I suppose he must be signing on behalf of General Hulin, Commandant of the division.'

'Perhaps he is replacing him. I heard that General Hulin was ill.'

But why waste time over these obscure generals? The signatures were there. That curious stamp, a handwritten L, was probably the personal stamp of Lanjuinais, secretary of the Senate, used provisionally while waiting for a new one, without the imperial eagle.

No eagle, no Empire: Napoleon was dead, and so was the Empire: would France collapse again into political and social disorder? Thank Heaven there was already a government, appointed by the Senate, and he, Frochot, was a member of it.

He scanned the list of the Senate decree: there were generals, aristocrats, and ex-Jacobins, but he, who represented the capital, who provided the assurance that Paris could be held, they must have included him in that government which would have the hard task of succeeding Napoleon. Not only must he be included in it, but it must be he who would instal it, there, in his Hôtel de Ville, and organize its operation.

Frochot, who a moment earlier had seen himself on the threshold of destitution, envisaged the possibility of becoming the arbiter of the new government, the man capable of reconciling intransigent republicans like Carnot, Florent-Guyot and Jacquemont with monarchists like Mathieu de Montmorency and Alexis de Noailles. A man like him, who had escaped the Terror, who had come to the fore after the 18th Brumaire, acting always in full accordance with legality thanks to his complete familiarity both with the laws and with the mentality of the officials and magistrates who applied them, had every chance of emerging secure from out of that huddle of heterogeneous personages to whom France was entrusting herself after the death of her hero in a distant land with his armies scattered in the farthest corners of Europe.

The best proof of the important role he was naturally

destined to assume in the new government could be seen in Savary's hurried visit. If the Duke of Rovigo, the proud and all-powerful Minister of Police, had taken the initiative to come in person to see him, it was a sign that he urgently wanted to reach an understanding with him, perhaps to negotiate the support of the army, of Napoleon's loyal followers, for a government which, except for him, consisted of avowed anti-Bonapartists.

From the first moment when he heard of Napoleon's death to his perusal of those documents, Frochot had felt himself assailed by a rising alarm, so much so indeed that before going to his office he had ordered a light phaeton to be harnessed ready to carry him off in haste if need arose. But now he began to breathe again and resume the natural equilibrium of a man who knew how to conceal his own importance and authority behind a courteous demeanour.

'Colonel, I am here to assist you in the execution of your orders. Tell me what you want.'

'M. le Préfet, as specified in the written instructions, I am to prepare the necessary quarters for the new Government, and in particular a place for the Ministers' meetings and for the General Staff.'

'The Ministers can meet in the main hall of this building, and I think the ground-floor rooms will be perfectly suitable for organising the services of the General Staff. I'll arrange it at once.'

He rang the bell and an usher appeared.

'Call the steward and all the chief service staff.'

Like all soldiers, Soulier had no great belief in the efficiency of civilian officials; but this time he had to alter his opinion. Frochot issued orders with the energy and clarity of a good military leader, and his dependents, all those clerks in their dark clothes, reacted like soldiers, turned round smartly and went off to carry out their instructions.

Desks and chairs were brought out from the store-rooms, long tables covered with green baize were quickly set up in the rooms indicated by the Prefect, while the ushers hastened to set out inkstands and sheaves of white paper. In less than half-an-hour all was in readiness for the new Government and its General Staff to begin their activities.

At this point Count Frochot took leave of Commandant Soulier. 'I think your instructions have been carried out in every detail. I'll leave you to your military duties. If you have no further need of me for the moment, I will withdraw to my apartment. The emotions of this terrible morning have exhausted me, and I feel I need to regain my strength for the rest of the day. Let me know as soon as the members of the Government begin to arrive. Till later, then, Commandant.'

Soulier clicked his heels in acknowledgement and went down again to the Place to assure himself that his troops were on guard outside the building, keeping back the crowd that was beginning to seethe around the square, and were ready to do the honours when the new Ministers should arrive at the Provisional Government's headquarters.

Chapter 7

Place Vendôme No. 22

Only the 1st Company was left with him, but General Lamotte marched as firmly and as quickly as if he had been at the head of a whole division. Left, right, left, right, along the rue Saint-Honoré to the Place Vendôme, and the footsteps kept pace in his head with what still remained to be done: the last actions necessary to complete the work, the perfect edifice which since dawn had been rising up stone by stone, and which in a few moments would make him the new leader of France, a France free and democratic, a France eager above all to heal the wounds she had inflicted on herself and on other peoples.

The new leader: he, General Malet, who would appear on the balcony, before the crowd, casting aside the temporary mask of the imaginary General Lamotte behind which he had concealed himself to carry out the first steps of his enterprise – Malet, the old enemy that Napoleon believed he had got rid of for ever.

The General marched, and his chest swelled with pride. Everything that had happened since earliest dawn, everything he was about to do to achieve complete success, that bloodless revolution which was to end twenty-two years of bloodstained revolution, *coups d'état* and wars, was his work, proof that the reality born of a brain capable of vivid imagination and iron will was no less valid than everyday reality born of facts.

Napoleon was dead because he had declared it so and proved it with his documents, and if everyone believed in those documents it was exactly as if Napoleon was really dead, and he and all the others must continue to behave as they would behave if the news of Napoleon's death were authentic and not invented. And he, Malet, was in fact the first to believe in it and to regulate his conduct in accordance with that conviction: I act in this way because Napoleon is in effect dead, not because I have made everybody believe it to be so.

Had not everything in fact happened up to now just as if a cannon-shot had really killed Napoleon beneath the walls of Moscow? What he, Malet, had conjured up, firmly believing in the force of his own imagination and his genius for organization, had been translated into documents, proclamations, marching orders for the troops, precise instructions for the authorities. And the soldiers had marched, the commanders had obeyed; prison gates had opened, closed, and reopened; former prisoners became chiefs, and chiefs left their officers and ministries to be shut up in cells. They were all marionettes: the soldiers and officers who obeyed, the authorities who let themselves be put in prison. One man alone pulled the strings, he, Malet, with his invincible imagination and will stronger than any banal reality rooted in concrete facts.

He no longer felt conscious of his fifty-eight years, of past vicissitudes, bitterness and imprisonment. He marched in time along the cobblestones of Rue Saint-Honoré and heard behind him the soldiers' feet beating the rhythm of their pace, the squeaking of their leather belts, the rattle of their mess-tins fastened to their haversacks, the breathing of all those men who followed him obedient to his orders, from the elderly captain marching behind him down to the youngest recruit.

Perhaps for the first time in his life Malet felt happy, sure of himself, of his own strength, of the mission he had taken upon himself to free France from the tyrant who was draining her life-blood and putting Europe under fire and sword. The instrument that his will had succeeded in utilizing so effectively was the complete command of the military organization, from the orderly rooms to the General Staff and the Ministry. And just as he knew every detail of the whole organization, the endless papers, how to draw up orders, adorn them with convincing seals, and address them to the correct headquarters in accordance with the particular military logic so different from the logic of civilians, so also he knew the mind, brain, and natural reactions of the soldiers to whom those orders were addressed, in whom by their whole fashion and the time-honoured bureaucratic liturgy of their mode of expression such orders at once set in motion the spring of obedience, with the result that commonsense, doubts, hesitation, questionings were all stifled at birth, like a candle suddenly deprived of air.

All those years of subordinate commands, of garrison quarrels with superior officers, years of frustration over disappointments in his career, of envy for all the ex-corporals who became dukes and marshals of France, years of disgrace and prison, had matured in him a perfect knowledge of the military machine, a knowledge that represented the essential requisite for destroying it from within, causing it to collapse, and gaining control of it, the chief instrument of the Napoleonic tyranny. Minute by minute, hour by hour, shut up in his cell and later in that less stringent prison to which they had recently transferred him and from which he had so easily escaped a few hours earlier, he had gradually built up the plan which he was now putting into action that October morning.

First, on his own, he had put together in his mind piece by piece the groundwork of the scheme that was now proving vital. Then he had found an incomparable companion, Abbé Lafon, as different from himself as a churchman could be from a soldier, but identical in their mutual hatred of the tyrant and their determination to overthrow him. From that day General and priest had worked together to build up that 'truth' composed of false documents indistinguishable from real ones and therefore beyond dispute for those who believe that it is documents that legitimize truth, and not vice versa. What had happened so far that morning seemed to prove the priest and General right.

Where was the good Abbé who had been so useful to him? It was unfortunate that he had twisted his ankle in jumping down from the wall of the Dubuisson clinic, the mild prison for inoffensive enemies to which Savary's unwary police had transferred him from the real goal from which it was not so easy to escape. But though the Abbé had not been able to follow him to the Popincourt Barracks and La Force, he had certainly been busy in the meantime and would by now have made contact with those friends of his whose power Malet had indirectly tested. Their immediate aim was the same as the General's, to overthrow Napoleon, although a further reason motivating Lafon and his friends was the liberation of the Pope, now a prisoner at Fontainebleau, and his return to Rome. As their views coincided in the first objective, they could fall in with his plans and ally themselves with an old Jacobin like himself, a soldier of the Rhine army, and with that priest who besides the Pope had nostalgic memories of the King.

Once matters were settled at the headquarters in Place Vendôme, Abbé Lafon would certainly present himself without delay before the new Commandant to offer him advice and the powerful support of his friends, and to help him in the difficult task of uniting, in a government capable of opposing Napoleon's return, both the Jacobins of yesterday and the followers of the Pope and the King. The important thing now was to exercise great care in placing the last stones on the edifice to crown all that had been accomplished in those few hours. Lahorie and Guidal must have carried out their missions by now : besides Savary and Pasquier, the Arch-Chancellor Cambacérès, Duke of Parma, the Minister of War, Clarke, Duke of Feltre, and all the rest should be in prison. Their medieval offices and foreign titles had all dissolved that rainy morning: there would be no more Arch-Chancellor or princes and dukes fabricated by imperial decree.

The people of Paris would need only to realize the ridiculous aspects of their misfortunes to dismiss scornfully for what they were worth those titles and offices and the authority of him who had conferred them. With them the Empire would crumble: the Russian snows and the allied armies would take care of the rest. Before Napoleon would be in a position to attempt a reaction, even supposing he could – for all the peoples of Europe would revolt against him, and his own soldiers would refuse to march against their brethren – a new free and democratic regime would be safely installed in France, a regime that would proclaim peace and put an end to the slaughter, and all would acclaim his name, the name of General Claude-François Malet, as liberator of the world.

To achieve all this only one act had still to be accomplished – not an easy one, certainly, but by no means impossible. This last mission he had entrusted to no one else reserving it for himself. This was to gain possession of General Hulin, commandant of the Paris Garrison, and prevent him from being able to take any action: once this obstacle was overcome, Paris and France itself would be in his hands.

Hulin was a hard nut to crack, Malet did not conceal it from himself: always in the front line when decisive action had to be taken for the past twenty years, ever since, as a simple guardsman, he had been the first to penetrate the Bastille, up to the day when, as a violent Jacobin turned zealous Bonapartist, he had presided over the council of war that had condemned the Duke of Enghien to death. Always on the hunt for spies and enemies of the Emperor, he soon became a Count of the Empire, Grand Cross of the Legion of Honour, General and Commandant of the Paris

Division. Now that General Junot, Duke of Abrantès, was at the wars, he was in effect Governor of Paris.

This, then, was the man who had to be got rid of, the more so since Malet, in all those decrees and orders of the Senate which had so far worked miracles, was himself appointed Commandant of the Paris Division in succession to Hulin. Therefore, come what might, Hulin must disappear.

Malet reviewed his plan as he approached Place Vendôme and the hour for action.

* * *

They had almost reached the Place in front of the church of St Roch (did Malet perhaps recall that it was on the steps of that very church, with his 'whiff of grapeshot' of the 13th Vendémiaire, that Bonaparte's political career began?) when Malet halted his troop and went over to the shop of of a vintner of his acquaintance, a certain Briand, to ask him to tell his shoemaker, Ladré, to come and see him later at headquarters to measure him for a pair of boots. Was this an agreed sign to an accomplice, or did he really need a new pair of boots? In that case, at any rate, it afforded proof of the absolute certainty of success that accompanied Malet throughout this decisive action.

After a moment's pause the march was resumed, and the General sent off his aide, Rateau, who was walking two paces behind him with his bagful of papers, to take a letter to an old friend of his, General Desnoyers, who lived near by, asking him to put on the uniform that was in a big parcel entrusted to a soldier and join him at once at headquarters.

The first company of the 10th Cohort of the National Guard finally emerged in Place Vendôme, the centre of which had for the past two years been adorned by Napoleon's triumphal column.

Malet gave the order to halt at the entrance to the Place and called the company's three officers to him: the Commandant, Captain Steenhower, a fifty-year-old Dutchman who had advanced but little in his career during his many years in the French army, and the two section Commanders, Second-Lieutenant Gomont Saint-Charles and Lieutenant Prévost.

Malet had his plan of action clear in his head and it took only a few minutes to give the three officers their orders. The first section, under Second-Lieutenant Gomont Saint-Charles, was to station itself before the house in which General Hulin lived, No. 22, on the side of the Rue des Petits-Champs. The second section, Lieutenant Prévost's, was to take its stand in front of the Garrison Command headquarters, in the opposite corner at No. 7. Lieutenant Prévost, having drawn up his men so as to block the entrance, was to go to Colonel Doucet, Chief of the General Staff, and give him the letter and folder of documents addressed to him. Prévost was then to go down to the gateway, while Colonel Doucet would carry out the instructions he had received, and there await the General, who would join him as soon as he had dealt with General Hulin, and in the meantime he was to prevent anyone from entering the building.

The two section Commanders saluted and with a quick about-turn ran off to put themselves at the head of their troops. Captain Steenhower was close behind the General, ready to follow him drawn sword in hand and very conscious that he was carrying out perhaps the only important mission of his dull, monotonous career.

Malet felt calm and self-assured, especially as Hulin did not know him by sight, though it was he who had pointed out Malet as a dangerous enemy of Napoleon and had had him sent to prison four years earlier. To encounter an enemy who does not know your face is a great advantage, and Malet meant to make the most of it, at any rate in the initial stages of the meeting, while at the same time holding himself ready to take direct action if necessary; for this dangerous obstacle had to be eliminated, and in addition there was his own personal hatred for a man he regarded as his persecutor.

Even without the presence of those soldiers under his orders drawn up before the house, nothing could have stopped him at that moment. He advanced firmly towards the entrance, Steenhower still following sword in hand. The General signed to four men to go with them. His decisive manner and soldierly authority sufficed to make the concierge, himself an old soldier, draw aside and in a few strides Malet, the Captain and the four soldiers were at the head of the stairs and outside the door of the General's private apartment.

* * *

Hulin had the habit of staying snugly in bed beside his wife for a little while after waking. After all, to get to headquarters, where he never arrived before nine o'clock, he had only to cross the Place. They were now far off, those days of dawn risings, of charges at the gallop against the enemy, of adventurous *coups de main* to rout an adversary, the days when from one minute to the next a chance bullet could put you out of action. Now he no longer need expose to risk his great six-foot-tall body and the powerful muscles that swelled his uniform; now he had to use his head – that proud head, adorned with sidewhiskers, firmly planted above his braided collar – to keep the enemies of the Empire at bay, ensure order in the capital, and give the distant Napoleon the certainty that all was well at home.

At that moment, reclining on the pillows beside his wife in her nightcap, his appearance was not particularly martial, although the sheets and blankets that formed a mountain on his side of the bed testified to the gigantic proportions of his body.

Malet left the four escorting soldiers on the landing and boldly entered the anteroom of General Hulin's private apartment, followed by Captain Steenhower. ('Tonight I'll have something to tell my wife', thought Steenhower to himself, 'something different from the usual barracks gossip.') To the servant who hurried up to him Malet said that he must speak to his master at once, he had an urgent communication from the Senate.

'At once', he insisted when the servant objected that the General was not yet up, and followed on the man's heels to the bedroom.

It was a huge room like a drawing-room, with a half-hidden alcove in the rear. The servant had barely time to announce the arrival of a General with a message from the Senate before Hulin, leaping from his bed in a nightshirt that made him look even taller and stouter, found himself face to face with an unknown General escorted by an officer with a drawn sword. Through the window came the clatter of armed soldiers. The alcove seemed deserted: Countess Hulin at the unexpected arrival of the two men had hidden her head under the bedclothes.

Malet, without introducing himself or giving Hulin time to recover from his surprise, embarked with assurance on the little speech he had prepared.

'General, the mission I have been entrusted with is a very painful one. The Government has decided to dismiss you and appoint me in your place. Unfortunately it has also given me the task of arresting you and ordering you to hand me your sword and the seal of the First Division.'

Hulin, barefoot and in his nightshirt, in the middle of that great room, seemed for a moment near to tottering. Then he pulled himself together but only managed to utter one bitter comment: 'They've done this to me, me, the Emperor's most loyal soldier?' Malet interrupted icily: 'The Emperor is no more. He has been killed beneath the walls of Moscow. Here is the decree of the Senate establishing the new Government and giving me the orders by virtue of which I am here.'

'A decree of the Senate? But if the Senate had met I should have known it. It's impossible.'

'The Senate met last night and proclaimed the end of the imperial regime. I have all the documents to prove it.'

Hulin hesitated, not knowing what to say : perhaps it was true, and they had kept him in the dark just because he was the Emperor's most faithful follower. Malet, tall though he was, seemed a small man beside that gigantic figure draped in white; yet at that moment it was he who was the dominant one who was gaining the upper hand.

From the alcove came a woman's voice, and above the sheets the nightcapped head of Countess Hulin emerged:

'My dear, the gentleman says he has documents. He will no doubt have the service order for your dismissal and his appointment.'

Hulin braced himself. She was a clever woman, his wife.

'Show me your service order.'

'Certainly, General. If we can go into your study I will show you the order and all the other documents.'

Countess Hulin's voice was heard again: 'Put on your dressing-gown and slippers, you'll catch cold.'

Hulin obeyed this time too and went into the alcove to put on a high-collared velvet dressing-gown and embroidered slippers.

At that decisive moment Malet felt sure of himself, master of every word and gesture. Final success was now within his grasp, he must not hesitate for a second but profit to the uttermost from the confusion that still dominated Hulin and that so far had prevented him from calling for help from the servants, the concierge, and the officers at headquarters nearby.

Wrapped in his dressing-gown, Hulin preceded Malet into the study next door to the bedroom and signed to him to enter. Malet advanced only two paces towards the

General who had gone up to his desk, and drawing a pistol from his belt fired at him, aiming at his head, saying as he did so: 'There you are, that's my order!'

Hulin crashed to the ground like a great tree felled. Steenhower, still on the threshold, gazed at this incredible scene pale to the lips, still clutching his ridiculous sword. Countess Hulin rushed screaming into the study to her husband lying on the ground in a pool of blood. With complete calm Malet let her go in, then left the room closing and locking the door and made for the anteroom, signing to Steenhower to follow him.

The Captain, showing anything but the General's sang-froid, tottered behind him into the anteroom. He had barely the strength to stutter, even then feeling it was a breach of discipline: 'But don't you think, General, that he had the right to ask to see the order?'

Malet felt as if he could move mountains. He answered with a shrug: 'Orders indeed! In a case like this one acts on verbal orders.'

And he went down the stairs. The four soldiers, who had heard the shot from the landing, asked themselves what could have happened but gave up trying to understand: anyway, that day who understood anything? But Steenhower felt faint and before following the General to headquarters on the other side of the Place he went into the concierge's lodge and asked for a glass of something strong.

With a firm step Malet crossed Place Vendôme to go and assume command of the First Division and the Paris Garrison.

The *coup* had succeeded.

Chapter 8

Place Vendôme No. 7

Place Vendôme No. 7 was dreaded more than the plague by the officers of the Paris garrison. It was not just the natural antipathy of all soldiers for the higher commands. The men who sat in those offices in there, holding in their hands the armed forces of the entire capital, wore the uniform of the army, but in reality they were police-spies, clever, experienced, tough police-spies. Their chief was the old *sabreur* Hulin, but his colleagues, though nominally colonels and adjutants, were what the common people would call bloodhounds or, quite simply, copper's narks. They had seen no war service, and from their desks that they had occupied for years they scrutinized the secret life of Parisians, soldiers and civilians alike, and controlled the maintenance of order, manoeuvring gendarmes and dragoons, issuing warrants for arrest, and imprisoning suspects in their fortress of Vincennes, a prison from which escape was difficult.

The career of every officer, even of the highest rank, was virtually in the hands of these police-spies, who in addition had the job of uncovering the activities of all opponents of the Imperial regime. The most greatly feared among them were Colonel Doucet, who, as Chief of the General Staff, bore the title of Adjutant-General, and, even more, his right-hand man, Adjutant Laborde. The latter was a repugnantly ugly man with, it was said, a scandalous private life, but a crafty and implacable police-spy, head of a vast network of spies and informers, who had been a gendarme in youth and for the past fifteen years concerned in military and political police work.

Towards this building Lieutenant Prévost was making

his way, followed by his men, mentally repeating to himself the General's orders. If he did the thing properly and distinguished himself by his zeal and precision in a mission like this, it might well earn him promotion.

Prévost therefore drew up his men before the building (the man on guard at the door paid no attention since he supposed it to be the first squad come for the weekly review of the garrison) and went up to the gateway. From the courtyard two stairways ascended, on the right the main staircase leading to Colonel Doucet's apartment, on the left more humble stairs leading to the mezzanine floor, the offices, and Adjutant Laborde's dwelling. Lieutenant Prévost presented himself without difficulty to Colonel Doucet, who was still at home in his apartment at the top of the main staircase.

He clicked his heels and, taking care to maintain the correct regulation position, held out the letter and documents to the Colonel, who stared at him wondering what this little unknown officer could want.

'M. le colonel, General Lamotte has ordered me to give you these papers which contain instructions for this command.'

General Lamotte? Doucet's astonishment grew as he weighed the papers in his hand. Then he took the letter, unsealed and opened it, and read its contents with ever-increasing amazement. The letter ran:

From the Divisional General Commander in Chief of the armed forces of Paris and the troops of the first military division, to M. Doucet, Brigadier-General, second in command of the General Staff.

General Headquarters, Hôtel de Ville,
October 23, 5 a.m.

M. le Général,

You have been promoted to the rank of Brigadier-General; this promotion is due both to your long service and to the exceptional probity that has always distinguished you during the revolutionary upheavals. Let us hope that the present upheaval may be the last: to this end we shall need the support and aid of all brave soldiers like yourself: I therefore count on you.

I convey to you the decree of the Senate announcing the death of the Emperor and the abolition of the Imperial Government, the order issued by me indicating the generals to be employed in the Division, and my proclamation to the troops. You will please read these documents to your colleagues of the General Staff and your guard and service personnel. This measure is necessary in order to avoid incidents that might arise from ignorance of what has happened.

I am sending a detachment of soldiers to take possession of the person of General Hulin. Though this is a purely precautionary measure I felt you should not be asked to carry out this order, for reasons of tact, in view of the service relations you have hitherto had with this General. It is my intention, however, that you should oppose no obstacle to the execution of this order.

As to M. Laborde, he is so much hated by the military that I judge it prudent to avoid that he should show himself. To prevent unpleasant incidents or worse, you will at once order his domiciliary arrest, placing a sentinel at the door. I will send you General Desnoyers, designated to the office of Chief of the General Staff. This is a provisional appointment, after which you will resume your functions in full.

In the meantime, prepare to carry out the following orders. . . .

There followed two pages of detailed instructions for the occupation of public buildings by detachments of the Paris garrison, the strengthening of guard posts at the city gates, and the establishment of a messenger service. These instructions were followed by the announcement that an order for 100,000 francs for special expenses would be sent shortly.

The letter ended on a note both firm and deferential:

> You will certainly understand, M. le Général, the importance of all the measures I have indicated. I have no doubt they will be carried out with all the prudence and speed they call for, and of which I know you are capable.
>
> I have the honour to salute you.
>
> signed: MALET

Malet! That name sufficed to dismiss any doubts from Doucet's mind. Malet, the old enemy, the old conspirator who had already, four years before, in conjunction with General Servan, fabricated a plot of this kind and had finished up in prison before he could carry it out. And he should be in prison still, should Malet – unless he had escaped and tried again.

Doucet looked out of the corner of his eye at the lieutenant, who was standing at ease awaiting orders: he looked a good lad, pretty harmless, probably an innocent fallen into the trap.

Before acting the Colonel glanced rapidly at the documents that the young officer had brought, examining the seals and signatures rather than the text, and everything became clear: it was a forgery, a clever but obvious forgery. Had he had any remaining doubts Malet's proclamation to the troops would have sufficed to disperse them, a *rechauffé* version of the old Jacobin rhetoric: 'The tyrant has fallen under the blows of the avengers of humanity! . . . They have deserved well of the country and the human race. . . .' And that final cry, the same that had echoed through the Place de la Révolution as the heads fell on the scaffold: '*Vive la nation*!'

At this point Doucet exploded: 'This is pure madness!'

'M. le Colonel, I don't know what to say. I've just carried out an order.'

'But who gave you these papers!'

'I've told you already, M. le Général Lamotte, who led our Company. He should be coming here soon, and then you can hear direct from him. In fact, look, there he is.'

From the window Prévost pointed to Malet, who was crossing the Place. Doucet recognized the thin, self-assured figure at the first glance. That was Lamotte – Malet himself.

'Has he other troops with him under his command?'

'There's my section, and on the other side of the Place the first section of the company under Second-Lieutenant Gomont Saint-Charles, M. le Colonel.'

'Lieutenant, rejoin your detachment. I will talk to the General.'

Prévost went off in confusion: he smelt disaster rather than promotion and was happy to bring that conversation to an end. Better go back to the ranks with the soldiers.

Doucet ran out of his apartment and down into the courtyard, where he made for the left-hand staircase leading to the offices to give the alarm to Laborde. Not an instant's doubt or hesitation entered his shrewd policeman's head – promotion to General cut no ice with this old hand. Doucet was not a man to be taken in by words and documents, however well faked. As he hurried to Laborde's room he had already thought up a plan of action. Malet would have to reckon with the two of them.

* * *

As he approached the headquarters Malet felt assured of success. With Hulin out of the way, Doucet was not the man to rebel against an order that had all the appearance of legality, based on a Senate decree: notoriously attached as he was to his career, he would be quite content to swallow yet another change of regime and emerge with promotion and 100,000 francs in his pocket which needn't be accounted for to anyone. It would suit Doucet down to the ground to get rid of that bad-tempered Laborde: Malet would decide himself later what should become of Laborde, he might either have him promoted or put in prison, according to how he behaved; the main thing for the moment was to get him out of the way. He felt mathematically certain that at the sight of those impeccable orders, those instructions drawn up in such perfect form, the good soldier Doucet would at once react according to the promptings of discipline and blind obedience, just as all the other soldiers had done that morning. What Malet forgot, however, was that the only soldierly thing about Doucet was his uniform: his brain was that of a police-spy, and it was not easy to make him stand to attention and say, 'Yes, sir', if he found his orders unconvincing.

The Place was filling up with people come to see the parade, but the soldiers of the 10th Cohort had chattered to some of those near them, and the news had spread among the crowd, gaining in detail as it went from mouth to mouth. So much so, indeed, that a distinguished-looking gentleman who asked a passer-by what was happening got the reply: 'Nothing serious, citizen. The Emperor is dead and they're restoring the Republic.'

Whereat the gentleman, hearing himself called 'citizen' like twenty years ago in the terrible days of the Revolution when he had only saved his skin by a hair's breadth, hurried on with the thought that it might be high time to leave Paris for a safer refuge.

Malet threaded his way through the knots of people, accompanied by Steenhower who, ashamed of his momentary weakness, was now trying to impress the General by his energy. Just before they reached the headquarters Rateau came up at a great pace, his bag under his arm. With some embarrassment he informed Malet that he had seen General Desnoyers but the General had refused Malet's invitation to join him.

'So much the worse for him,' retorted Malet with a shrug.

'If he won't accept, there are a hundred others ready to come forward and offer themselves for the post. Let us go and instal ourselves at headquarters.'

Lieutenant Prévost did not feel much like running up to report Doucet's reaction and so confined himself to giving Malet a correct military salute from his post at the head of his section. So, thought Malet, everything was going well. Allow half-an-hour to make sure that Doucet would get the instructions carried out, and then he could appear on the balcony to announce to the crowd the death of Napoleon and the advent of the new republican regime.

Malet believed he was thoroughly familiar with the headquarters building. He made straight for the main staircase leading to Doucet's apartment, but an orderly on guard on the landing informed him that the Colonel was in his office, at the top of the other stairs. Malet turned on his heel and made for the stairs on the left, Steenhower and Rateau close behind him.

Halfway up the stairs Malet found himself confronted by the bulldog countenance of the most hated man in Paris, Laborde. Malet barred his way and addressed him in the tone of a superior who would stand no nonsense.

'Why aren't you in your room, M. Laborde? I ordered General Doucet to put you under arrest!'

'To be under arrest in my room I have to cross the courtyard,' answered Laborde quite unruffled and seemingly unsurprised at this encounter.

Malet just gave him a stern look and went on up the stairs. There were guards about and he marched straight into Colonel Doucet's office, Steenhower behind him. Rateau remained on the landing from which the corridor opened leading to the offices.

* * *

Doucet was sitting at his desk and made no movement to rise when he saw Malet enter escorted by a captain of the

National Guard. This undeferential attitude caused Malet to raise his voice and speak curtly and peremptorily.

'As I informed you, you have been promoted to Brigadier-General. I have assumed command of the First Division. I have sent you my orders; see that you carry them out.'

At that point Doucet should have sprung to attention and said: 'Yes, sir.' Instead he answered:

'I obey only the orders of the legal Government. Your orders are issued in the name of a Provisional Government of whose existence I know nothing, and they bear signatures I do not recognize. If it were a case of a legal government I should obey immediately.'

'It was I who signed the orders and I am responsible for them to the higher authorities. Obey or it will be the worse for you!'

Doucet rose and placed both hands on his desk.

'Never,' he answered decisively. 'I will never obey orders of that kind.'

Steenhower was following this exchange, his eyes moving from Doucet to the General, with rising amazement at what he was witnessing – a colonel refusing to obey a general, whatever next! Malet stood motionless before the desk. For a moment he remained silent, seeming to meditate his next step. He had only to give an order to Steenhower, to Rateau standing outside the door, to summon with a cry from the window Prévost and his men and the other section of the company stationed in the Place. He knew that here at headquarters there were hardly any forces available, only a few gendarmes and two or three dragoons who served as messengers. But he seemed undecided. Doucet never took his eyes off him. In a large mirror hanging on the wall behind Malet he could see his every gesture and anticipate any move.

Then Malet appeared to make up his mind. 'Obey!' he cried once more, and in the mirror Doucet saw his right hand move towards a back pocket and glimpsed in his fingers the butt end of a pistol.

He sprang round the desk, seizing Malet's arm and twisted it so sharply that the pistol fell to the ground, at the same time shouting at the top of his voice, 'Laborde, *à moi*!'

Laborde burst into the room. Between them he and Doucet, both of them strong men experienced in operations of this kind, seized Malet and held him tight with his hands behind his back.

Steenhower, completely taken aback, had no idea what to do: the two must have gone mad to treat a general in that way.

'You're making a mistake, you don't know what you're doing,' he exhorted them in tones more imploring than indignant. 'Don't you understand, there's a new government!'

Laborde cut him short, barking out: 'Coward, traitor, be silent!'

Malet seemed quite overcome, as much by unbelief at this check to his plans as by his opponents' strength. Doucet continued to grasp him firmly, while Laborde ran to the door and shouted: 'Dragoons, *à nous*! They're trying to murder the chief!'

Everything must have been arranged beforehand, for only a few seconds elapsed before a subaltern and three dragoons rushed into the office to lend their aid.

Malet still tried to resist:

'Dragoons, the Emperor is dead! There's a new government!'

'It's a lie,' yelled Laborde, trying to shout him down.

'I am the new commander! You're acting illegally and you'll answer for it!'

'Hold your tongue! Gag him!'

A dragoon entered running with a rope in his hand and in no time Malet was bound tightly unable to move with his hands tied behind his back. There was no need of a gag to shut his mouth: he was struck dumb at the incredible spectacle of those men who refused to obey his orders, his instructions, to believe in his impeccable documents – in a word, in him himself.

Steenhower stood motionless, thunderstruck by these happenings too big for him to grasp, with which, unprepared as he was, he felt quite unable to cope. He started when Doucet curtly ordered him to put himself under arrest. Mechanically he answered, 'Yes, sir,' almost glad to be given an order that he could carry out, and to begin with he put back in its scabbard that useless sword he had been grasping for the past hour.

In the midst of this turmoil of dragoons, subalterns and gendarmes, Rateau grasped only one thing: he must escape, escape as soon as possible from this headquarters that was a death-trap. He threw into a corner the bag stuffed with papers which till a minute before had been the symbol of his office as aide-de-camp and tore down the stairs to make off as fast and as far as his legs could carry him from Place Vendôme.

As Rateau fled, a thin man some forty years of age with a priest's collar and three-cornered hat elbowed his way through the crowd, entered the headquarters gateway, and in the midst of the hurly-burly of soldiers made for the offices. He found himself face to face with Adjutant Laborde, who was running towards the gateway. What could this civilian, this odd sort of priest, want in all this confusion?

Abbé Lafon grasped in a flash that something had gone wrong.

'Excuse me, sir, I came to ask for information about a relative of mine with the army in Spain. We've had no news of him for a long time. . . .'

'This is a bad moment. Come back another day – we're all very busy at present.'

The Abbé did not wait to be told twice; with a deferential word of thanks to the officer he made off hurriedly. To judge by his rapid pace it would seem that all trace had disappeared of that sprained ankle he had got jumping over the wall of the Dubuisson clinic, the prison for privileged detainees from which he had fled the night before with General Malet. He went in the direction of the Tuileries, and from that moment no policeman, civil or military, ever succeeded in tracing him.

* * *

The first thing to be done, Doucet reflected, was to prevent the false news of Napoleon's death from spreading and leading opponents of the regime to seize the occasion to rise and attempt to gain control of Paris in conjunction with Malet's accomplices: so far nothing was known about the numbers or names of those accomplices or the extent of the conspiracy. To Doucet's first hurried questions Malet merely responded with a speechless stare. But the plot must be nipped in the bud at once seeing that by good fortune its leader was already in the hands of the authorities. That Malet was the leader seemed clear from those documents of his on Doucet's desk.

From the hubbub of voices from the crowd now thronging the Place and the demeanour of the soldiers he could see from the window, it was clear to Doucet that the Emperor's death was regarded as good news: the voices sounded gay, and an occasional cry could be heard of 'The Empire's finished, the war's finished!', 'Now there'll be peace', 'They'll all come home'. And the soldiers of the National Guard with their little lieutenant seemed to be making common cause with the townspeople and vociferating with them.

Doucet moved towards the balcony, opened the window, and stepped out, raising his arms to call for silence: 'Soldiers, your Emperor is not dead. You have let yourselves be taken in by an absurd story. The man we have arrested is a simple imposter. Judge for yourselves.'

And turning back into the room he dragged Malet by force, bound, on to the balcony – that same balcony from which he was to have announced to Paris the end of Napoleon's regime. Malet did not even look at the crowd, but he heard the cry that rose up from them, a cry he had believed he had stifled for ever: 'Long live the Emperor!'

Now he could not help glancing down at those people who would certainly have acclaimed him with the same warmth if he had presented himself before them with the news that Napoleon was dead in Russia: even the soldiers of the 10th Cohort, even Lieutenant Prévost, stood there open-mouthed acclaiming, like the rest, the Emperor more alive than ever.

* * *

They brought him back into the room and tied him to a chair for greater safety, while Doucet set about taking the situation in hand to make sure that the conspiracy was really snuffed out. Messengers were sent off to the various commands, and others to the Ministries to get news.

In a few minutes Laborde, who had been to Hulin's residence, returned. 'Malet attacked Hulin and shot him. Thank Heaven Hulin isn't dead. He is wounded, and it may be serious, but there's hope of saving him. The doctor is with him now.'

The wound was indeed serious, a bullet in the jaw which had entered so deeply that no doctor ever succeeded in extracting it. So for the rest of his long life the unfortunate old soldier Hulin went about with that projectile in his mouth, which earned him from the Parisians the half-admiring, half-derisive nickname of General Bouff'-la-balle.

Malet, bound to the chair, could not even put his hand in his pocket to get at his watch and find out the time, and he wondered frantically where Lahorie and Guidal could be and what stage they had reached in their missions. He had ordered them both to rejoin him there at headquarters with a detachment of troops when they had carried out his instructions: they might even now be near at hand and arrive to outwit Doucet, Laborde and their four dragoons and set him free. Perhaps all was not yet lost, it might be only a temporary setback, a delay in the time-table of operations.

It must be more or less nine o'clock by now, and the action had begun five hours earlier, at the gates of the Popincourt Barracks, but he and the Abbé Lafon had escaped some four or five hours before that when they jumped over the clinic-prison wall. They had made their way from the Dubuisson clinic in Rue du Faubourg Saint-Antoine to the little house of the Spanish priest in the Passage Saint-Pierre. An extraordinary person, that Abbé Cajamaño, a valuable discovery of Lafon's. He had spent many years in French prisons, dragged by the gendarmes from one town to another as a dangerous foreigner and suspected agent of the Vatican, though he didn't know a word of French; finally he had been set at liberty thanks to the intervention of Lafon, who had even managed through his ecclesiastical acquaintances to get him taken on as sub-deacon in the parish of Saint-Gervais, where they had given him a lodging in the tower. Lafon had thought of Cajamaño when, on meeting Malet as a fellow-prisoner in the clinic, he had realized that here was an ideal companion to prepare with him a *coup* to put an end to Napoleon's tyranny, and they had begun together to work out the plan for the conspiracy. Through Cajamaño they would arrange to rent a quiet, discreet apartment – Cajamaño was deaf and stupid, or perhaps he merely seemed so because apparently he could not understand or speak French, so he would ask no questions and there was no danger of his talking – and use that house as the base of operations for the plot. They would have no accomplices; only the two of them, Lafon and Malet, knew everything, so there was no risk of betrayal. The two fellows whom Lafon had recruited through his friends among the congregations, Corporal Rateau, who was to play the role of adjutant, and

Boutreux, the pseudo-commissioner of police, knew nothing, they were mere nonentities who had been promised a fine career thanks to a *coup d'état,* one of the many such that had happened in France in the past twenty years.

Was it months, days, or only hours ago that, dressed for their parts in the clothes sent by Madame Malet to the Spanish priest's lodging, the General, Adjutant Rateau, and Commissioner Boutreux had emerged from the little house in the Passage Saint-Pierre and set forth in the rain for the Popincourt Barracks?

Lafon did not go with them. As we know, the unfortunate Abbé had hurt his ankle jumping from the clinic wall and he certainly could not arrive with them limping at the gates of barracks and ministries, it would have looked too odd. But they would meet later, when it was all over.

Malet felt he was almost falling asleep with fatigue, kept upright only by the ropes that bound him tightly to the chair. It was simply not possible – it couldn't finish like this. There were the regiments on the march, there were Lahorie and Guidal installed in the Ministries – they would come and free him and everything would start to move again as he had planned. They'd see which of them was right, those policemen who declared Napoleon was alive or he, Malet, who pronounced him dead: it could not be otherwise, for he himself had decreed it.

* * *

Monsieur Pâques, in his capacity of Inspector-General of Police, regarded himself as one of the best informed men in Paris. In particular, his direct chief, Minister Savary, had entrusted him with the supervision of the political detainees and suspects, and he was therefore in the best possible position to know anything new, any item of news great or small, relating to the opponents of the Imperial regime, whether in prison or not.

He was therefore even more ashamed than amazed when, arriving at the Place Vendôme headquarters to organize the transportation of General Guidal from La Force prison to Aix-en-Provence for his trial there, he perceived in Colonel Doucet's room one of the detainees under his charge, General Malet – tied, indeed, to a chair, but a long way from the Dubuisson clinic where he had been confined and where he, Pâques, had seen him with his own eyes only two days before.

Doucet rapidly put him in the picture while continuing to give orders to the messengers: the prisoner, that inveterate conspirator, had escaped and tried to bring down the Government. So far nothing was known about his accomplices or the extent of the plot: it was a waste of time to ask Malet, and there was no time to waste. Since he had been in Pâques' charge Doucet would hand the prisoner over to him: Pâques must guard him well and have him brought in a few hours' time, when the situation would be clearer, to the Ministry of Police so that the Minister himself, the Duke of Rovigo, could interrogate him. In the meantime Doucet himself would go and inform the Minister and get further news. He had already sent a letter to Arch-Chancellor Cambacérès, the head of the Government, informing him of what had happened, so as to set his mind at rest and permit him also to set at rest the fears of Her Majesty the Empress Regent at Saint-Cloud.

Bound to his chair Malet listened to them. For the first time in those five hours he heard mentioned the name of the Empress Regent, a name that signified not only the wife of Napoleon but the mother of Napoleon's son, the little King of Rome, heir to the throne, to whom none of those who had been shown the famous Senate decree appeared to have given a thought as the natural and legitimate successor of Napoleon.

Chapter 9
Out and about in Paris

Malet was saying nothing: it was a waste of time to question him about the conspiracy. This Doucet had already realized, but even if Malet would not talk, the papers spoke for him, his famous documents brought by Lieutenant Prévost and still lying scattered on the desk, and even more the papers found in the bag left behind by Rateau. A careful reading of them sufficed to reconstruct the itinerary of Malet and his accomplices and discover the stages of their plan of action: the various barracks, the La Force prison, the Prefecture of Police, the Ministry of General Police, the Hôtel de Ville, and headquarters command in Place Vendôme. And since Malet's action had been cut short precisely there, at what appeared to be the final objective of the conspirators' assault operation, Doucet cherished the hope verging on certainty that his intervention had been decisive, enabling him to strike at the fountain-head. For Malet, the man sitting bound there before him, was the real head of the conspiracy, and all that remained to do was to lay hands on the accomplices and demolish the work wrought by the conspirators in those few hours. But at the same time orders must continue to go out to the various military corps, and detachments of the Imperial Guard must be summoned to the city so as to create a security apparatus strong enough to prevent or discourage attempts by any other forces whose complicity Malet might have secured. Doucet himself would remain at headquarters to direct operations, while Laborde and Inspector Pâques should go at once on horseback to the Ministry of General Police to make contact with Minister Savary, or to arrest the man who, according to Malet's written orders, might have usurped his functions.

The Police Ministry building at Quai Voltaire was still guarded by the 10th Cohort of the National Guard. Captain Piquerel, in command, at once recognized Adjutant Laborde, and his sudden arrival on horseback with a civilian in tow sufficed to make him feel there was trouble ahead and the only thing to do was to submit to his orders.

'Assemble the company at once in the courtyard!' ordered Laborde dismounting, and in a few brief words he explained to the officers and soldiers that they had been the victims of an imposter, and that the Emperor was not dead at all. Therefore the orders they had received from the pseudo-General were revoked and the Captain was to return at once to barracks with his men.

Officers and men responded to these words with the regulation 'Long live the Emperor!' and Piquerel at once gave the order to return to barracks.

A careful look at these men would have shown that, far from being glad, they seemed downcast and disappointed: if Napoleon was alive, the same old life as before would begin again, with military service and the risk of being sent at any moment to Russia or Spain.

Laborde signed to one of the gendarmes of the Ministry's permanent guard to follow him, and with Pâques he went up the stairs to the Minister's apartment.

* * *

Lahorie had certainly not imagined that his first morning as Minister of Police would have been spent in that way, in solitude and inaction. Except for his useless drive to the Hôtel de Ville he had seen no one but Boccheciampe, who had come about the order for release, and he had had nothing whatever to do. No official had appeared, for no one had a pass, and worse still, Malet had sent no messenger with news about the progress of the plan. Guidal had left him after they had together taken Savary to La Force, and, in the drunken state he was in then, it was doubtful how far he would have got with his mission, which was to arrest Councillor of State Réal, the War Minister, and the Arch-Chancellor.

Lahorie was all alone, sitting at that imposing desk, and he didn't know what to do. He would have liked to send a note to Sophie Hugo to tell her that he had been set free and they could meet soon. He was also anxious to resume contact with Malet since there was no news from him. He took a sheet of paper and began to write: 'My dear Malet, I have arrested the Minister of Police and the Prefect. To be on the safe side I am compelled to. . . .'

He stopped writing at that point for three unknown persons suddenly entered the room—an officer, a civilian, and a genarme.

'What can I do for you?,' asked Lahorie with his customary courtesy.

But the officer pointed a pistol at him and in very different manner shouted to the gendarme: 'Arrest this scoundrel! Search him to make sure he isn't armed. As for you,' he added, turning to Lahorie, 'I warn you, the game is up, it's lasted too long as it is!'

Lahorie stood motionless. He seemed completely thunderstruck. He merely stammered in bewilderment: 'What? Malet was not. . . ?'

His sentence, like his letter, remained unfinished. Other gendarmes entered the room, and Laborde had him taken away to be shut up under strict surveillance in an isolated place. He did not yet know what forces the conspiracy could command or whether accomplices might attempt to set Lahorie free.

On a seat in a corner there still lay some of Savary's clothes, left behind when he had hurriedly dressed a few hours before when they came to arrest him. This fact may have given rise to the subsequent legend that Lahorie had spent the morning trying on the Ministerial uniforms and had even sent for the Minister's tailor to measure him for one.

* * *

At the Ministry Laborde had encountered an important official, Secretary-General Saulnier, who had been keeping himself hidden until he saw how things were going. Laborde asked him to accompany him to La Force prison to set the Minister free. Saulnier eagerly agreed: he would never find another chance like this to get into the good graces of the Minister, who would regard him as his liberator. He ordered a carriage and prepared to follow Laborde. But before going to the prison, where after all the illustrious prisoner could be left a little longer since he was in no danger (Laborde did not yet know about Pasquier and Desmarets), there was a more urgent task to be carried out—to clear up the muddle created by Malet at the Hôtel de Ville and disperse the crowd which, so Laborde had learnt from his couriers, was massing in ever-increasing numbers in Place de Grève to acclaim the new Government. The next port of call must therefore be the Hôtel de Ville.

Commandant Soulier had done everything correctly on this last occasion when he would command the cohort before getting his general's stripes. His men of the National Guard had taken up their rifles and were now standing lined up in ranks in front of the building awaiting the arrival of the members of the new Government. Close by the Commandant, the bugler was ready to sound the command for the troops to stand to attention ready to present arms, a ceremony that Soulier was determined to carry out in the best martial manner.

From the direction of the Seine he saw a carriage approaching, preceded by an officer on horseback, and as he drew nearer he recognized the face of Laborde, that police official who to all the officers of the garrison signified inquiries, punishments, transfers, and close arrests. He had barely time to think: 'That confounded Laborde has managed to get in with the new Government already!' when Laborde dismounted and, disregarding his own inferior rank, curtly informed Soulier that he had allowed himself to be taken in by an imposter, that Napoleon was more alive than ever, and that he should therefore withdraw his troops and return to barracks.

Return to barracks? Admit that he had let himself be tricked? Soulier couldn't swallow that so easily, it stuck in his throat. (Goodbye to his important mission, his promotion to General! and whatever would he say to his wife?) In the end he decided to refuse: since the order had been given him by a General he could not accept a counter-command from a mere officer, even from Garrison Command. It was a question of hierarchy and discipline, and in matters of that kind Soulier knew no compromise: a General had got him out of bed with a temperature and made him march at the head of his troops; a major like Laborde could not cancel by word of mouth the order of a higher-ranking officer.

Laborde was not a man endowed with patience, least of all on such a day. The discussion between the two officers in the entrance to the Hôtel de Ville, in the presence of the troops and only a few paces away from the crowd thronging the Place, created quite a scene, largely because of Laborde, for Soulier confined himself to saying, in reply to Laborde's raucous shouts, that he would withdraw his troops only if the previous order were countermanded in writing by the General who had given it.

'General Lamotte gave me the order: he must countermand it himself, otherwise I shall be committing a serious breach of discipline.'

'Lamotte, indeed! There's no such person as General Lamotte: the man who gave you the order is that traitor

General Malet, who escaped from prison and has just been caught by me. Continue to resist and I'll have you arrested as an accomplice!'

The dispute was interrupted by a courteous and authoritative voice: 'I see there is a difference of opinion between these gentlemen. May I ask the reason?'

It was the Prefect of the Seine, Frochot, who had heard from an official what was going on and had rushed out to see for himself: at times like this it was necessary to keep oneself fully informed and not be taken by surprise if one wanted to be on the right side. Standing aloof from the excited soldiers was a civilian whom he knew, Saulnier, the Secretary-General of the Ministry of Police: a high-up official like him would certainly know what was happening.

'What is going on, my friend? The sad news has been confirmed?'

'What news, M. le Préfet?'

'The death of the Emperor in Russia.

'It was all a mistake. His Majesty is alive. There's not a word of truth in it. The conspirators have been arrested.'

'Thank God!' exclaimed Count Frochot, raising his hands to heaven and turning to embrace Saulnier. Then as further proof of his delight at the good news he embraced Laborde too.

Frochot's eyes glistened and he spoke at the top of his voice to emphasize his rejoicing, but he felt cold drops trickling down his spine and a thought sharper than a dagger penetrated his brain: how can I ever make them forget that even for a moment I was taken in by the conspirators and believed Napoleon dead? If I don't act at once I am lost: I must be the one to tell Paris that the Emperor is alive, I must show myself as the very symbol of loyalty and the man who publicly unmasked the conspirators.

In the eyes of Soulier, Frochot, though a civilian, was somebody of high rank, the kind of personage who until that day he had never had the luck to approach: as Prefect of the Seine he could give Soulier the protection of his authority. Soulier therefore approached him and said diffidently: 'I see, Your Excellency, that we really can believe this good news. If your Excellency will confirm it and give me the order, there is nothing more for me to do here and I will return to barracks with my men.'

Frochot was eager to put an end to this scene and answered hurriedly: 'Return, return, Commandant. I myself will at once inform the people of Paris of the glad news that His Majesty is alive – they will rejoice as we do.'

Laborde intervened curtly, as if to convey that the affair could not end thus in fine words and an exchange of embraces. 'Take your men here back to barracks, and recall the other detachments of your corps that obeyed the conspirators' orders. You will remain in barracks and await instuctions from Garrison Command. You are personally responsible for carrying out this order precisely.'

Soulier appeared to forget that Laborde was a mere major and he a colonel, not to say a general *manqué*, and answered promptly, 'Yes, sir.'

Frochot went up to the first floor, accompanied by Saulnier, to go on to the balcony and give the assembled crowd in the Place the good news that the Emperor was alive and the conspirators had been arrested.

Laborde did not follow him: instead he made a tour of the building, and a glance into the main hall, with its tables, chairs, inkstands, and even paper, sufficed to show that everything had been set ready to receive Malet's imaginary Provisional Government.

From the Place cries of 'Long live the Emperor!' arose as the crowd greeted Frochot's announcement, but Laborde's countenance retained its bulldog expression. 'He had got everything ready for the new Government, that old Frochot. His embraces and speeches to the crowd won't be able to wipe that out', he thought, and the idea lodged in his mind as if he had already written it down in his report on the day's events.

Had he remained in that hall a few minutes longer he would have seen a crowd of ushers and clerks rushing in to clear away everything, tables, chairs and all, with the same speed with which an hour before Frochot had set on foot the preparation of the room as seat of the new republican Government.

* * *

The tribulations of Monsieur Bault, concierge of La Force prison, were not ended with the liberation of Lahorie, Guidal and Boccheciampe and the incredible arrival under arrest of such personages as Savary, Pasquier and Desmarest. Not long after that last event another carriage stopped before the prison gates and yet another personage got out: the Secretary-General of Police, Saulnier. He was accompanied by Laborde, on horseback.

When they began excitedly explaining to him that he had been the victim of a trick, that everything that had been done from dawn onwards must be undone, and that to start with Savary and any other persons shut up by order of Malet must be set free at once, poor Bault at first understood nothing and stammered excuses, then burst into imprecations against his deceivers, and finally seemed completely to lose his head. For an honest gaoler accustomed to the quiet, methodical life of a prison, events of this kind were simply too much: Laborde grasped that he would be wasting time with him. He ordered a warder to take him to his quarters and put him to bed and in the company of another warder went off to see Malet's unfortunate prisoners.

Saulnier stayed close beside him and thus was able to be the first to enter the cell where the Duke of Rovigo was imprisoned and announce to his chief that he was free and the conspiracy had been uncovered.

Savary was overjoyed to find his misfortunes ended in this

way, but while the handclasp he gave his liberator-colleague expressed gratitude, it conveyed even more a plea for complicity, a tacit understanding that 'this will just remain between us two, won't it?' Meanwhile Laborde had ascertained who were the other personages whom Malet had had arrested and had arranged for them to be freed.

Thus the Minister of Police, Savary, the Prefect of Police, Pasquier, and the police-spy Desmarest found themselves at liberty in the entrance-hall of the prison, shaken by the brief adventure they had experienced and anxious to emerge from an affair that, after its dramatic opening, seemed now to be ending on a note of absurdity that might prove even more dangerous for persons of their calibre. All three gladly accepted Saulnier's invitation to get into his carriage, while Laborde, after assuring himself that the whole operation had been carried out successfully, mounted his horse and set off to continue his tour of Paris to undo Malet's work.

The three sat side by side in the carriage, and Saulnier, facing them, told them how Malet's attempt to gain control of Paris had foundered. Each of the three related eagerly, as if by way of excuse, the dangers he had incurred, the threats and bayonets, but it was obvious that the one idea of all of them was to get back behind their desks and somehow blot out the thought that a *coup* engineered by a few hotheads had sufficed to put in prison the chiefs of the French police.

Some movement of troops was to be seen in the streets, and when the carriage crossed Pont-Neuf and approached Quai Voltaire Savary saw with satisfaction that detachments of grenadiers of the Imperial Guard were preparing to go on guard at his Ministry: with soldiers like them one felt safe, unlike that collection of rabble, the National Guard, who had let themselves be duped by the conspirators.

There were already grenadiers on guard in the entrance

of the building, and they stood in rank and presented arms when the Minister left the carriage and walked towards the staircase in the same solemn little ceremony of every day, just as if nothing unusual had occurred that morning. Pasquier and Desmarest refused his offer to send them on in the carriage: a short walk was just what was wanted to settle their nerves.

Savary first reassured his wife, who had barricaded herself in her rooms anxiously awaiting news, and then quickly made for his study. On the desk still lay Lahorie's unfinished letter, and on a chair were the clothes the Minister had left lying there a few hours before. These traces of the recent events were yet another reminder to Savary that the most urgent thing to be done was to draw up an official version of the affair, with the dual object of tranquillising public opinion and informing the Emperor of what had happened in a way not too discreditable to himself, the Minister of Police who had allowed himself to be taken off to prison by a handful of conspirators.

Savary was not simply a soldier; the years spent at Napoleon's side, first as Gendarmerie Commander, then as Chief of Police, had taught him to manipulate words with the same skill that he used to manipulate gendarmes and policemen. He took a sheet of paper from the pile left blank by Lahorie in his few hours of ministerial leisure, and the result was the following text, which can still be admired today as a *chef d'oeuvre* of the art of minimising unpleasant occurrences:

> 'Ex-Generals Malet, Lahorie and Guidal have practised a deception on some National Guards and directed them against the Ministry of General Police, the Prefect of Police, and the military commandant of Paris. They have exercised violence against them, spreading false news of the Emperor's death.
>
> 'These ex-Generals have been arrested and their im-

posture has been unmasked: they will be brought to justice.

'Complete calm reigns in Paris. The three buildings entered by the brigands were the only places to be affected.'

Saulnier could not help admiring this faultless communication drawn up by his superior, and he undertook to have it printed and affixed at once to the walls of the capital, while the text would be distributed throughout the country by heliograph, the ingenious invention of Abbé Chappe which had done such good service in those years in making known to France the Emperor Napoleon's great victories.

Savary now devoted all his energies to investigating the plot and giving orders for the arrest of the accomplices still at liberty, such as Guidal, the two young men who had played the parts of the commissioner and adjutant, Abbé Lafon, and all those who might have aided the conspirators in any way, beginning with Madame Malet, the General's wife, who lived in a small hotel in the Rue de l'Université. All the police forces were mobilized. It was discovered that in the same hotel in which Madame Malet lived there also lodged a real General Lamotte whose name, unknown to him, had been taken by the leader of the conspiracy. Despite his protestations of innocence he too was arrested.

* * *

On leaving La Force Prison Laborde had but one idea: to go as quickly as possible to the Prefecture of Police in hopes of surprising there Malet's accomplice who had installed himself as Baron Pasquier's successor after the latter's arrest. At a brisk trot he rode through the narrow streets of the Marais and the Saint-Antoine district, along the Seine, and so to the Ile de la Cité and rue de Jérusalem.

At the Prefecture of Police, in accordance with Malet's

instructions two companies of the Paris Guard had replaced the detachment of the National Guard, with the strict order to let no one leave or enter unless he had a pass. For this reason, when Laborde dismounted and prepared to enter the building he found his way barred by the Commander of one of the two companies, Lieutenant Beaumont.

He had barely begun to give him orders to return to barracks with his men when the Lieutenant interrupted him curtly: 'If you have orders for me you must show me your pass.'

Laborde still felt seething within him the rage engendered during his recent encounter with Commandant Soulier. He shouted in reply, with that familiar bark that should have been recognizable even to the blockhead before him: 'Me with a pass? Do you dare to ask me for a pass? So you're on the side of the conspirators! I'll have you arrested!'

But the guards gathered around him threateningly, and the sergeant-major who commanded the other company shouted that anyone trying to enter without a pass must be arrested at once.

Laborde's protests and threats were of no avail: Lieutenant Beaumont, feeling he had the support of his men (there were threatening cries of 'They think it's still the Empire!' 'They can't frighten us any more – it's the republic now!', 'They've finished him off, the Little Corporal!') told Laborde firmly that he would be compelled to arrest him and send him under escort to Garrison Command.

'You're mad!' yelled Laborde. 'You're risking your head.'

But Beaumont pointed his sword at his breast and Laborde was forced to follow on foot a picket of soldiers of the Paris Guard who led him foaming with rage to the headquarters in Place Vendôme.

Even had he succeeded in reaching the office of the Prefect of Police, Laborde would not have found Boutreux there: for the past hour since Abbé Lafon's visit the young man had been completely alone and without news, and beginning to feel some alarm had decided to go off. Since he had a pass he had encountered no difficulties at the gate and had simply vanished. By that time he was already far away. He was not quite so worried as he might have been because no one knew his real name: they all, from Pasquier downwards, believed he was called Balancié.

* * *

The agitation among the soldiers of the Paris Guard at the gateway of the Prefecture of Police had not completely subsided when a civilian approached the entrance with measured step.

A guard stopped him and Lieutenant Beaumont, full of importance at having arrested a superior officer, asked him what he wanted.

'To go in,' he replied; 'to go up to my office.'

'Show me your pass or I shall have to turn you away.'

Baron Pasquier was not expecting this sort of welcome on the threshold of his own Prefecture after being set free from prison. He tried to explain with his customary politeness. From the courtyard some men of the National Guard left behind to hand over to the Paris Guard came running up; they recognized at once the Prefect whom they had seen carried off under arrest a few hours earlier.

'It's the old Prefect! He's escaped from prison, arrest him!'

There was a momentary hesitation and Pasquier profited by it to obey his instinct and make off at top speed. He was fifty paces away when the guards started in pursuit, brandishing their rifles, but the Prefect, out of breath, luckily found a shop open and ran in, begging the assistants to bar the door and save him from the madmen outside.

He had landed in a shop where he was well known, Sillan the chemist's, and so he was treated with due respect. While the soldiers banged on the door threatening to break the shop windows the chemist consoled the Prefect with a glass of cordial of his own making, well suited to such cases.

As to the conclusion of this last misadventure of Baron Pasquier's that day, the chronicler finds himself in some uncertainty, having discovered various conflicting versions in the memoirs and books he consulted. According to Pasquier himself and some historians, the siege of the chemist's shop lasted over an hour, ending only when the situation at the Prefecture was clarified and obsequious officials arrived to free their chief from his second imprisonment. On the other hand, according to the story that went around Paris the next day and became the subject of songs and *vaudevilles,* the Prefect made his escape by a back door disguised as a woman, with his head concealed beneath Madame Sillan's red wig, which wig he subsequently forgot to restore to the chemist, who sued him for it.

* * *

Laborde, returning in an inglorious state of arrest to headquarters at Place Vendôme, found there both Colonel Doucet and Colonel Rabbe, commander of the Paris Guard, who had gone there in accordance with the orders signed by General Malet. The good Colonel had discovered that he had let himself be grossly deceived and was striving to to show particular zeal in collaborating with his colleague Doucet to blot out the memories of his stupidity.

He thus became the scapegoat for Laborde's rage. Laborde was, in fact, a personal friend of his, but he found in this involuntary accomplice of Malet's the object on whom to let loose all the pent-up wrath engendered by his ridiculous arrest. To pacify him Rabbe offered to go back with him to the Prefecture of Police to get his subordinate Beaumont to see reason and to clear up the situation.

Beaumont was not so rash as to demand a pass from his corps commander when the latter rode up with Laborde.

He had to believe what he was told and in addition to stand to attention and submit to a tremendous ticking-off from Laborde, ending with the ritual phrase: 'Return to your quarters and put yourself under close arrest.'

The two companies of the Paris Guard which hurriedly assembled to return to barracks were the only military detachments that morning who failed to acclaim the news of Napoleon's survival with the cry of 'Long live the Emperor'.

* * *

Arch-Chancellor Cambacérès was in his bedroom in the Rue Saint-Dominique being shaved when a messenger brought him Doucet's letter informing him of the abortive conspiracy and Malet's arrest. His face was still covered with soap when Councillor Réal entered, who was able to give him more details about the first phase of the conspiracy, the arrest of Savary and Pasquier, than about its failure.

These two important personages, confronted by the news we know, were still not wholly reassured and sent off messengers to get further information, while the Arch-Chancellor had the guard at his residence reinforced.

For more than twenty years Jean-Jacques Régis de Cambacérès, now Duke of Parma and Arch-Chancellor of the French Empire, himself a man of law and order, had lived among *coups d'état,* and from each *coup* had managed to derive profit by showing himself indispensable to the winning faction. This time, however, it was not a case of advancing and gaining fresh honours but of retaining the position he had won, the highest position next to the throne, corresponding to that of Prime Minister, a position that made him Napoleon's man through thick and thin, linked with his fate by a thread now perhaps as slender as the fine interminable thread that linked Paris with the far-off army and the Emperor, in the wastes of Russia. If Napoleon should fall, or even should his authority be impaired or endangered, what would Cambacérès' dukedom be worth, or his grand if slightly absurd title of Arch-Chancellor? If anyone had need to fear and oppose the conspirators, the enemies at home while Napoleon was occupied fighting those abroad, it was he, the head of the Government today, the Second Consul of yesterday, Deputy of the Convention and member of the Committee of Public Safety in the years of the Revolution, the man who had made his way up thanks to difficult times and *coups d'état* and who must now devote himself to defending what he had won.

These thoughts troubled him so much that he did not at once bethink himself of the Empress Regent, but then, fearing that someone else might get in first, he hurriedly sent off a messenger to inform her that there had been an attempted conspiracy which had at once been checked and all was now calm in Paris.

An hour later Cambacérès, his fears set at rest, finding that he could venture forth without risk into the city decided to go in person to reassure the Empress. His servant carefully dressed his hair, arranging the big curls above the ears in the fashion of twenty-five years before, and donning the semi-state uniform prescribed for private audiences with Her Majesty he had his four-horse carriage brought round.

Arrived at Saint-Cloud, he entered the presence of Marie Louise and in a few words supplemented the news he had sent, describing the affair as an attempt carried out by a few brigands who had been promptly arrested by the authorities.

The Empress listened with an air of aloof calm tinged by astonishment: 'I wonder what your brigands could have done to me, the daughter of the Emperor of Austria.'

A lady-in-waiting who was present relates in her memoirs that Cambacérès, annoyed at this display of regal serenity, answered stiffly: 'I am glad to see that Your Majesty takes it so philosophically, but I cannot disguise from you that if

Malet's plans had succeeded the King of Rome would have been put in a foundlings' home.'

It was learnt later that the other august ladies of the Imperial family, Madame Mère, mother of the Emperor, and the ex-Empress Joséphine, learnt of the affair with considerably less indifference than the Empress Regent, who seemed to have forgotten that twenty years earlier the fact of being the Austrian Emperor's daughter had not saved Marie Antoinette from the guillotine.

* * *

The cabby Nicolas Georges had the habit around midday of drinking a couple of glasses of white wine and taking a short rest after a morning spent on his box driving people here and there or, what was worse, on bad days waiting for clients who never came. That day, at the wineshop of Nicolas Tacherat in Rue de la Fonderie everyone had some tale to tell: some had seen the troops go by led by the conspirators, others swore despite the denials that Napoleon was really dead, and yet others knew nothing at all about it but declared they were better informed than anyone else. Georges the cabby too had something to contribute, a comical story that certainly had nothing to do with the conspiracy; indeed it sounded more like some amorous adventure, but an authentic story and really amusing, of the kind that only happens to Paris cabbies.

That morning, he said, waiting in Place du Louvre he had been approached by a young officer who asked to be driven to a certain blind alley in the Marais quarter. They were nearly there and Georges was pulling up his horse when he heard the sound of one of the cab windows being broken from within. He stopped, for they had by now arrived, and before he had time to complain about the broken window his fare jumped out presenting a startling appearance: he had undressed in the cab and must have broken the glass by accident with his sword. Now he was quite literally undressed, without uniform, boots, shako, or even shirt, and just as he was, barefoot in his underpants, was preparing to enter the house to which he had been driven.

He threw the cabby his fare plus a five-franc piece to pay for the broken window, and with his clothes bundled up inside his shirt disappeared into the entrance of the house, a squalid, shabby little place with a dark courtyard beyond. The cabby had got down from his box and had a good stare at the entrance to see where the half-naked young man had gone.

'It's my belief that officer was mad, I mean madly in love and wanted to turn up at his girl's ready undressed so as not to waste a minute. There are some crazy people about, and we cabbies get 'em all.'

On that he had another drink, but as he was about to leave a man came up to him dressed in a cloak with a high collar, on his head one of those tall hats narrower at the top than at the bottom often worn by plain-clothes police, and took him aside.

'Cabman, would you like to earn a bit of money without driving a yard? If so, come and tell your story at the police station near by.'

In this way cabby Georges earned a hundred francs, and the police, who were searching all over Paris for the young man who had played the part of Malet's aide-de-camp, were led to discover the conspirators' secret hide-out, the apartment of the Spanish priest Cajamaño in Passage de Saint-Pierre, in the Marais quarter, not far from the Popincourt Barracks.

The lieutenant in such a hurry to get out of uniform was in fact Rateau, whose one idea now was to be rid of the uniform of which he had been so proud and revert to being Corporal Rateau of the Paris Guard. In order to do this he had to go and fetch his corporal's uniform which he had left in the house of the Spanish priest. He was so panic-stricken that in his blind haste he had idiotically undressed in the carriage and broken the window with his sword, thus attracting the cabby's attention.

Cajamaño might not speak French (all he knew was the slang of the underworld learnt in prison, eked out with a bit of ecclesiastical dog-Latin) but he grasped the situation at a glance. He handed the young man his corporal's uniform and with a gesture conveyed that he would take care of the compromising officer's clothes.

In fact he took good care to destroy every trace of the conspirators' nocturnal meeting: the uniform was burnt in his fireplace together with the papers left behind by the General, and the sword, shako, and epaulets were thrown into the bottom of the well in the courtyard.

Which did not, however, prevent the police who invaded the house a few hours later from finding after a prolonged search the uniform buttons among the ashes; and in the end they emptied the well and found the sword and all the rest as well. So although the priest continued in his peculiar language and with eloquent gestures to protest his innocence, he had all the same to return to one of those French prisons that he knew so well.

Corporal Rateau was mistaken in thinking he had got off scot-free: the corps to which he belonged, the Paris Guard, had participated, if involuntarily, in the conspiracy, and though no one from the detachments of the Guard had actually seen him with Malet, some of Rateau's fellow-guardsmen had seen him flaunting his uniform in the streets of Paris beside the General who led the conspirators. Back in barracks, before he even had a chance to think up some excuse to explain his absence to the subaltern on duty and get off with a light punishment, he found himself the butt of his companions' jeers at his rapid demotion after those few hours as an officer. Consequently the company Commandant, while awaiting higher orders, shoved him at once into the punishment cell, where next morning the gendarmes found him and took him off in handcuffs.

* * *

According to the orders given him by Malet, Guidal should have taken a detachment of the 10th Cohort to arrest those exalted personages, the Minister for War, the Arch-Chancellor, and Councillor of State Réal.

As we have seen, however, he ended by accompanying Lahorie to arrest Savary where, under the influence of wine and his own desire for revenge, he had behaved more like a madman than like the cold, intelligent executant of a meticulous plan such as Malet had prepared.

He was so drunk and crazy with rage that Lahorie had left him at La Force to let off steam against his goalers of a few hours before. He had left the prison after a while, not however to go in search of the detachment of troops allotted to him for the accomplishment of a mission so decisive for the success of the conspiracy, but to continue his peregrinations from inn to inn.

He had finished up in the neighbourhood of Place Vendôme where, despite his sozzled state, it had dawned on him that Malet had run into disaster. Thereupon he regained some degree of lucidity, but for the time being found no better solution than to continue to roam about Paris in search of a possible refuge.

Even in a big city like Paris it can happen that two people wandering about in the same quarter with no definite goal and with the same worries on their minds may run into each other and join forces. Thus it happened that at a certain point Guidal found himself on a crowded pavement face to face with someone who had shared prison with him and should have shared with him the honour of acceding to the new class of leaders if Malet's *coup* had been successful: the Prefect *manqué* of the Seine, Boccheciampe, who was traipsing through the streets with his mythological manuscript under his arm and no idea where to go. This encounter and the exchange of first impressions on the obvious failure of their common enterprise led them to unite in seeking a solution for themselves.

In Boccheciampe's view, the only thing to do was to go back to prison and say: 'We were deceived. We meant no harm. Put us back in our cells and forget the affair.' But for Guidal it was not such a simple matter: for him, however things went, return to prison meant facing an execution squad, either as an accomplice of Malet or on the earlier charge of betrayal to the English. Therefore he must make every possible effort to evade arrest.

He bethought himself of a friend of his from Marseilles, a certain Paban, who was now a shopkeeper but who in the past had been much concerned with politics and was linked with left-wing anti-Bonapartist circles, people like Tallien, all-powerful in the days of Thermidor but now reduced to living as a private citizen and confining his opposition to Napoleon to bitter confidences among friends. Guidal hoped through those same friends to find a safe refuge for himself and Boccheciampe.

It seemed to have been a good idea, for Paban received them warmly and at once set about finding a refuge for them both. After some thought he believed he had hit upon the right solution.

'I can't keep you here – I'm too well known as an opponent of Napoleon, and the police would find you easily. But I've got a good safe friend, a man called Lefèvre, a clerk at the Bourse, who shares my views, but the police don't know about him and it would never enter their heads to look for you with him.'

They followed Paban to the house of this Lefèvre, in the neighbourhood of the Faubourg Poissonnière. He was out, but the servant agreed to let the two in and even to give them something to eat, for they were starving after all their wanderings on foot through the city. Meanwhile Paban was to go to the Bourse and arrange matters with Lefèvre.

What happened next is not very clear. The most likely thing is that Lefèvre, on returning home and taking a good look at the two fugitives whom he had somewhat light-heartedly agreed to conceal, repented and to avoid trouble went straight to the police and denounced them.

Be that as it may, the police descended so promptly upon the house in Faubourg Poissonnière that they found Guidal and Boccheciampe still at table attacking the roast. It was the first and last meal they were to eat at liberty.

The same police also went later to Paban's house. There they found neither him nor his wife, who had both fled, but instead they discovered hidden arms and traces of documents to do with the conspiracy, which Guidal had tried to burn in the fireplace. Paban himself was traced two days later and taken off to prison.

Still at liberty, however, were the young man known as Balancié, otherwise Boutreux, and Abbé Lafon, who remained so invisible that he might never have existed.

* * *

Of all the events of that disturbed day and its abortive conspiracy, the only thing, apart from rumours, of which most Parisians were aware was the unusual movement of troops, detachments on their way to occupy ministries or guard the city gates, a constant commotion of soldiers going hither and thither on foot or on horseback, giving an impression of disorder and chaos like a first rehearsal for a ballet when the dancers have not yet learnt to obey the producer.

At Command headquarters, Doucet and Laborde were completely at sea. Some troops had moved in accordance with their instructions, others had followed orders given by Malet, but for those in command of the detachments all orders were equally valid, since all appeared to emanate from Garrison Command. It was a crazy situation, with no one wanting to admit that he had let himself be tricked or obeyed the conspirators.

Even Laborde and the other officers from the Command could not disentangle the chaos, though they rushed about all day from one detachment to another trying to bring order into the confusion and distinguish between legitimate military obedience and the mechanical execution of faked orders. The worse complication arose from the fact that some detachments which had acted on the basis of orders from Doucet had previously also received similar instructions from Malet, so that legality and imposture became inextricably intermingled.

At last, after innumerable scenes and fruitless attempts at explanation, Laborde, who had exhausted even his powers of rage and invective, decided the best thing was to send all the troops back to barracks – especially since the danger seemed to be at an end. Only the Imperial Guard remained on duty in the city, ready to help the gendarmerie and police in case of need.

At this point, with the conspirators in prison and the troops back in barracks, the scene began to be dominated by a new figure who took the situation in hand, punishing those responsible, whether deceivers or deceived, and revealing the weaknesses of the authorities, actuated by the secret but overriding aim of impressing on everyone, and most of all the distant Emperor, his own stainless personality as the one man who had not let himself become involved in any way in that unhappy and ridiculous adventure.

This new figure, on whom the conclusion of the story will depend, was General Clarke, Duke of Feltre, Minister of War, the man whom the drunken Guidal was to have arrested and who was now preparing the final act of the drama.

Chapter 10
L'Abbaye Prison — 1

Those who have experienced it say there is nothing worse than the first morning's awakening in prison: to find oneself suddenly in the sordid reality of a prison after the brief parenthesis of sleep, the hopes nurtured in dreams extinguished, with the light of dawn filtering through the bars of the darkened window, the straw palliasse, the fetid bucket, and gaoler periodically looking in through the spy-hole in the locked door.

Malet was at least spared that wretched awakening in the cell at L'Abbaye where they had shut him up late at night, at the end of that day that had begun with his victorious march through Paris, only to end so ignominiously in the hands of the military police. He was spared it for two reasons: first, because for the past four years he had never awakened as a free man either at La Force or later at the Dubuisson clinic, a more comfortable prison but nevertheless a place of detention; and secondly, because throughout the hours of night he had not slept at all and so had never lost consciousness of the realities of his present situation.

He had no hopes or illusions left. When questioned by Councillor Réal at the Ministry of Police where they had taken him with his hands still tied behind his back, and surrounded by gendarmes, he had tried to convey that he, Malet, had believed in the authenticity of the Senate decree which, so he said, had been delivered to him at the Dubuisson clinic, and had therefore imagined he was acting legally in accordance with the orders of a new government formed after the news of Napoleon's death.

It was a threadbare story that could not stand up to Réal's most obvious objections, but Malet had stuck to it tenaciously for hours, almost as if he still hoped for some help from outside, perhaps from Lafon's mysterious friends or from the innumerable enemies of Napoleon, those people who that very morning had applauded the news of his death.

From a distance he had seen going down a corridor of the prison the handcuffed figures of Lahorie and Guidal, and he cursed their feebleness that had caused his perfect plan to founder. There was plainly nothing to be hoped from them or from the troops he had put in their charge, but as far as he could make out Lafon was still free and might do something for him.

Moreover, if he had refused to give in to Réal and continued to insist on his own good faith, on his conviction that Napoleon was really dead and there was a new government which had entrusted him with the military command, this was not just a simple expedient, an attempt to get away with it easily. He could not bear to renounce his belief in the truth of the structure he had built up, in which the officers and soldiers who had obeyed him had also believed. It was this that had tormented him throughout the long sleepless night on his wretched palliasse: the idea that a mere grain of dust, the petty brain of a police-spy like Doucet dressed up as an officer, had sufficed to throw out of gear the perfect, powerful mechanism that he, Malet, had constructed and made to function.

Réal had not learnt much from his questioning: Malet denied having had any accomplices. Though his own good faith might be in doubt, there could be no question about that of his followers, from the two Generals he had freed from prison to the various army officers who had believed they were obeying legitimate orders.

Réal, whom the Minister of War, Clarke, had entrusted with the conduct of the inquiry, was well aware of the authority accruing to him as one of the few police chiefs to emerge unspotted from that adventure which could seriously affect the future of those who had let themselves become involved in it. This reassuring conviction as to his own career spurred on his zeal and made superfluous General Clarke's recommendation to 'act with inflexible severity and with the utmost speed'. Obviously, the uppermost thought for each one of these ministers and officials, whether implicated in spite of themselves like Savary, Pasquier, and Frochot or emerging blameless like Clarke, Réal, or the Arch-Chancellor Cambacérès, was that Napoleon would have to know the facts once the curtain had come down on the conspiracy and its authors.

Notwithstanding his zeal and his consummate ability, from that first interrogation Réal failed to learn much more about Malet's plan than was already common knowledge. In the end he gave up and sent Malet off to prison without more ado.

For the first time in that interminable day that had begun before dawn, the man who for a few hours had held Paris in the hollow of his hand could now take some nourishment. Before shutting him in his cell they gave him a plate of soup and a slice of meat in the prison canteen. But while they gave him a spoon for the soup, so dangerous a prisoner was not to be entrusted with a knife. Malet was protesting to the warder about such treatment when an official came in who that morning had distinguished himself in the operations for restoring order – Secretary-General Saulnier. Probably he had been sent by his chief, Minister Savary, to see what progress was being made in the inquiry that his colleague and adversary, the Minister of War, had taken out of his hands.

The astute Saulnier seized the opportunity afforded by the little incident of the knife to start a conversation with Malet and try to get him to talk in what might euphemistically be termed a slightly more convivial atmosphere. He had him given a knife, sat down beside him, and from the ensuing conversation managed to discover what Malet's plans would have been had the *coup* succeeded.

According to the prisoner, the attitude of the troops who had obeyed his orders that morning was clear proof of the widespread feeling against Napoleon in the army. If the cowardice and inefficiency of Lahorie and Guidal had not ruined the victorious progress of his action, Malet would have easily succeeded in gathering around himself the numerous dissatisfied officers and the troops who wanted to see an end to war. Thus he could quickly have got together an army capable of encountering Napoleon, who on learning of the events would certainly have left Russia and the Grande Armée at once and made for Paris. They would have stopped him halfway, on the Rhine, at Mainz, and shot him without trial, thus putting an end to the whole bloodstained imperial venture. Any attempted reprisals by the imperialists would have been quelled and then, with his army reassembled round Paris, Malet would have signed peace with the allies and at last sent on leave the soldiers who had been absent from home all those years. In this way he would have earned the gratitude of France and of mankind.

* * *

Mainz was the place where a volley of rifle-fire should have ended the career of the man who had cut short the Revolution to make himself an empire, there on the Rhine where he, Claude-François Malet, had begun his career as a soldier of the Revolution. Memories of that far-off time mingled in his head with his present bitter ruminations over the decisive day he had just lived through. In the darkness of his cell, lying on the straw bed where he had thrown himself still clothed, the years vanished, their events intermingled, and his disappointed ambitions became identified with his lost revolutionary hopes. Before all that, before the Jacobin war, his youth as a son of the lesser nobility had been spent at Dôle, in the Jura, where he was born, and there had been a time when he had worn the uniform of the King's musketeers, in Paris, and he had then been proud that his provincial name was preceded by an aristocratic 'de' which enabled him to enrol in that crack corps.

In the army of the Rhine, at Strasbourg, he had sung for the first time a song that was to become famous as the 'Marseillaise' : a cousin of his from the same province, Rouget de Lisle, had written it, and that song had accompanied them on their marches against their enemy, the Austrians. He was not the only one of noble birth among those republican officers : their leader was Prince Charles of Hesse, and among the Generals were Luckner and Beauharnais and the Lameth brothers, all born with a 'de' to their names but now at the head of the victorious battalions of Republican France; while in Paris, in the former Place Louis XV, the heads rolled of those incorrigible aristocrats who refused to march with the times and recognize the equality of men.

With the army of the Rhine he went to war, and war offered the great opportunity for a soldier to rise rapidly in his career : within a few years he was promoted to the command first of a battalion, then of a brigade, becoming a Colonel. If the Republic continued to conduct victorious wars against its enemies he would go far. But then Malet discovered that his real enemies were not the men he fought against in battle who wore a different uniform from himself. His were enemies who spoke his own language and stayed at home behind their desks plotting his disgrace and ruin while he thought only of the war : at that time they were known as Committees of Safety, tomorrow they would be called prefects, director-generals and ministers.

He felt them all around his bedside in the cold darkness of the cell watching him lying there beaten and crushed, the men who had forced him to turn his military career into a sort of interminable private war in which today he won and secured a command, tomorrow they, his enemies, were victorious and he found himself suspended from service and put on the retired list if not actually in prison.

It began while he was on the Rhine and they became suspicious of him because of his noble birth and his past as a King's Musketeer. So, goodbye to the army, goodbye to the victorious campaigns to the sound of the 'Marseillaise'. He went home to Dôle to eat out his heart and watch the green waters of the Doubs flow beneath the arches of the stone bridges. Then, after five months, they ceased to regard him as suspect and sent him back to fight in the name of the Republic.

So the seesaw went on : eighteen months later they sent him home again, shelved because of army cuts. This time he went not to the provinces but straight to Paris, the only place where with brains, shrewdness and push it was possible to make one's way even in disgrace. Malet tried to see which way the wind was blowing, to find some support to get out of his wretched position of semi-retirement and secure a new command.

In the army now the only talk was of the new man, that Corsican ex-artillery Captain who had made a name for himself by shooting down the royalist conspirators of the 13th Vendémiaire on the steps of Saint Roch and whom the Convention had rewarded by making him commander of the army in Italy. He himself had never known that General of the lightning career, that Bonaparte. Malet had certainly not been among the small group of men, nearly all of humble birth, ex-sergeants or dragoons, who had rushed to follow the fortunes of the new man, relying on the special protection he enjoyed as husband of the recent mistress of the omnipotent Barras.

What a confusion of names, dates, and faces passed through his head as he tossed and turned on the palliasse. This favourite, or former favourite, of Barras', this wife a good deal older than the youthful General, destined within ten years to become Empress of the French, was none other than Madame Joséphine de Beauharnais, formerly married to a companion-in-arms of his on the Rhine, General Alexandre de Beauharnais, guillotined in '94. Through her he might have become friendly with the new head of the army in Italy, standing out from among the rabble of ex-N.C.O.s who surrounded him and were worth so much less than himself. Who knows what he might have become by now, certainly a duke or a marshal like them. But no, he himself had refused to mix among such people, choosing instead to remain faithful to the republican principles he had adopted with so much enthusiasm. That thought still sustained him now, helping him to withstand the nightmares of his sleepless vigil: he had lost, but he had refused to sell his ideals as others had done for ambition and wealth.

His past seemed like a seesaw, up and down, alternating between promotion and disaster. Now his mind went back to another occasion. His labours in Paris had borne fruit: a decree of the Minister of War recalled him to service with the rank of Adjutant-General and sent him to the headquarters of the sixth division, at Besançon, in the Jura, not far from his native place. Now he no longer seemed to be caught up in the swing of a seesaw but in the gyrations of a merry-go-round, a merry-go-round of faces set above high embroidered uniform-collars, faces now smiling and helpful to him, now viewing him with hatred and working to destroy him. That face there, adorned with thick sidewhiskers, was Clarke: now he was hostile to him and kept him a prisoner in that cell, but then he was his friend, and indeed it was Clarke, already powerful at the War Ministry, who had procured the decree that had brought him back into active service. At Besançon, whether it was his native air or the friends he found there, dissatisfied like himself about the way things were going and about the Government, that Directorate that seemed increasingly to forget its revolutionary origins and veer towards reaction and opposition to those still loyal to its Jacobin past – whatever the reason, everything seemed to draw him towards politics, into the struggles and intrigues that seemed so much more exciting than the quiet life of garrison duty and office files that suffocated his ambitions.

His military duties left him plenty of free time and he became more and more involved with the opponents of the regime who, as was fashionable at the time, formed secret societies with neo-classical names, again following the fashion for the neo-classical in furnishings, art and dress. Their own particular provincial freemasonry was called the Philadelphians' Society. Malet took the name of Leonidas, while his orderly was called Philopemene. He was elected a deputy with the aid of opposition votes, but naturally his enemies caused the Government to intervene and the election was annulled.

Malet continued his private war with the authorities whom in his official capacity he was supposed to be representing. There followed denuciations, memoranda, disputes, and more rockets from the Ministry.

While General Bonaparte and his army advanced in Egypt in the footsteps of Alexander the Great, and under the shadow of the Pyramids the legend of the hero Napoleon was born and gained strength, Malet was removed from the Jura, where he was regarded as dangerous, and sent to another military command, to Grenoble.

It might have been worse, indeed that set-back seemed to mark the opening of a new era in which a breath of martial air dissipated the miasma of petty provincial intrigues and garrison officialdom. In Italy, with Napoleon far away, the war had started up again; things were going badly there after the defeat of Novi, and the new commander, Championnet, needed more men and generals. Malet, at Grenoble, was available: he had found fresh sources of support (there were still a good many in the army who like him cherished links with the Revolution, and possibly the Philadelphians also had a powerful faction in Paris) and in view of the urgent situation he was promoted Brigadier-General and sent to Savoy. It fell to him to cross the Little St Bernard and be the first to enter Aosta. Now the only obstacle between him and Piedmont was the fortress of Bard, a sinister stronghold that seemed to seal off the Val d'Aosta but which in the end proved an illusory defence.

Nevertheless General Malet's Italian campaign came to an end at Bard: the swing of his fortunes descended once more, and for reasons which remained obscure even to himself he was suddenly removed from the command, replaced by a colleague, and sent back to France. He was, however, now a General, and he was posted to the second reserve army quartered at Dijon under the command of Brune.

It was perhaps from that time in Dijon that dated Malet's profound hatred for the security officer Desmarest, the inspector-general whom that same morning he had made a point of eliminating by shutting him up in La Force. There were no witnesses to that far-off conversation in Dijon between him and Desmarest, indeed it might never have happened. But it needed only the arrival of Desmarest in Dijon, sent by his chief Fouché, for a vague plan of the Philadelphians there, in which 'Leonidas' and his aide 'Philopemene' were certainly involved, to be nipped in the bud before it could come to anything. Bonaparte had come back from Egypt, and a month after his return, on the 18th Brumaire 1799, he abolished the Dictorate and proclaimed himself First Consul, thus destroying what was left of the republican regime. Six months later General Bonaparte, who was preparing to reconquer Italy, was coming to Dijon to inspect Brune's army. What more favourable opportunity could offer for the true republicans (and what stauncher republicans than the Philadelphians?) to get rid of that man so dangerous to freedom, to prevent him from consolidating his personal power? What had Desmarest found out? What had Fouché's envoy and the republican General, the Philadelphians' 'Leonidas', said to each other? Malet never spoke or wrote a word about it, nor did Desmarest. Bonaparte inspected Brune's army, set out for Italy, and that was all.

It is not even known whether the young conqueror of the Pyramids, now master of France and preparing to be master of Europe, and the obstinately republican soldier ever met, saw, or spoke to each other that day at Dijon. But one thing is certain: Malet was convinced that that man, whom the French already greeted as their saviour destined to restore the country to its past greatness, was in fact the gravedigger of the revolution and of freedom. There were henceforth two armies in France, two different brands of soldier: on the one hand the republicans, *sans-culottes,* or former aristocrats who had created an army from nothing, conquered at Valmy, and with their drums and bayonets had spread the call of revolution throughout Europe; and on the other the new group of soldiers gathered around the man of destiny, basking in the glory of the campaigns in Italy and Egypt, unscrupulous *arrivistes* ready for anything to enrich themselves and advance their careers, while at the same time their leader assumed the pose of an oriental sultan, protector of the arts and sciences.

Malet now had but one idea: if France and the Revolution were to be saved, the enemy to be struck down was General Bonaparte, Napoleon, as the people with dangerous simplification had begun to call him.

* * *

Twelve years had gone by since then, since the days when Bonaparte had begun to transform himself from an ordinary mortal into a legend and, having reconquered Italy at Marengo, was on the way to becoming Consul for Life, the first step to the Monarchy.

Malet, on the other hand, was still a Brigadier-General, with no Italian laurels, no lightning career, shifted about from one French garrison to another, today Montpellier, tomorrow Bordeaux, the next day Angoulême, an anonymous pawn moved on the chessboard of the military bureaucracy by the indifferent hand of a minister or mere official. They never asked him what he thought of these moves, what sacrifice they represented for him and his family. But had a pawn like him a family – a General who existed only in so far as his name figured in the army list? Yes, he had a family, a wife and son, and all he had to provide for them was his meagre pay as a Brigadier-General on home service, with no extra allowance for foreign service, or those other allowances, not strictly defined but quite substantial, which those 'others' had managed to secure for themselves in the conquered countries – the brilliant Generals around the First Consul who followed the example of his brothers and brothers-in-law in filling their pockets. Their leader, Bonaparte, shut his eyes to these perquisitions: in enriching themselves and purchasing fine houses and estates his companions caused their origins to be forgotten, became respectable, and he had need of respectable people about him.

To Malet each of those moves meant not only a blow to his pride but a whole series of problems to be solved, paying off old debts and contracting new ones, establishing himself in new surroundings, with his chin held high, trying to maintain the position due to his rank, and withstanding the petty tyrannies of the civil authorities, the direct emanation of the First Consul.

His private war continued, in the office, at headquarters, in drawing-rooms, in struggles with prefects and mayors. But at home he was at peace – the incredible, wonderful peace that was his through having married the best, the tenderest and most loving of wives, who stood by him, helped and encouraged him, and could always find a way out when lack of funds made it difficult to keep up the necessary appearances, the very opposite of those wives who in such a situation merely reproach their husbands for their ineptitude and inability to make themselves felt.

Now that the picture of his wife, of Denise, had come into his mind, the troubles that assailed him, the faces of enemies crowding in the darkness of his cell, vanished and dissolved. But far from finding peace, he plunged into a depth of anguish untempered by rage or hate.

Their son was with good friends, but where was Denise, what might she now be suffering at that moment through his fault? She must certainly have been arrested too and put in prison: indeed Réal had said as much when questioning him, trying to trap him by challenging him with confessions attributed to Denise, but Denise had not spoken, he was sure of that, even though she knew everything and was indeed his sole accomplice besides Lafon. Denise knew how a good wife should conduct herself, she came like him from an old family of the provincial aristocracy, educated by nuns, and if she had always supported him in his political ideas even when she did not share them, it was simply because she knew it was her duty, a proof of the love that united her to him ever since at seventeen, and against her parents' wishes, she had insisted on marrying him, a penniless ex-officer of musketeers twice her age.

She had had little satisfaction, poor Denise, from his laborious and chequered military career. She had shared its bitterness, restrictions and disappointments. Looking back over those years between the Consulate and Napoleon's accession to the imperial throne (Malet had set his teeth and adhered to the Empire, in a letter seemingly inspired by eloquent and dignified patriotism) he recalled, alternating with periods of territorial commands troubled by everlasting disputes with the civil authorities, long months of waiting, with the constant fear of finding himself out of the army and without his officer's pay, his only means of livelihood.

While Napoleon's armies ranged over Europe, conquering at Ulm and Austerlitz, and the sergeants of yesterday became dukes and marshals, the three of them, he, Denise and their little son, lived in Paris in a small apartment in Rue Taranne, waiting for the result of his requests and supplications to be taken back into active service and so be sure of his regular pay.

Then the seesaw swung upwards again: once more there was need of troops and generals to command them; as in Championnet's day, his salvation came through an appointment to command a brigade in Italy. It was not a front-line unit, but consisted of a battalion of customs officers and a negro regiment from San Domingo, one of the first formations of coloured troops in the French army. Later on he was given other troops, reserves of Corsican legionaries and Italian dragoons. With this heterogeneous collection, while Masséna was fighting the Austrians, he was allocated to a quiet garrison command in the neighbourhood of Verona, a post behind the lines where troops were trained.

But the seesaw rose higher: this time Malet's fortunes seemed to coincide with those of Napoleon. The Bourbons were turned out of Naples, and Napoleon's brother Joseph went to occupy their throne; in Rome relations with the Holy See went from bad to worse. Therefore the French troops extended their occupation to the whole peninsula, and even a General like Malet came in useful, first in a subordinate position and then as commander of the division on the Mediterranean coast stationed between Rome and Civitavecchia.

Pay for officers and troops was slow to arrive, but they were living in a conquered country where it was possible to manage. The civilian population had to provide alike for Fra Diavolo's brigands in the countryside and for the French in the towns, and the officers were the cleverest of all to profit from the situation.

In his apartment in Palazzo Rinuccini, on the Corso, Malet for a brief time forgot his hatred of the tyrant: he adapted himself to his colleagues' habits and savoured the advantages of being an important person in an occupied country. Opportunities were not lacking: sea-traders were ready to pay large sums if the coastguards closed an eye to the movement of ships violating the anti-British Continental blockade, and keepers of gaming-houses offered a percentage of their gains for the permission to open cardrooms where *zecchinetta* or faro were played. Bribery and pillage; they all did it, generals and colonels alike, and more than all the others Marshal Masséna. *La madre magna, la fija se gratta* (the mother itches, the daughter scratches herself), said the lampoonist Pasquino, giving his own translation of the inscription beneath the statue of France erected in Rome, which said in fine Latin characters, *Matri magnae, filia grata* (A grateful daughter to a great mother).

He would soon be able to send for Denise to come to Palazzo Rinuccini and enjoy for the first time the advantages of being a General's wife; privations were over, and a military career, even without glory, had its compensations. But how long would the upswing of the seesaw last? As in France he had quarrelled with the prefects, so here all too soon he quarrelled with the French Ambassador to the Holy See, and his dealings with the traders of the port of Fiumicino and the gaming-house keepers of Terni, Narni, Albano, and even Rome were discovered by that diplomat, now a personal enemy on grounds of competition, and denounced to the Viceroy of Italy, Eugène de Beauharnais.

Denise would not after all leave the Paris apartment (now in Rue des Saints-Pères) for the Palazzo in Rome. What was permissible on a much greater scale for 'them', the officers of Napoleon's clique, was in his own case, as a republican serving the Empire against his will, reprimanded as a shameful crime without precedent. He was hauled up before the Viceroy in Milan, deprived of his command, and sent back to France pending inquiries.

The seesaw had never swung lower: after a year and a half on service in Italy he was back in Paris with the threat of being sent to prison or at the least discharged with the minimum pension. Denise resumed her role of comforter, Malet his role of opponent of the government.

* * *

It did not take him long to re-establish contacts with his old friends the Philadelphians. They were people from his own region, the Jura, old republicans who lived as best they could, consoling themselves for the political difficulties of the times by speaking ill of Napoleon and seeking ways to overthrow him and restore freedom.

Among them were men like Lamare, an ex-priest and later a leading republican, who now kept a private school, or Demaillot, an actor and author, who enjoyed a certain notoriety for a play of his where the chief character was the fishwife Madame Angot, made famous nearly a century later in an operetta. They included an anarchist agitator, Rigomer Bazin, former adherents of the Convention and old accomplices of Babeuf, and a landowner named Corneille who wrote poetry a good deal worse than his celebrated namesake.

All these people lived in Paris, and their reunions, which took place mostly at Lamare's school, had but one aim, to carry on the struggle against Napoleon and bring together all the forces of opposition, so that on the tyrant's death, hastened possibly by assassination, the republican regime should be re-established with no question of imperial heredity or Bourbon restoration.

The Jura Philadelphians were not the only ones to speculate at that time on what would happen when Napoleon died: others too, more important than them, considered the problem, people in official positions, senators, high officers of the state. Without betraying the Emperor to whom they had sworn loyalty, they asked themselves what would happen if in one of the countless battles in which he exposed his life a bullet were to hit him. He had no sons by the Empress Josephine, and none of his brothers seemed worthy to succeed him. There was a danger that the Bourbons might profit by the situation, and none of them, Bonapartists today but still sons of the Revolution, wanted that.

These discussions among senators and officials, sufficiently frequent, anxious and circumspect to give them the air of conspirators' meetings, were naturally common knowledge with Fouché, the Minister of Police, and he let them alone. He let them alone because he shared their anxieties and fears. Who, indeed, had more reason to fear a return of the Bourbons than he, who had on his conscience the slaughter of royalists and moderates at Lyons at the time of the Convention, and who had voted for the death of Louis XVI?

Fouché also knew something more. He knew that another person was speculating in the same way but more concretely and dangerously – General Servan, Minister for War in the days of the Girondins and now influential among the republican opposition. He also knew that between the anxious senators and the republican General some contact had been established and a common plan of action might be in preparation.

Fouché watched and did not intervene, not even when it seemed that the moment had come for Servan and his friends to act: the campaign in East Prussia and Poland had driven Napoleon too far from France, to the borders of Russia, and the battle of Eylau seemed more like a half-defeat than a victory. The question of the succession was becoming more real, and the links grew closer between Servan and the anxious senators, the so-called 'liberals' in the Senate. Then the victory of Friedland and the peace of Tilsit removed the senators' anxieties and Servan's hopes of an opportunity to act. But he continued to plot and plan until his unexpected death in May 1808, ten months after the peace of Tilsit, when Napoleon was already involved in another war, this time in Spain.

Servan's friends looked round in search of another leader, a republican general who would be prepared to take his place at the head of the conspiracy.

No one knew that Malet was under a charge of peculation committed in Italy; they all supposed him to be in disgrace, the victim of his obstinate attachment to republican ideals. He seemed to all of them the very man to succeed Servan.

Such a position, though it involved serious risks, attracted Malet both because it assuaged his oft-wounded pride and also because he feared the imminent decision of the commission of inquiry, and the only alternative to prison or dishonourable discharge from the army seemed to lie in a victorious conspiracy. From that moment the hitherto nebulous conspiracy, or rather the two-fold conspiracy, that of the 'liberal' senators and that of the Philadelphians, became Malet's own conspiracy, linked with an idea that had gradually been developing in his mind during the months of anxious wating for the commission of inquiry's sentence.

* * *

As he looked back now, in his cell at L'Abbaye, to those days, it seemed impossible that four years had passed since then. He seemed to be enclosed within a unity of time, as in a classical tragedy, in which those events represented the first act and present events the last, or perhaps only the last but one.

Unity of time and, even more, unity of thought: today, even after all those years in prison, after those two resounding failures, far from renouncing his original idea, his point of departure, he believed more firmly than ever in that discovery. There was no need to destroy the Empire in order to remove it, for the Empire did not exist, had never existed: all that existed was the physical person of the Emperor, of Napoleon – the rest was a fictitious construction, made up of ambitions and greed, based on and held together by decrees, senatorial ordinances, and stamped documents. Were the Emperor to disappear or be said to have disappeared or even merely been dethroned, the same materials that had served to build the Empire – decrees, senatorial ordinances, and stamped documents – would suffice to destroy it and put in its place another edifice, more solid and lasting because it would seek support in the will of the people, the desire for peace and the abandonment of conquests.

This had always been his idea ever since he was put at the head of the conspiracy in 1808: it was no good wasting time on an attempt to destroy Napoleon physically, merely adding another to the series of unsuccessful attacks on his life. It was enough to profit by his remoteness from Paris, the physical impossibility of his intervention for several days, to destroy the imperial edifice of laws and decrees by means of other laws and decrees which would appear formally valid and would allow the conspirators to assume power on a substantial basis before Napoleon could react.

The problem was therefore twofold: to assemble an apparently unquestionable legislative machinery, and to coordinate the timing perfectly. No one, Malet felt, could be better qualified than himself for these tasks: he was completely conversant with bureaucratic forms and parlance, both military and civilian; and as an expert in logistics and army organization he was in a position to calculate exactly how long it would take for news to reach Napoleon on the Spanish borders, and for him to assemble sufficient troops to move to reconquer the capital. It would then be a question of calculating how strong a position the conspirators would meantime have managed to achieve in the country, and taking the necessary measures to make it effective.

Napoleon was at Marrac, near Bayonne, close to the

Spanish frontier: there was no heliographic connection between Paris and the Pyrenees. News of the conspiracy would have to be sent from the capital by means of couriers on horseback, which would take at least two days riding day and night. A further two days would be needed to bring back Napoleon's orders for dealing with the conspirators, and a good deal longer for the Emperor to put himself at the head of an army corps and move on Paris to regain the upper hand. Therefore the conspirators could count on at least four days in which to seize power, destroy the Napoleonic Government's ability to act, and prepare to hold out against Napoleon himself. The plan seemed feasible, especially since two other factors could be reckoned with: insurrection by a people weary of conscription and wars, and intervention by outside enemies, the allies, to put an end to Napoleon's domination of Europe.

So they must all set to work to carry out the first part of the programme, the preparation of the false decrees and laws necessary for the destruction of the paper edifice that was the empire.

What sort of government should it be? Better to say nothing about a republic for the present, so as not to alarm those whom that word reminded of the years of the Terror. It would be called a provisional government, a dictatorship, with important names that would satisfy everyone, and among them his own, Malet, as Minister of War, promoted at last by his own hand to be Divisional General. A seal would be needed to give an appearance of legality to those papers; he must get it cut, and to be on the safe side he would order the engraver to make a stamp with the obscure word DIOTATURE. A bit of filing would suffice to transform the 'O' into a 'C' and thus provide the dictatorship with the necessary chrism. Meanwhile, in preparation for the rifles they would find in the Ecole Militaire, they bought daggers, 1,200 daggers: the classic weapon to destroy a tyrant.

There were many accomplices, drawn from different social ranks: besides the Philadelphians and those who maintained contact with the senators, there were two former generals dismissed from the army, as he himself might also be as a result of the commission of inquiry.

Too many accomplices, in fact. Someone talked, perhaps Demaillot, who had a tongue as long as his theatrical heroine, the fishwife Madame Angot, or perhaps one of the ex-generals confided in a colleague turned out of the army like himself.

Anyway, that last was the one who warned the police to win merit for himself, but he was shrewd enough not to go to Minister Fouché, who probably once again knew all about it and was letting it ride, but to the Prefect of Police, Dubois, an enemy of Fouché and anxious to show himself in a good light with the Emperor.

Dubois took action, put them all in prison, sent a report to the Emperor, and only then informed his Minister.

Malet for the first time in his life heard the sound of the key turning in the lock behind him and knew what it was to be in prison. So began the long monologue that was still going on that night, four and a half years later.

Chapter 11

L'Abbaye Prison — 2

Regrets for his military career or the conspiracy, both such failures, were not the burden of the monologue initiated then in a cell of La Force Prison and prolonged now in greater anguish and hopelessness into that first night in a cell at L'Abbaye.

Then, as now, he regretted nothing, nor did he accuse himself of having gambled his life on a wrong card and a cause lost in advance. The dominating idea in his mind was the same then as now: Napoleon must be eliminated to save France, or rather, to secure that salvation it sufficed to convince everyone that Napoleon had ceased physically to exist. The events of that morning showed that he was right, that the empire was so closely linked with the person of Napoleon that it could not survive his death or even the mere news of his death, since it itself had no real political, administrative, or military existence, no life of its own.

Why, then, had his success lasted only those few hours, why had his 'truth', accepted unhesitatingly by everyone, at a certain point been rejected, refuted, destroyed? Was he to blame, had he made mistakes or neglected some detail in the careful, meticulous preparation of his plan which he believed had taken account of all possible factors, both practical and psychological? Was it the fault of his accomplices, too many, too foolish and talkative the first time, so few the second time, the bare minimum needed, but they too had proved incapable of carrying out to the end the tasks assigned to them?

Over the years, for this man of action confined in a cell,

to act had meant to think, invent, build up in his mind piece by piece the imaginary facts that in the future would transform into reality that elementary, explosive idea of his which could overthrow at a breath the whole Napoleonic edifice.

His thoughts and his imaginings dominated his existence, and when after an initial period of segregation he was allowed once more to see his fellow-conspirators, also prisoners in La Force, he began again to plot, make plans, and seek contact with those who had eluded Dubois' police.

Outside the prison there was Denise to act for him, try to help him, mitigate his sufferings and seek for any means of saving him. In those days he learnt really to know her, to discover the energy and capacity for action in her which till then had found expression in complete devotion and a loving acceptance of the difficult existence she had always known at his side and which had become precarious now that he was a prisoner. There was in her a humble dignity coupled with stubborn obstinacy which enabled her to petition those in power without humiliating herself, a natural nobility unobscured by poverty which allowed her to turn to her husband's enemies, to those who desired his downfall, and ask them to intervene on his behalf.

She wrote letters of appeal and petitions, presented memoranda, requested audiences, and undiscouraged by refusal faced long hours of waiting in antechambers, trying to profit from the rivalries of politicians and high officials to secure some amelioration of her husband's fate and prepare the ground for a remission or even a pardon.

Her first success was to obtain the end of his segregation and permission for him to see the other prisoners, but that was not enough for her. While her husband's case was still undecided she received only a third of his pay, and so to economize she left her apartment and went to live in a little hotel in the Rue de l'Université. She spent very little for herself and her son, so as to send food and anything he might need to her husband in prison.

She tramped unwearingly from ministry to ministry, and every day at visiting time she was at the prison gate with a parcel in her hand and with the news for which her husband was even more eager than for the food she brought.

* * *

News began to arrive, and quite interesting news too. Fouché, accused by the Emperor of negligence and lack of vigilance, defended himself by trying to show that there had really been no conspiracy, it was all gossip and the café title-tattle of malcontents and petty opponents that should not be taken seriously. By a fortunate chance the interests of the Minister of Police and the prisoners seemed to coincide: perhaps there might be some hope of an amnesty.

Fouché conducted matters extremely cleverly at the Council of Police which was called to decide, without trial, the fate of the conspirators: he arranged that the Council, instead of taking the conspiracy as a collective whole, a single crime against the Empire, should consider the individual conspirators case by case. He even succeeded in suppressing any mention of the 1,200 daggers procured in advance by them.

Thus the conspiracy lost its more serious and dangerous aspects: the fate of the arrested men became a matter of ordinary administration for those times, a question of police procedure against suspected persons. Ten of them, the most notorious ones, among them Malet, the other generals, and some of the Philadelphians, were declared State prisoners; for most of them this did not mean imprisonment but removal from Paris to forced residence in a provincial town. For greater security one of the generals, Guillaume, was sent to live outside France, in Genoa. One of the compromised officials was given a job in the customs at Arras. In short, Fouché succeeded within certain limits in showing that he had been right in regarding these people not as conspirators but as malcontents, harmless grumblers whom it was better to keep away from the capital.

But in spite of all Denise's efforts and appeals, not even Fouché succeeded in securing clemency for Malet and four others. By will of Napoleon they were to remain State prisoners for a period unspecified until such time as the Emperor should decide otherwise. Or perhaps, in Malet's case, it was Fouché himself who did not press too insistently for his prison sentence to be commuted into removal from the capital: he knew from Desmarest, his most trusted servant, that the General would never give in but would continue to plot, thus belying his efforts to minimize the affair and reduce to mere gossip the danger represented by this obstinate opponent.

* * *

Fouché was right. What might not Malet have attempted at liberty, if still in prison he never abandoned his fixed idea of destroying the Empire? Instead, it had become the very reason for his existence, stronger even than the hope of freedom. Since he was unable to act, he could do nothing but think and imagine, and the fruits of his imaginings were translated into words in interminable conversations with his fellow-prisoners.

At all times it has been a custom of the police to keep in prisons some men in their own service who have the job of listening and reporting, usually prisoners who hope thereby to improve their own prospects. In French prison slang they are called *moutons,* sheep, because of their innocuous manner and their habit of seeming to mind their own business, paying no attention to their companions' talk or to gossip and rumours while in fact they listen avidly and memorize everything.

The 'sheep' who went around gleaning news among the prisoners in La Force was an Italian, Sorbi by name, held in prison on suspicion of spying for Spain. Whatever he heard he reported periodically to Desmarest, hoping thereby to hasten his own release.

Thus it came about that one day he thought he had got hold of an important titbit to pass on to the police: Malet was preparing from prison a fresh *coup*. He was planning to escape with a group of companions and with them, aided by outside accomplices and a display of flags and drums, to appear unexpectedly outside Notre Dame at the moment when all the highest authorities would be assembled in the cathedral to celebrate with a Te Deum the capture of Vienna. The nub of the plot was to be the same: the sudden proclamation of Napoleon's death; all the authorities shut up in the cathedral would be taken prisoner, while Malet would call upon the people and the army to rise and help him to overthrow the Government thus deprived of its leaders, and make himself master of France before Napoleon could intervene.

Desmarest, as a model colleague of Fouché's, did not attach much weight to this revelation, which amounted at most to a confirmation of Malet's intentions and the fantasies seething in his brain. But since Malet was in prison, it was as well that Sorbi should stay there too to carry on with his job and keep the General under his eye.

Thus the revelation produced neither Sorbi's release nor any punishment for Malet.

* * *

Sorbi – his was another face that floated up upon the mirror of Malet's memory where prisons, gaolers, and fellow-prisoners mingled with no sense of time in those featureless days that gradually mounted up to weeks, months and years. A dim, obliging sort of creature, who used to stand there listening as if he did not understand when in a low voice Malet expounded his plans to his companions.

Malet never took any notice of him, until one day a gaoler, an old republican who had seen service on the Rhine, said: 'Be careful of that chap, General, he smells of sheep', and after that if poor Sorbi wanted to bear tales to Desmarest he had to invent them.

But at that stage the General's activities remained confined to dreams, words, and plans – plans still based on the principle of initial surprise, but which as time went on became more and more complex and detailed. This imaginary activity at least helped to mitigate the enforced inaction that is the worst trial of prison life.

* * *

Denise continued in her role of tireless suppliant; she even managed to persuade her husband to sign petitions for pardon to the Emperor. A man convinced as he was that he had a historic task to perform could not but accept the principle that the end justifies the means. Thus in asking pardon from Napoleon and protesting his loyalty to him he was not betraying himself or in any way renouncing the design that was the reason for his existence: rather he sought thereby to facilitate its accomplishment – freedom alone could enable him to act and by careful preparation to avoid falling into the same errors.

Denise secured one small victory: her insistent prayers succeeded in bringing about her husband's transfer from La Force to Sainte-Pélagie, also a prison but formerly a monastery, which allowed the prisoners greater freedom and a less strict regime with better possibilities of communicating with the outer world. The 'sheep' Sorbi remained at La Force.

For Malet, greater freedom meant more opportunity to conspire, discuss his plans, and seek outside support, and this was facilitated by the fact that two of the Philadelphians arrested with him, Gindre and Gariot, were also transferred to Sainte-Pélagie. Then his two companions left him. Gindre was sent to one of those private clinics in Paris where, under pretext of health, prisoners who were regarded as less dangerous, or who had friends at court, were sent to less severe detention where the police could still keep an eye on them. Gariot was actually sent home to the Jura, though forbidden to show his face in Paris.

From that moment Denise, unable to secure her husband's release, concentrated her efforts on getting him transferred from prison and sent to one of these clinics.

Despite refusals she would not admit defeat, and maintained her efforts throughout eighteen months, during which Malet, left alone at Sainte-Pélagie, resumed his silent obsessive monologue with himself, working out in his mind every detail of his plan, just as other prisoners work at the bars of a window to prepare their escape.

All other recollections of that period vanished in Malet's memory before the picture of a transformed Denise as she appeared one day in the parlour of the prison with shining eyes and cheeks flushed with joy.

She made herself speak low so as not to be overheard, but it was easy to see that she longed to shout from the rooftops the news that had brought her running early to the daily interview.

'Wonderful news: Fouché has been dismissed. It won't be official till tomorrow, but I know it's true.'

'And who is to succeed him at the Police Ministry?' asked her husband, delighted at the news but too cautious to indulge in transports.

'The Duke of Rovigo. The decree has been signed by the Emperor.'

Savary, the gendarme, the man known for his tough enterprises, captures of dangerous opponents, and nocturnal shootings in a fortress moat. A stern, inflexible customer, but not a subtle and intelligent police-spy with whom it was useless to match wits or seek accommodation unless it were to his own advantage. Denise had grasped, even before her husband, the weak point to attack.

'If I can manage to convince Savary that you are a victim of Fouché's intrigues, I may be able to get you a pardon or at any rate have you transferred to a clinic. Savary doesn't know you, does he?'

They had never met in the army. Savary, much younger than Malet, was always at the Emperor's elbow. He had occasionally seen active service, but for the most part his duties had lain in the gendarmerie. Napoleon had even tried to make him an ambassador, but without success. At any rate it was worth while trying what Denise suggested with such enthusiasm and conviction.

The attempt was made. Denise sent the Minister one of her elegant, dignified letters, typical product of an aristocratic convent-school education, in which she depicted her husband as the victim of manoeuvres by Fouché, a personal enemy of his, who was arbitrarily keeping him in prison.

'Malet? Who is this General Malet? I seem to have heard the name, but I don't know anything about him,' said the Minister when a secretary presented the petition to him. The Ministry was in great confusion: Fouché had covered his retreat by destroying files and ordering his henchmen left behind to keep their mouths shut in order to make his successor's task more difficult and show Napoleon that Fouché was irreplaceable.

They presented the Minister with a vague report, based on a few precedents. Savary did not want to take the responsibility of releasing a State prisoner. He chose the halfway solution of authorizing his transfer to a clinic under police surveillance on the pretext of his age, ill-health, and relative harmlessness.

Thus it came about that after two years in prison Malet one day found himself between two gendarmes in a carriage which bore him to the far part of the Faubourg Saint-

Antoine, in the region of the Barrière du Trône, where was the nursing-home of Dr Dubuisson.

That day seemed to him to mark not so much a first step towards his complete freedom as a first stage towards the accomplishment of his grand design against Napoleon.

He had few clothes in his bag, but in his brain was his plan, by now mature and worked out in every detail.

* * *

Thinking back to his first days in that nursing-home where no one was ailing except from bitter hostility to the imperial regime, his recollections became mixed with much more distant memories of the court at Versailles, when he was a King's musketeer. In the dining-room, corridors, and garden of that extraordinary clinic one encountered, as at court, only people of quality, famous old French names, dukes and marquises who had escaped the guillotine and survived through the various phases and transformations of the Revolution up to that monarchy, unacceptable to them, which was the Napoleonic Empire. There were Armand and Jules de Polignac, the Marquis de Puyvert, leader of the southern monarchists, Bertier de Sauvigny: all enemies of Napoleon, but all protected by exalted connections, by relationship with personages who had adhered to the regime and acquired important positions, whose ancient titles of nobility seemed to lend an air of authenticity to more recent titles, hastily conferred by the dozen to create a court for the new sovereign.

The conversation at table and in the garden was brilliant, even if the subject was always the same: the misdeeds of Napoleon and his followers, and how best to get rid of them. Thus far they were all agreed, these Bourbon loyalists and Malet the republican. Their opinions differed about the regime to be introduced in France once Napoleon was overthrown, but they preferred not to talk about that. It was premature and unsuitable to discuss it. Or was perhaps Malet beginning to feel less Jacobin, to think that a good king, a constitutional king, was at least preferable to the adventurer who held Europe under his bayonets and France under his police-spies?

Certainly among those cultivated people, accustomed to practising an ironical and gentlemanly type of opposition, for whom to be in disgrace with the sovereign and under detention seemed to form part of an old tradition going back to the Fronde and beyond, Malet felt himself being reabsorbed into the class in which he was born: it was as if the 'de' before his name, abolished in the days of the Rhine army, had inadvertently reappeared.

The days went peacefully by in the mansion of the Faubourg Saint-Antoine; conversations among the 'patients' were spiced by the news and gossip brought each day by friends and relatives, who were freely admitted up to dusk, when the entrance gate was closed and they began to play cards or chess.

The house was run with discretion and courtesy by Dr Dubuisson, who was more like a State hotel-proprietor than a doctor, and who owed that profitable position to highly-placed friends and firm support from the police. Naturally, as in other hotels, the account had to be paid each week, and this after some months became an increasingly serious problem for Malet and especially for Madame Malet, who continued to cope with everything, provide the payments out of the third of her husband's pay that she still received, and make untiring efforts to ensure that his privileged position should last as long as possible.

She also continued to send in petitions for pardon. She sent one to the Emperor on the occasion of his marriage with the Archduchess Marie-Louise. She sent others, still unsuccessful, to Savary and to Napoleon invoking as a reason for clemency the birth of the long-awaited heir, the little King of Rome. It was all of no use. With growing concern she felt the day draw near when Malet would be definitely struck off from the army and even that wretched but blessed third of his pay would cease to come in at the end of the month. For her husband that would mean return to an ordinary prison, and for her and her son stark poverty.

At that point a new guest arrived in the nursing-home, somewhat different from the others in character, if not in ideas: Abbé Lafon.

* * *

He remembered their first meeting very clearly, as something separate from his recollection of their daily converse and the friendship that followed. Malet looked rather dubiously the first evening at this new arrival who, with his round collar and tricorne, seemed to be an ecclesiastic, though his dress was more that of a professor than a priest. He felt those blue eyes fixed on him as they gleamed from beneath bushy eyebrows in a sallow face. Lafon showed no reticence or hesitancy towards Malet. With the others, the aristocratic *pensionnaires* in the nursing-home, Malet had had to explain on arrival who he was, why he was there, and what were his political views, before being admitted to their circle. With this Abbé it was very different. Lafon opened his arms in an affectionate embrace. His voice with its Gironde accent was sonorous and cordial, and he seemed to be aware of everything as if they had always known each other.

'General Malet, I knew I would find you here, and I was anxious to meet you. I am sure we have a lot to say to each other.'

From that moment life for Malet in the Dubuisson clinic became a long uninterrupted dialogue with Abbé Lafon. By very different ways, one and the same hatred had brought them to that place, and that hatred, that common enemy, quickly made them friends, ready to confide everything to each other and unite their projects, plans and hopes. It made no difference what lay behind them, what was the ultimate goal that inspired them. The immediate aim was the same, Napoleon's overthrow and the end of the imperial regime. Malet could keep to himself his republican ideals – which had in any case of late been somewhat watered down – and all his frustrations and disappointments. Lafon had no need to relate in detail the reasons that had brought him, after some months at La Force, as a prisoner to the clinic: that he formed part of a vast organization based on a large section of the French clergy, which planned to liberate Pope Pius VII and restore him to the seat of St Peter in Rome.

The bull of excommunication which the Pope had issued against Napoleon three years before, when the French invaded the Papal States, and which had caused him to be exiled from Rome, had never been published in France, but it had become known in clandestine ways through prelates, priests, and the faithful.

The French clergy were now divided, a majority remaining faithful to their obedience to the Holy Father, while a minority had acquiesced in the imperial decision. Bishops and archbishops who made known the bull, thus revealing to the French that their sovereign was excommunicated, were arrested. The Pope himself, for fear of attempts by the British Navy to liberate him, had been brought a few months earlier from his place of exile in Savona to Fontainebleau, while various Italian cardinals in his suite were put under arrest in the fortresses of Vincennes. Lafon, reckoned as small fry, had been shut up in La Force but had not stayed there long; someone had managed to get him transferred to the hospitable clinic of Dr Dubuisson.

'I have many friends, powerful friends,' said Lafon, 'and my friends will become your best allies if we join forces and act together.'

Happiest of all about this meeting was Denise, who at last saw her husband united in friendship and objectives with a worthy man of the church instead of with all those doctrinaire fanatics, relics of the Jacobin club, cardboard Brutuses capable merely of betraying themselves by their rash talk. This was a serious, powerful man worth having as an ally. Her Christian upbringing revived within her, prompting her desire to associate her husband's salvation with the salvation of his soul.

Lafon also liked Denise, this active and intelligent woman who had managed to retain some old friendships in the army world, valuable sources of indispensable information for translating into practical reality Malet's plans, now become the plans of them both: for the Abbé's political and ecclesiastical subtlety complemented the military and administrative experience of the General. Whether later the Bourbons, defenders of the Church, should return to the throne, or whether the republic, supporter of freedom, should be re-established, could be decided later on: for the time being the important thing was to combine efforts to eliminate Napoleon and his sham Empire. It never entered Malet's head that the man whom he regarded as a tyrant to be destroyed had been greeted by many people in Europe as the bringer of freedom who with his codes and laws had spread abroad the best principles of the Revolution, equality between all men, the end of feudal privileges, whereas Lafon's friends were fighting not so much for the Pope's liberation and the independence of the Church as for a return to the days of the inquisition, absolute monarchies, and an ecclesiastical gag for all free expression of thought.

Lafon was attracted by Malet's fundamental idea of convincing the army, authorities and people that the far-off Napoleon was dead and seizing the opportunity to gain possession of Paris and instal a provisional government. The important thing was to organize matters in such a way as to give the greatest verisimilitude to the news and to make their operation appear perfectly legal.

Napoleon's political and military designs seemed to have been made on purpose to further their plans and convince them that the moment had come to act. The country was weary of war and sacrifices, the soldiers had had enough of absence from their homes, and young men called up to the colours were ready for any risk to avoid military service: deserters and defaulters already numbered some four hundred thousand, and the gendarmes could not manage to hunt down everyone to enrol them by force. The blockade that was supposed to ruin the British economy had ended instead by ruining the French traders. Everywhere there was talk of bankruptcies, of people who had lost everything on the falling exchange, and at each street-corner of Paris beggars held out their hands.

Napoleon with his Grand Army was more than 3,000 kilometres away from Paris, in the heart of Russia, involved in a campaign which was to have marked the culmination of his great political design, but of which no one in the country understood the need. That vast distance, that country remote as the moon, had swallowed up him and his men, and his bulletins, arriving at long intervals with their news of victories and advances, did not suffice to tranquillize public opinion.

Indeed the few people who were able to consult a map and decipher those unpronounceable names found that Napoleon was merely going further and further off into the depths of that country which seemed to have no eastern limits. There were hardly any effective troops left in Paris and the rest of France. Reserve armies of conscripts had had to be formed and concentrated in Germany, and troops had been sent to Spain where things were going badly, with the popular insurrection receiving support from Wellington and the British. In France, apart from the gendarmerie and the regimental depots, there were only the cohorts of the National Guard – soldiers rejected for active service but enrolled of necessity, who had been promised that they would not be posted outside France but who felt no trust in such promises and feared they too might be sent to be killed in far-off countries.

The bulletins from the Grand Army spoke of victories but they were victories like that of September at Borodino, on the River Moskva, which, as everyone now knew, had been a tremendous holocaust, the most bloody battle of all Napoleon's eighteen years of war. There had been a bulletin announcing the conquest of Moscow, the enemy capital, but was it really a victory to celebrate with a Te Deum, as when the Emperor had conquered the other enemy capitals?

Lafon and Malet, in the nursing-home which had become for them like a staff headquarters, knew all this and followed events closely. Denise redoubled her efforts to secure useful information, and Lafon received visits from certain friends of his, priests in ordinary dress or young Oratorians, who also brought news and other particulars and names of officials who could be counted on.

The time for action was approaching: they must work out practical details. In Denise's anxiety Malet recognized his own anxiety, the personal reasons that combined with political causes to counsel speed. Denise had learnt from one of her friends at the Ministry of War that the measure was imminent which would strike her husband off the army list, thus ending their source of livelihood. It meant return to prison for him, and starvation for the family.

The Abbé and the General prepared the details of their action with the same care with which they moved the pieces of the chessboard each night. 'No accomplices,' Malet had declared from the depths of past experience, 'by eliminating accomplices we avoid the risk of informers and gossipers. We must ensure that we have only such people as are indispensable for the operation of the plan, but no one must know what the plan is, indeed they mustn't even know that there is a plan at all. The few collaborators necessary for the initial stages must themselves be the first to believe in the truth of what we shall proclaim.'

Lafon had all kinds of resources and could lay hands on the people needed. Boutreux, a mild man, religious, a bachelor of law and an arcadian poet, wretchedly poor, asked for nothing but the help to get a job of some sort that would enable him to live. There was no need to ask him to play the part of the police commissioner when the time came for action: it was enough to assure him that circumstances were maturing in which he might at any moment be taken on in the police with the duties of commissioner and the prospect of a good career. In this way they could be sure that, being unaware that he was playing a part, he would give a thoroughly convincing performance as commissioner.

That other lad who came to pay respectful visits to the Abbé, young Rateau, a corporal in the Paris Guard, also aspired to improve his position. With him all they had to do was to make him believe that coming events would enable his powerful friends in temporary disgrace, Abbé Lafon and General Malet, to secure his promotion as an officer. Without needing to make him an accomplice, Malet was thus assured of the person destined to play the role of aide-de-camp, indispensable at his side at the moment when he presented himself to the troops to proclaim the death of Napoleon and assume command.

Lafon was ready to answer in every way for these two good lads who, despite the times, frequented the Oratory and never missed Mass. He had introduced them one after the other to the General, who had received them with kindly superiority: two humble, modest postulants, but sons of their time, who found yet another upheaval of the State perfectly natural, and considered themselves fortunate to be there in time to secure the support of those who would be in power tomorrow.

They did not ask much: Boutreux wanted a job, if possible in the police, the safest career under any regime, so as to be able to marry the girl to whom he dedicated madrigals under the poetic name of Eulalia. Rateau, who had been educated by the priests but who liked to enjoy himself and have a good time, hankered after an officer's epaulets which would guarantee success with the girls and a good salary, whether under king, emperor, or republic.

Lafon assured them that the powerful General to whom he had introduced them, and who was soon to be entrusted by the Senate with a highly important mission, would give them what they wanted if they obeyed blindly. The two declared they asked for nothing better.

Malet was enthusiastic about Lafon. With such a collaborator he felt safe: he neglected no detail and always found the best solution for every problem. The old army martinet in Malet admired the Abbé's ingenious devices, his shrewd, brilliant intuitions, his mysterious and inexhaustible resources. They would need somewhere to meet after escaping from the nursing-home, a secret base in which to don their uniforms and set out to conquer Paris. Lafon at once found the very man to arrange for the meeting-place, a poor devil of a Spanish priest, Cajamaño, innocuous because of his inability to speak French, but shrewd and clever enough to discover the most suitable place and make sure of it by renting it: an apartment in a blind alley near Place des Vosges, the Passage Saint-Pierre. The house was old and dilapidated, the alley-way sordid, but it was quiet and lonely, and not far from the Popincourt Barricks, scene of the first act of the great drama that they were preparing to stage. La Force Prison and the Minimes Barracks, where the next scenes were to take place, were not too far off, between the Marais *quartier* and the Faubourg Saint-Antoine. They would also need a stamp to give the seal of officialdom to the documents they would concoct. After the failure of the DIOTATURE stamp ordered from an engraver at the time of the 1808 conspiracy, it was better to be prudent and eschew craftsmen. Lafon was ready with a solution: a seal of his own with a fine letter 'L' which could be taken to mean all sorts of things, 'Liberty', 'Law', 'Legislature', or even 'Lanjuinais', the name of the secretary of the Senate, and which for nostalgics of the monarchy might signify 'Louis', the name of the exiled pretender.

They drew up a list of the documents to be forged, the Senate decree, the proclamation to the troops, orders to the corps commanders, passes; and they studied carefully the various moves and their timing which would enable them to gain possession of the key points in the city, to secure in a few hours the mastery of Paris and so of France.

Two important elements were still lacking, two men with the habit of command to put at the head of the troops that were to arrest Savary, Pasquier and Cambacérès, the chief members of the Government. Where were they to find the necessary collaborators without uncovering the plan too soon and creating dangerous accomplices or potential informers? The ideal thing would be to find them among people like themselves, imprisoned for political reasons. Hatred of Napoleon, together with the desire to obtain their freedom, would encourage such men to break out at the right moment, while their present isolation in prison would prevent any careless talk on their part.

There was still imprisoned at La Force the unfortunate Demaillot, author of *Madame Angot,* who had neither the money nor the influence to get himself transferred to a more supportable prison. Malet was in touch with him through a young woman, a corset-maker, who for some reason or other had free access to the prison parlour. One day when the preparations for the *coup* were already well advanced this young woman brought the General a somewhat cryptic note from the imprisoned author: 'I have three treasures. There are perfect conditions here which I will cultivate if you permit.' The corset-maker explained these enigmatic words, which prudence dictated in case the note might be discovered by some gaoler whose zeal to search might be prompted by the desire to get his hands on that personable young woman. The three treasures that Demaillot proposed to cultivate in prison, as other prisoners might cultivate a pot of basil, were three State prisoners, General Lahorie, General Guidal and a mysterious Corsican called Bocche-ciampe who was said to be a secret agent of the allies.

'Go ahead and cultivate your treasures,' was the message sent by the General in reply. He added nothing more, and he did not reveal his plans: but he now knew that there were two generals available at La Force animated by the same hatred of the Emperor. Lahorie he knew well, though he had not seen him for many years, and he knew him to be a good soldier and a perfect gentleman. Of the other, Guidal, he had heard only that he had sold himself to the English and was liable to be shot; he would therefore be ready to take on any enterprise that might save his skin.

Lafon approved his answer and made a mental note of the two names.

Not long afterwards a young lady heavily veiled came to see Lafon in the clinic. She had a brief talk with the Abbé and went away without being seen by anyone.

'Your corset-maker was right', said Lafon to the General. 'Her information was quite correct. The lady who came to see me just now is the separated wife of a general who is fighting in Spain. She tells me that there is imprisoned at La Force someone very dear to her, General Lahorie, and she assures me that we can count on him if there is any serious operation in view to overthrow the Empire. Naturally her motive is love rather than politics, and what she is most anxious about is that Lahorie should stay in France and not be deported to America, as it seems Savary intends. In this case even love can be useful to us.'

Lafon rubbed his hands: clearly he knew women and what they would do for love at least as well as he knew men and their political passions.

It was now time to start on what the two called their 'clerical work', the meticulous and careful preparation of all the documents needed for their undertaking.

* * *

The half-light of dawn now entering the cell at L'Abbaye did not interrupt the frenzied plunge into the past that had peopled Malet's night with figures. Closest of them all to him was always Denise, whom he imagined sleepless like himself in some other prison cell. Denise was near him now, as she had been throughout those days with her more and more frequent visits – so tiring for her since, as well, she had to go all over Paris in search of the information anxiously awaited by her husband and Lafon in their nursing-home in the Faubourg Saint-Antoine, far from the centre of the city. She must have walked miles each day, unwilling to spend any of their small store of money on carriages, and sustained in her interminable journeyings by the love that bound her to her husband and by her hopes for the success of his venture.

The information she brought each day was both accurate and valuable. She was helped by an old friend, General Desnoyers, who hesitated to become involved himself in the conspiracy but willingly supplied her with the information she needed. Thus they knew the exact composition of all the military corps in Paris, barely 7,000 men and nearly all of the National Guard, and the names of all their officers down to the platoon commanders. They knew the state of mind of the men, and which corps was the least disciplined and most discontented, having a less energetic commander, and which therefore became the chosen target for their first effort to secure initial success – the 10th Cohort of the National Guard, quartered at Popincourt Barracks. They also knew that the toughest nut to crack was Garrison Command, Hulin and his men, and Malet therefore reserved this most difficult and decisive part of the business for himself.

Denise also told him that an old retired general had come to live in her hotel, a certain Lamotte or Lamothe, she wasn't sure of the name. No one in Paris knew him, and his name would be useful as cover in the first stage of the operation, when it was advisable that Malet should not yet declare himself.

It was naturally Denise, too, who procured the necessary uniforms of a general and aide-de-camp, with swords, cocked-hats and epaulets, and the police commissioner's sash, and she got Boutreux to take them in a trunk to the house of the Spanish priest ready for the moment of action, and another general's uniform for Desnoyers in case he should decide to join Malet when it came to the point.

There had been no news from Russia for a week or ten days. They had heard of the conquest of Moscow and the conflagration in the city, but since then nothing. This silence filled France with disquiet: it seemed as if that fabulously remote country had swallowed up Napoleon and his men. It was the first week in October, and the time for action drew near.

For hours and hours each night, Malet and Lafon filled sheet upon sheet of paper, drawing up in their handwriting of the orderly-room and the seminary copies of the Senate decree, the proclamations to the army and the people, and the orders for the commanders. The style was Malet's, the style of the Rhine army, full of patriotic ardour and revolutionary rhetoric. They left the dates blank to be filled in at the last moment.

The provisional government they had thought out was to satisfy all the malcontents: at its head a famous general of the Revolution now in exile, Moreau, and then left-wing and aristocrat politicians, a great soldier and scholar such as Carnot, jurists, an admiral, two senators, and, of course, Malet, promoted Divisional General, as Minister of War and military commander of Paris. None of them had been consulted. If the *coup* succeeded they would all be only too eager to accept their appointments.

Lafon had had an excellent idea: 'Let's put Frochot, the Prefect of the Seine, in the provisional government too. He's an official of Napoleon's but he is so keen on his career that after shedding a tear for Napoleon he'll put himself and his whole Prefecture at our disposal. He believes he is indispensable to maintain order in Paris: we'll let him go on thinking so and profit by it.'

On one of those last evenings they got Rateau to tell them the password given every day by Garrison Command to the sentinels in barracks: it was an ill-supervised secret, but useful to lend verisimilitude to the first scene of the first act, the General's arrival at Popincourt Barracks.

All was in readiness and Malet fixed the date of the action for the night of Saturday-Sunday, October 10-11. The emptiness of the streets on a Sunday morning would facilitate operations. If things should go badly, Denise too would be arrested: they therefore decided to entrust their son, now fourteen years old, to the care of a woman friend who was to take him forthwith to a castle in the north of France.

Thinking it over now, that night seemed to him at once a nightmare and a farce, a sort of dress-rehearsal gone wrong. At the beginning things went well, and they had found it quite easy to get away from the nursing-home by climbing the garden wall, a possible undertaking even for middle-aged people like Abbé Lafon and the General. They had reached the house in Passage Saint-Pierre in half an hour. Boutreux was waiting for them with Cajamaño, who had got ready something to eat to pass the time. Rateau had still to come, and they spent the interval in putting the dates on the documents. An hour, two hours went by and he did not appear. They began to get worried. Better stop dating the documents and return to the clinic before being surprised by the police who might have somehow been put on their tracks. Boutreux was also told to go away and await fresh orders. No use wasting words on Cajamaño: he had grasped at once that the whole thing would have to be started all over again.

It had been simple enough to climb the wall from the garden side, but it was nothing like so easy from the street, and after some fruitless attempts the Abbé and the General had to resign themselves to ringing the bell to have their prison door opened. It was answered by Dr Dubuisson in person, and he gave them a fine scolding, complaining that they put him in a most awkward position and he would have to denounce the escapade to the *quartier* police. Malet kept in the shadows holding tight to his folder stuffed with documents. But Lafon had one of his bright ideas. Lowering his eyes and gesticulating with his hands he said in a subdued voice: 'Try to understand, doctor. We are men of the world. One can't spend every evening playing chess or écarté. If you denounce us, they will send us away from your delightful house.'

Dubuisson held open the door for the two contrite culprits to go in. The doctor made no promise, but no denunciation reached the *quartier* police, thanks to the fellow-comradeship that pertains in France among gentlemen in matters of gallantry.

They learnt next day that Rateau had not kept the appointment for the simple reason that he had returned to barracks drunk the night before, and the sergeant on duty had shoved him in the cells – so he had not been able to let Boutreux and Cajamaño know in time. They breathed again, but from that moment they looked somewhat dubiously on the would-be aide-de-camp who was too ready with his glass.

There was still no news of what was happening in Russia to Napoleon and the Grand Army, and they therefore decided to make a second attempt without loss of time, making sure this time that none of the necessary characters should be missing at the last minute. They chose the night of October 22/23: the 23rd was a Friday, the day of the weekly review of the garrison in Place Vendôme, and troop movements in the streets would not appear unusual up to the moment when the news of Napoleon's death was publicly proclaimed. Boutreux was told to go and wait outside the barracks for Rateau, who was to ask for leave of absence for the night.

Rateau had told them the password for that night. Was it a coincidence, a warning, or an augury of success? The password chosen by the Paris Garrison Command for the night of October 22 was 'conspiracy'. They decided to regard it as a good omen.

Malet still felt on his cheek the kiss that Denise gave him on the afternoon of the 22nd when she came to say goodbye and wish him victory; he saw again the sad smile in her grey eyes as they sought in his own eyes the certainty to sustain her in the long hours of waiting ahead. When would he see her again? Or would he ever see her again, before Napoleon's men, Savary or the others, avenged themselves upon him with a volley of rifle-shot for having played that trick on them?

From that moment when the action began everything functioned perfectly. They left by the garden window and climbed the wall, first the General, then the Abbé, who complained with a stifled groan that he had twisted his ankle as he jumped down. They made off, the General striding ahead and the Abbé limping behind. He waited for him at the first street-corner and they went on together.

It was raining, and the streets were empty. The General felt sure of himself, calm as always in the moment of action. The Abbé looked at him for a minute from beneath his bushy eyebrows and said in a low voice: 'I can't help wondering what the Emperor will say when he knows. . . .'

'You forget, the Emperor is dead,' replied the General brusquely. 'The proofs of his death are with us here.'

And he struck with his hand the folder containing the documents they had fabricated with such care. Therein lay his 'truth'.

* * *

This time they all turned up in the house in Passage Saint-Pierre. They set to work at once adding the dates to the documents, making it appear that Napoleon had died on October 7th, the news had reached Paris on the 22nd, and the Senate had issued its decree that same night. Malet then prepared the envelopes with the orders to be given at the right moment to the various commanders. He and the Abbé worked on for some time. Lafon kept rubbing his ankle which, he said, was swelling. Then they had something to eat and drank a glass of wine, taking care that Rateau didn't have too much. Malet looked at his watch: the appointed hour for action was drawing near.

He drew Boutreux aside: 'Young man, earlier on I promised you to see about your future. Would you like to be a police commissioner?'

'Of course I would, General, but I don't see how. . . .'

'But I do. From this moment you are a commissioner. The mission entrusted to me by the Senate is about to begin, a historic mission in which I am giving you the good fortune to share. You merely have to accompany me and carry out my orders carefully. Your career is made and will take you far.'

Then he called Rateau: 'I know that you, Corporal, hope for promotion.'

'I won't deny it, General.'

'If you are ready to obey my orders, I promote you now to be an officer and my aide-de-camp.'

Rateau felt as if he must have got drunk again, and he could hardly manage to stammer out his thanks.

They opened the trunk that Boutreux had brought and took out the uniforms, the swords and the commissioner's sash.

Malet took the General's uniform, handed the adjutant's to Rateau, and went into the next room to dress. He reappeared a minute later resplendent with gold brocade, epaulets, gold-embroidered sash, sword, and plumed hat. They gazed on him with respect, and Rateau, who was flaunting himself in his officer's uniform that had seemed beyond his wildest dreams, stood to attention. Boutreux had tied on his commissioner's sash which showed beneath his cloak.

Malet had put in his pocket all the money he had, only twelve francs, but he already felt himself master of Paris and even of France. Pressing his sword to his side he turned to Boutreux and Rateau and said in a solemn voice: 'You are the first to hear the announcement I am about to make to the troops and the citizens of Paris: the Emperor is dead.'

From the expression in their eyes, from their mouths falling open in amazement, he measured the paralysing effect this news would have. He ordered Rateau to wrap up the other General's uniform that was in the trunk and to make a parcel of the documents that were not in his brief-case.

'You will come back later to fetch these packages with the men I shall give you as escort, and you will bring them to La Force Prison, where you will find me with a detachment of the 10th Cohort. We are going now to Popincourt Barracks to embark on my mission.'

He looked again at his watch. It was nearly three in the morning. 'Come, Abbé. It is time.'

'Unfortunately I can't come with you,' said the Abbé. 'My ankle is hurting me, and I'm sure you don't want to appear before the troops with a lame man limping beside you. I'll rest a bit and join you later. In the meantime I will communicate with the friends you know of.'

Malet, caught up in his active role, made no objection. He wrapped his cloak about him and set out in the rain, followed by his two companions, for the Popincourt Barracks and the sentry-box where Hippolyte-Boudin, known as Polyte-Flatfoot, stood sentinel.

* * *

When day came and the warder entered the cell with the mess-tin of coffee, the prisoner Malet was lying on the palliasse with his eyes wide open, his mind teeming with recollections of the day he had lived through, the day on which Paris had been his, the day on which he had conquered and annulled Napoleon and cancelled him from the world.

Throughout the long hours of questioning to which he had been subjected, he had consistently given negative replies, maintaining that he was in good faith and had really been entrusted with a mission by the Senate. Now, after that night spent in going over the past, he had taken an irrevocable decision. When they next questioned him he would take on himself the entire responsibility, saying that he and he alone had thought up the whole thing, that the others were not his accomplices but were the first to believe in his truth, a truth that no one could destroy and that represented his victory: that with Napoleon dead, or even merely thought to be dead, the Empire ceased to exist and dissolved of itself. Whether or not Napoleon returned alive from Russia, his edifice had no foundations and would sooner or later collapse like a house of cards, and of this he himself had given factual demonstration, he, General Malet, the victor.

They could question him again as soon as they pleased, condemn him, and shoot him: but no one could deny that truth or obliterate his victory.

He said to the warder, who stared at him in amazement: 'I am ready to follow you to the judge. Why are you wasting time?'

Chapter 12

Rue du Cherche-Midi — 1

Abbé Lafon had not told Sophie Hugo on which day the *coup d'état* would take place which was to restore Lahorie's freedom; but from certain cautious indications and partial admissions Sophie had convinced herself that the event was planned for the second half of October. For days she had been living in anxious expectation, not daring to leave her house in the Passage des Feuillantines in case a messenger might come or even, who knows, the beloved figure of the 'man with the diamond eyes' himself, and she not be there.

Lafon had been interested to hear the news that Lahorie could certainly be counted on in the event of a decisive *coup* to overthrow the regime; and he had promised to restore the imprisoned General to freedom and enable him to rejoin the lady who had loved him for so long. He had only laid down one essential condition: Lahorie was not to know what was on foot, and the names of Malet and Lafon must on no account be mentioned to him. It would be enough for her to tell him to be of good courage, to await confidently events that would soon restore his freedom and obviate his deportation to America, that bitter concession that Savary had decided to make to his old friend and former companion-in-arms.

To have Lahorie free again, to avoid his deportation which would mean their permanent separation and the end of any possible reunion with the man for whom she had sacrificed her social position and reputation – Sophie could think of nothing else. She was not in the least worried that liberation procured in such a way might prove illusory or full of risks and possibly mortal dangers. Born in the Vendée and accustomed from childhood to guerrilla actions and conspiracies, she found it perfectly natural that Lahorie should regain his freedom in this way, by outwitting his enemies and countering force by guile. All she wanted was to have him free and back with her in the little temple at the bottom of the Feuillantines garden, to love and care for him as in those months when, because he was in hiding and sought by the police, he lived only for her, cut off from the unfriendly world, his whole existence enclosed by the trees and walls of the secret refuge in which his beloved sheltered him.

She wanted the *coup d'état* to succeed because that would mean safety for him and for them both, the defeat of their enemies and an end to their tribulations, not because she had any desire to see Lahorie become an important personage, perhaps a member of the new Government: for then he might be too busy to think of love and she might lose him yet again.

She never left the house. News would be brought to her at the right moment by the closest and safest of their friends, Pierre Foucher, an official at the War Ministry, who was always well-informed, cautious and discreet. Naturally to Foucher, a government official, she had said nothing of her meetings with Lafon, less still of the fact that she was counting on the success of an anti-Napoleonic conspiracy to restore her lover to her; she had merely got Foucher to promise to keep her immediately informed of any news concerning Lahorie. Foucher had promised, and she could trust him. He came to see her nearly everyday, bringing with him his daughter Adèle, who for years had been the favourite playmate of the Hugo boys. Victor was now ten years old, Adèle a year younger; they had almost given up their childhood games of running races or inventing terrifying and fascinating stories beside the old well where lived the imaginary monster called 'the Deaf One'.

Now they sat composedly side by side on a seat, and Victor in a low voice read Adèle his poems from an exercise-book.

'Look at them, Sophie : aren't they like a pair of lovers?'

'They are too serious, Pierre : they're more like husband and wife.'

Sophie's instinct had not deceived her. Only a few years hence, having rounded the cape of adolescence and entered on the open sea of youth, Victor Hugo and Adèle Foucher, he twenty, she nineteen, would be united in marriage. A most unhappy marriage, as any history-book of French literature will tell us, and one which shows yet again that first love is rarely the love of a lifetime.

* * *

About two o'clock on the afternoon of October 23rd Foucher sent her a note : 'Come to my house at once. I have news.' Sophie fastened the ribbons of her hat beneath her chin, threw on a shawl, and ran out.

Before becoming an official at the Ministry Pierre Foucher had for years been clerk to the War Tribunal, and he and his family still lived in an apartment in the gloomy old Hôtel de Toulouse, the military justice headquarters in the Rue du Cherche-Midi. It was a quiet, comfortable apartment with a large well-cared-for garden, and there was nothing to remind one that near by, under the same roof and separated only by a wall, were the halls where military trials were conducted, ending more frequently in death sentences than in absolutions.

Crossing the city with her heart in her mouth, Sophie looked around her, seeking for some sign of the remarkable event that was to restore Lahorie to her, a free man. There were groups of people about, passers-by and carriages moving much as usual. Only along the Seine she met detachments of soldiers marching in the opposite direction, separated from each other by a short interval. As the wife of a general accustomed to garrison life, she at once identified the uniforms and corps: one was a detachment of *chasseurs* of the Imperial Guard, with their busbies and their ponderous step, the other of the National Guard. The latter were marching even worse than usual, with their rifles on their shoulders at a far from regulation angle, and from their ranks a murmur arose, as if those makeshift soldiers, regardless of officers and sergeants, were chattering among themselves while they dragged their feet along in a disorderly 'left-right'. As they passed close to her she distinctly heard a guardsman in the last rank saying to the men in the rank ahead: 'We don't believe what they say. We know the Little Corporal is done for. . . .'

That phrase which seemed to augur extraordinary happenings gave Sophie fresh breath and strength to run along the *quais* beside the Seine and through the Faubourg Saint-Germain to the Rue du Cherche-Midi.

She arrived at Foucher's house overcome with fatigue and anxiety. Foucher and his wife were awaiting her with the air of persons prepared to convey bad news as tactfully as possible. But Sophie, flustered and out of breath, brushed aside their preliminary courtesies. Interrupting Pierre she gasped out: 'Tell me at once. Is there news to do with Lahorie?'

'Yes, indeed. Great news. General Malet escaped this morning from the clinic where he was being held and tricked the commander of a cohort of the National Guard, making him believe that the Emperor had been killed and there was a new government. He went at the head of the cohort to La Force Prison and set Lahorie free and also another general, Guidal, who was awaiting sentence.'

'Splendid, and then?'

'Then Lahorie went in command of a detachment and

arrested first the Prefect of Police, Pasquier, and then the Minister of Police himself, the Duke of Rovigo, who was still in bed, and took them to La Force.'

'Fine! He's made that infamous Savary who betrayed him pay for his treachery.'

Pierre took no notice of the interruption but continued in the same sober, reticent tone of voice.

'Malet then went himself to arrest General Hulin. Hulin resisted, and Malet shot him with his pistol. He is badly wounded and may die. . . .'

At this point Pierre stopped, searching for words. Sophie urged him on: 'But then, what happened next? Where is Lahorie now?'

'What happened next was that the officers of Garrison Command, Doucet and Laborde, weren't taken in by Malet's false news. They threw themselves upon him, bound him, and arrested him.'

'But Victor – I mean General Lahorie?'

Pierre's eyes took on the expression of one who would say 'Alas' but dare not.

'General Lahorie was arrested too, in the office of the Minister of Police where he had installed himself in place of the Duke of Rovigo.'

Victor arrested, back in prison again, and this time under the terrible charge of armed conspiracy. The danger was no longer of deportation but of something far worse. . . .

Sophie collapsed into an arm-chair. It was she and she alone who had dragged him into this venture to prevent his being sent into exile, and now what had she done to him?

'Are you quite sure about all this? How do you know? What will they do to him?'

'Since this morning, after Malet and his accomplices were arrested, the Minister of War has assumed the direction of investigations and given orders to proceed urgently against the conspirators. Obviously, for the Duke of Feltre this is a good opportunity to bring himself to the Emperor's notice at the expense of the Duke of Rovigo, who kept no special watch on Malet and got himself arrested into the bargain. A little while ago I saw my neighbour Captain Delon, the *rapporteur,* you know him I think, and he had already been called to the Ministry to prepare the charges.'

'Delon – I want to see him, to explain to him that Lahorie knew nothing of the conspiracy, it was I alone. . . .'

'Calm yourself and don't do anything foolish. Delon isn't at home now. As I told you, he was urgently summoned to the Ministry.'

'But Victor – where is he? What will they do to him?'

'The persons arrested have already been subjected to questioning by a commission presided over by Réal. Later they will be taken to L'Abbaye. The trial will take place in a few days, here, in this building.'

'I want to see Delon. I want to testify at the trial that Lahorie had nothing to do with the conspiracy. I can swear it. . . .'

The Fouchers tried to calm her, but Sophie was in despair – it was she, she alone, who had pushed him into this terrible position. It was her duty to strive to save him and prove his innocence, even if it meant herself appearing guilty and an accomplice of Malet and of that Abbé Lafon whose name had not even been mentioned by Pierre Foucher.

* * *

It was growing dusk, and for the past two hours and more Lahorie had been questioned by the Commission. Before him were ranged the heads of the French police, transformed for the occasion into interrogating magistrates: Réal, Pelet de la Lozère, Anglès and Desmarest, one of the protagonists in the morning's brief prison episode. Desmarest gave an embarrassed look at Lahorie when he was brought in (they had been at school together) but then the police-spy resumed the stern aloof expression that had become a professional habit with him. For hours on end they had questioned Malet, who had stuck obstinately to his intention of declaring he had acted in good faith, in accordance with an effective decree of the Senate which had been conveyed to him in the clinic by a mysterious person. Now they were about to put the screw on the man they regarded as his chief accomplice.

They had asked the Prefect of Police, Pasquier, to join them, and he had done so unwillingly. He was still shaken by his recent misadventures, but all the same it seemed to him unworthy of a gentleman to turn into the persecutor of men who had certainly caused him some anxious moments but had nevertheless treated him courteously on the whole and done him no physical violence. But, he reflected, neither he nor the other members of the Commission would have to perform an onerous task that day: it was the job of the chairman, Réal, to conduct the inquiry and try to make the accused contradict himself.

The Minister of War, Clarke, had explained to Réal personally how he wanted things done, and Réal, thankful to have evaded the conspirators' *coup* himself and so have nothing in his own conduct to be glossed over, reduced the questioning to a dialogue between himself and the prisoner, giving the other members of the Commission no chance to intervene.

The subjects of the inquiry were confined to a few points hammered home by constant reiteration. How could a man of Lahorie's military and political experience maintain that he had let himself be taken in by Malet? How could he have failed to realize that Malet was making outrageous claims if there was no prior knowledge or complicity on his own part? How could he possibly not have perceived that the whole procedure of his liberation from prison was irregular?

Lahorie answered firmly: 'There was no irregularity, gentlemen. Everything was carried out in a perfectly regular way. The head warder himself came alone to my cell and told me I was free and that a general was waiting for me in the parlour with a mission from the Senate. And in the parlour I found a general (he was not a personal friend of mine; I hadn't seen him for eighteen years) at the head of an army squad, who told me that the Emperor was dead, that the Senate had decided to establish a provisional government, that political prisoners were to be set free and in particular the army officers who had been detained for political reasons and who were now to be under his orders to help him in the execution of his mission as new military Commandant of Paris. And this General, not, I repeat, a personal friend of mine, showed me in support of what he said the written orders he had with him.'

'And did you not realize that these alleged documents were obviously false?'

'As a soldier I can tell whether the contents of an order is more or less acceptable. I am not a lawyer or an official who can verify the authenticity of a stamp. As to the contents of the orders, the facts themselves, I simply believed I was faced with a peaceful revolution, a *coup d'état* effected by the Senate, yet another *coup* to add to the series we have all experienced in France for the past twenty years. A new Thermidor, a new Brumaire. In my place would you, gentlemen, have been surprised or suspicious, you who occupy your posts and are preparing to judge me simply because thirteen years ago, on the 18th Brumaire, Napoleon Bonaparte with better organization and luck succeeded in doing what has not been brought off today by this rash and unfortunate General Malet whose accomplice I am not, but merely his first victim?'

Pasquier looked at him in silent admiration: this man of middle height, lean, with the bow-legs of a cavalryman, with his dark hair and sparkling eyes, was standing up to his inquisitor with the courtesy tinged with arrogance characteristic of the French officer of aristocratic birth. He was trying to oppose the clarity of his logic, the tempered elegance of his phrases, against the obtuse obstinacy of Réal who, confined within the limits of his instructions, strove to enrich the report of the inquiry with new facts, admissions, and flagrant contradictions by the accused.

'If you were not an accomplice but a victim, M. Lahorie, how could you proceed to arrest the Prefect and the Minister of Police and usurp the latter's title and functions? That proves your active and conscious participation in the conspiracy.'

'My sole care was that not a hair of their heads should be hurt of Baron Pasquier and the Duke of Rovigo. Malet's orders were simply to get them out of the way somehow. The only way to avoid personal danger and violence to them was to take them to a safe place, to a prison. In order to sign the order for their imprisonment I had recourse to the expedient of preceding my signature by the description "Provisional Minister of Police". I did not use it on any other document, either to free or to imprison anyone. And M. le Baron Pasquier, here present, can testify that I personally assured myself that no violence was done to him.'

Pasquier could not refrain from saying: 'It is my duty as a man of honour to declare that I was treated by this gentleman, and by the soldiers and the young civilian who accompanied him, with the greatest courtesy.'

'And your servant who was injured by the soldiers?' Réal interrupted brusquely.

'A faithful domestic who did not understand the situation and in his zeal tried to oppose the soldiers' bayonets unarmed. But that happened in the corridor, not where M. Lahorie was, and he at once sent the officer who was with him to quiet the disturbance and calm down his men.'

Baron Pasquier felt it behoved him to give this testimony; he was a nobleman of ancient lineage who had arrived at the high position he occupied under the imperial regime by managing to steer skilfully through the agitated waters of revolutionary France. He admired this man of similar background who had not adapted himself to cautious navigation but had always fought against his enemies. Even now – in this hopeless struggle in which he was already beaten because it had been so decided in view of the need to reinforce the Ministers' damaged position – he was expending all his physical and mental powers in an impossible defence to avert a sentence that had already been settled before the trial began.

Réal persisted relentlessly. He appeared to pass over what should have been the main subjects of the inquiry – proof of a prior understanding between Lahorie and Malet, names of accomplices, ramifications of the conspiracy – and instead became involved in captious questioning about the circumstances and details of Lahorie's actions during the few hours between his liberation from La Force and his re-arrest.

Pasquier was not the only one to have had enough of this. Pelet de la Lozère too could stand it no longer and drew the Prefect of Police aside to whisper in his ear: 'Réal is playing a positively cat-and-mouse game, don't you think? It's going too far.'

And turning to the chairman of the Commission he said curtly: 'I think we can suspend the interrogation for today. I am sure we shall discover nothing more from the gentleman than we have already learnt in these three hours.'

Réal had to give in and abandon his questioning. Lahorie, surrounded by gendarmes, was led away from the Ministry of Police where the interrogation had been held to the old prison of L'Abbaye in the Saint-Germain quarter, where Malet had preceded him.

By now night had fallen, the end of the long day that began before dawn arose on that 23rd October over the rainswept skies of Paris.

* * *

The Fouchers had not managed to persuade Sophie to calm down and return home to her three children. Sophie had made up her mind to speak to Delon and nothing would move her from this determination even if she had to wait half the night.

Pierre resigned himself, and when some little time later he was told that Captain Delon had returned home he went to ask him to receive Sophie. The Delons and the Hugos were, as a matter of fact, old friends: the Captain's son was the same age as Sophie's eldest boy and for years had come to play with the Hugo children in the Feuillantines garden. So Delon made no difficulty about seeing Sophie, and Pierre accompanied her to the door of his apartment.

Delon was an old magistrate and for years had been *rapporteur* to the military tribunal. From his calm countenance and serene, clear eyes beneath his grey hairs, one would never have guessed that in countless trials he had requested, and obtained, the death sentence for the accused – enemy spies, attempted murderers, or mere opponents of the regime – who had come up before him as Public Prosecutor. He wore uniform, but he was first and foremost a meticulous official and precise executant of the superior orders which in most cases, in a tribunal of this kind, took the place of the legal code.

Sophie ran up to him, still agitated but more in control of herself after her long and anxious wait.

'Delon, I am here not to ask for clemency but to prevent you from committing an injustice. Lahorie is innocent, he had nothing to do with Malet's conspiracy – I can prove it.'

'Prove it, Madame Hugo? How?'

'I am ready to bear witness that Lahorie knew nothing about what Malet was planning. No one knows it better than I. I want to prevent a crime being committed. . . . I knew everything, but he didn't: I want to be called as a witness. If necessary, I am ready to sit among the accused to declare, cost what it may, that I was aware of what Malet was planning, whereas Lahorie knew nothing of it. It was I who involved him in this affair without his being told anything about it, because I did not want him to be deported to America. Therefore I am ready to assume the whole responsibility provided he, who is innocent, can be absolved. I prefer. . . .'

Delon's clear gaze grew colder and he interrupted her: 'Madame, the only thing I can do for you is to forget your words, inspired no doubt by friendship and by grief. I will forget them, I promise you. Apart from that, I will not and cannot do anything which – forgive me – would impede the course of justice and cause me to neglect my duty. As for you, remember your children and your obligations towards them, even if you do not wish to remember that you are the wife of a French general.'

He took her back to the Fouchers without letting her say another word, refusing to profit from her grief to discover further details about the conspiracy. The instructions he had received personally shortly before from the War Minister, the Duke of Feltre, had, moreover, caused him to regard the trial as settled even before it began. The case was already decided.

Madame Foucher wanted to take Sophie home, but she refused: she was overcome, but she walked straight on without seeing anyone. Her eyes were dry. Even when she got home and found the three boys anxious at her absence she remained calm and mistress of herself.

'There's no need to worry, children, and above all no need to cry. Tears can only bring rust to a steel blade.'

This metaphor pleased Victor, and he made a mental note of it. He had grasped that only one thing could have aroused such deep, reticent and dignified grief in his mother: some misfortune must have befallen his godfather, who for so many months had been their secret guest and had taught him to read the Latin poets and love freedom.

* * *

The enmity and rivalry which for years had divided the two Generals whom Napoleon had made Ministers and honoured with an Italian ducal title – Savary, Minister of Police and Duke of Rovigo, and Clarke, Minister of War and Duke of Feltre – had exploded into open conflict over Malet's conspiracy. Clarke now felt he was the stronger. Unlike his colleague and rival he was not compromised, and having persuaded the Arch-Chancellor to entrust the inquiry to him he was conducting it in his own way. His indirect aim was to demonstrate the ineptitude of Savary's police, who had left a dangerous man like Malet in a clinic from which escape was easy, allowing the conspirators to prepare their plans and keeping no watch either on them or on their accomplices outside, and in a word had let themselves be taken completely by surprise. Savary, for his part, denounced the feebleness of the military authorities, the stupidity, not to say imbecility, of the commanders of the two corps entrusted with the defence of order in the capital, the seditious spirit shown by several officers and whole detachments, and the obvious enthusiasm with which the troops had received the news of the Emperor's death. Savary had not forgotten the aggressive and hostile attitude of some of the officers and men towards himself at the time of his arrest, the insulting remarks and threatening gestures which were certainly not just a part of their execution of orders but were dictated by dislike of the imperial regime and its exponents.

Towards Lahorie, Savary felt neither hatred nor resentment: he realized that Lahorie's presence had probably saved his life, and at the same time he was convinced that his old friend, whom he himself had had arrested in the past in unpleasant circumstances, was acting in good faith, believing that Napoleon was dead and a new regime had been set up by the Senate. He therefore took the step of intervening with Cambacérès to save the life of his brother officer before the start of the trial which was certain to end in a death sentence for the chief accused. It was a useless effort, but one which did honour to the Minister of Police.

But by then it had been decided that the inquiry should be put in the hands of the Minister of War. The police chiefs' Commission carried out some further questioning of the principals in the conspiracy and the army personnel who had allowed themselves to become involved in the *coup d'état*. In the meantime a Bench was appointed, presided over by a general, Count Dejean, and consisting of two other generals, a colonel and a major; the *rapporteur* of the Bench, in other words the public prosecutor, was Captain Delon, and he was entrusted with the task of continuing the interrogation of those arrested.

Of these there were quite a number. In addition to Malet and the direct accomplices, Lahorie, Guidal, Rateau, Boccheciampe and Cajamaño, by order of the Minister of War twenty-four officers and N.C.O.s of the 10th Cohort and the Paris Guard, including the two commanders, Rabbe and Soulier, had been put in prison, and a few days later seven more officers of the Paris Guard had suffered the same fate. Denise de Malet, the General's wife, had been shut up in the Madelonnettes prison, where she was to remain for more than a year, and with her had been arrested all those whose names had been connected in any way, however fortuitously, with the conspiracy – the shoemaker Ladré from whom Malet had ordered a pair of boots, General Desnoyers who had refused Malet's invitation to join him, and even General Lamotte whose name Malet had assumed without his knowledge. They also arrested or interrogated relatives and friends of the General, such as Rouget de Lisle, author of the *Marseillaise*, who was able to show that he had not left his village in the Jura for more than a year. And they arrested the young corset-maker who had brought Malet a message from Demaillot, and many other people whose sole offence was to have known Malet and occasionally spoken to him, an offence that cost them from eight months to a year in prison.

Neither the police interrogations nor those of Captain Delon produced much in the way of results. Malet at his second interrogation adopted the line he had evolved during the long sleepless night in the Abbaye prison: he and he alone was responsible and all the others, both the two Generals he had liberated from La Force and the military commanders who had placed their detachments under his orders, were completely innocent and had acted in good faith. They had believed in him and his 'truth': that Napoleon was dead, a new regime had been established by the Senate, and Malet was military Commandant of Paris, to be obeyed by all the armed forces of the capital. Therefore he alone was responsible, and to him alone was due the merit of having shown the world that the Napoleonic Empire did not exist as a political regime but was exclusively linked to the physical person of its founder, and that, moreover, the French people, beginning with its representative body the army, had had enough of that regime based on war, and of its leader. He therefore answered all questions by himself assuming the entire blame and exculpating all the others.

Lahorie continued in his original attitude, firmly and courteously maintaining his own good faith and his belief that he was experiencing just another of the historic 'days' to which his generation had became accustomed during the past twenty years. Only once did he become really roused. Captain Delon challenged him with having said to Guidal after their arrest: 'If you hadn't hesitated we shouldn't be here now.' Lahorie sprang to his feet and answered indignantly: 'I deny having used that expression, for two reasons. First, because I did not say it; and secondly because I cannot allow it to be said that I address General Guidal by the familiar "tu". No one is authorized to think that relations of that kind exist between him and me.'

From Guidal the captain learnt little. Guidal knew that however things went, either there or at Aix-en-Provence, the execution squad awaited him in the end, and on the whole he felt it was almost better to die as a conspirator than as a spy in English pay. However he too proclaimed his good faith and complete ignorance of the conspiracy and swore he had never seen Malet until he appeared at La Force to set him free. Nothing else emerged from his questioning.

Both the police and Captain Delon, on the other hand, learnt a good deal more from their interrogation of Corporal Rateau. From the moment of his arrest, the result of his extraordinary conduct in Cabby Georges' carriage, the young man declared that he wished to speak and tell all he knew to assist justice and prove his own innocence. Taken from the punishment cell in the barracks to the Abbaye prison, after a night in the cells there he came before the Commission of inquiry looking thoroughly bedraggled, a pale shadow of the ambitious little corporal of the Paris Guard who wanted to get on in life so as to wear a finer uniform and be a success with the girls, and who had deluded himself into believing he had suddenly and effortlessly achieved that ideal. The police on the Commission saw before them a panic-stricken lad, who kept on saying he held only two things in the world dear, his love for his mother and his devotion to the Emperor, and for that twofold filial motive he was ready to do anything, to tell all he knew and to collaborate with the Commission to the utmost of his poor powers.

Réal took him at his word and had no difficulty in eliciting from the unfortunate youth everything he was in a position to reveal. After first averring that he knew nothing of the conspiracy and had found himself by pure chance in the Spanish priest's house in the presence of an unknown General, Rateau declared that the General had told him the Emperor had been killed at Moscow and the Senate had charged him, the General, to assume the military command. As he needed an aide-de-camp and had no officer immediately available, the said General had there and then promoted him an officer and his aide, saying his appointment would be regularly confirmed as soon as he himself was fully in command. The young man also said, as if to add verisimilitude to his tale and convincing proof of his innocence, that the General, whose name he heard was Malet, wanted to attach the cross of the Legion of Honour to the officer's uniform he made him put on, but that he, Rateau, had refused, feeling himself unworthy to wear a decoration for valour since he had not yet had the chance to perform any action deserving of it. From that moment all he had done was to obey the General's orders and keep at two paces distance from him at Popincourt Barracks and on the marches through the city, performing no action whatever himself or on his own initiative.

Having made clear his own personal position and stressed his complete innocence, he then let himself go in revelations that Réal had no difficulty in extracting. He spoke of Abbé Lafon, whose responsibility in the conspiracy had not emerged from the previous interrogations. He told what he knew about him, his personal appearance, his clothes, and where he might be in hiding. He revealed that he had taken a note from Malet to General Desnoyers and brought back a negative reply (this revelation was to cost Desnoyers a year in prison).

He spoke at some length of the young man who had assumed the duties of police commissioner and then actually taken the place of the Prefect, and for the first time revealed his name, which was Boutreux, not Balancié, as the police had hitherto believed. He informed Réal that

Boutreux had at one time been tutor in the house of a certain M. de Bories, Mayor of Courcelles in the Seine-et-Oise department. It was therefore possible that he might have taken refuge in that quiet corner (and there, in fact, Desmarest's agents found him and brought him in, handcuffed, to prison).

The young man concluded on a pathetic note of appeal to the examining magistrate: 'You can judge of my innocence and my desire to collaborate with you in bringing punishment to the criminals whose victim I have been. Restore me to where I really belong, to my family – restore me to the Rateau family.'

After that oratorical effort he burst into tears and was still sobbing when the gendarmes took him back to prison.

* * *

Commandant Soulier found it almost impossible to believe that he had been put in prison and must prepare to appear before a military tribunal. In the few hours that he had spent in barracks awaiting orders after Laborde had told him to leave the Hôtel de Ville with his men, he had supposed that at most he would get a few days of house arrest, and he thought with distaste of the reproaches and criticisms he would have to put up with from his wife during those days of enforced stay in his home. His dependents, the officers and N.C.O.s of the cohort, who had taken part in the morning's operations under Malet's orders, were in the same state of uncertainty, anxious about probable discipinary punishments and the adverse effects they might have on their careers. The soldiers were less worried, hoping that as small fry they might get off scot-free. After all, they had only done what they had always done ever since they entered the army – obeyed the officers and sergeants, performed right or left turns, marched along the uneven pavements of Paris that hurt their feet, and carried out orders, some of them admittedly quite entertaining, like arresting a minister in his night-shirt and taking him to prison. A few pessimistic ones said: 'You'll see, it'll be us who have to pay for everyone. We'll be sent to fight in Russia or Spain – *adieu* Paris!'

The arrival in barracks of a squad of gendarmes with some officials brought the waiting to a worse end than they expected. The gendarmes took off under arrest ten officers of the cohort, among them the commander himself. The soldiers standing about in the courtyard were so stupified that they raised no cry of protest or even a murmur of surprise. The officers were led away by the gendarmes amid complete silence. What would happen to themselves, poor devils of privates with no one to protect them, if their officers were being treated with such severity?

When he found himself faced with Réal and Desmarest reproaching him for his unbelievable credulity, Soulier, looking more grey and worn than usual, could only justify himself by blaming his state of health when the General and his suite had arrived at his house in the middle of the night to find him in a feverish condition that had confined him to bed since the day before.

'I was feeling so ill, what with the fever and the emotion of General Lamotte's news that the Emperor was dead, that the sweat was running off me and I had to change my linen four times.' (The unfortunate man still, in fact, believed that he had had to do with a General Lamotte, not knowing that it was really Malet. It was only after being confronted with the unknown General Lamotte that he declared that he had never seen the man, whereas Malet he recognized at once. In spite of this, Lamotte remained in prison for some time.)

'Did you take the trouble to verify the authenticity of the documents this General showed you?' asked Desmarest.

'I was not in a position to verify anything. I did think for a minute of sending someone to find out from headquarters, but I had no one to send, and the General was most insistent that the Senate's orders must be carried out at once. So that when my Adjutant-Major, Piquerel, appeared at my house, as he had been told to do, I put everything in his hands and left him to carry out the orders. I simply wasn't equal to it in the state I was in.'

He seemed even then, as he stood before the Commission, to be still racked with fever, for he found difficulty in speaking coherently and not sounding sorry for himself. It was only when Desmarest insinuated that perhaps he had let himself be seduced by the prospect of promotion and the General's offer of a 100,000 franc voucher that Soulier became indignant and found the strength to refute the accusation of having acted for reasons of personal interest. In the course of questioning it emerged clearly that he had bothered so little about those 100,000 francs that he had never even noticed the date on the voucher, which was October 11th, not the 22nd – in other words the date of Malet's first attempt which came to nothing.

The police Commission learnt nothing more from him: it was all due to his fever, so he said, which had prevented him from checking the authenticity of the orders that a general in uniform, escorted by an aide-de-camp and a police commissioner, had brought him in the middle of the night.

To Captain Delon, the Public Prosecutor, next day Commandant Soulier merely repeated the same attempts to justify himself. He added only one more positive argument in his defence, which had perhaps occurred to him in the solitude of his cell: 'If I had been the conspirators' accomplice, I should have hastened to offer them the two barrels of powder and the ten thousand cartridges that I had in the barracks armoury. In that case it would have been a good deal less easy to cut short the conspiracy.'

They took him back to prison even more depressed and desperate after the second interrogation: by now he was sure that the Minister would not be satisfied with a disciplinary punishment but would make him appear before a military tribunal. What would become of his career, even if he could hardly be given a heavy sentence since at most it was a question of negligence? All hope of promotion was gone and he would have to retire with the miserable pension of his present rank. What would his wife say? For the rest of his days he would have to listen to her reproaches.

* * *

Colonel Rabbe defended himself in a very different way, by throwing the blame on his subordinates. He had received no direct orders either from the Senate or from Garrison Command: therefore he had had no means of checking whether their origins were authentic. He was at home, in civilian dress and about to leave on a mission, when the adjutant on duty had arrived to inform him of the orders that had come by messenger from the command of the military division. How could he have had any doubts about orders sent in a way so entirely in conformity with regulations and custom? Their contents seemed to be the inevitable consequence of so tragic and extraordinary an event as the sudden death of His Majesty the Emperor and King. Overcome with grief at the news, far from barracks, and, moreover, in civilian dress, Colonel Rabbe had no alternative but to let his subordinate officers carry out the orders from the command: it was they, therefore, who had assembled the detachments and sent them to their various destinations, who had assumed, in short, full responsibility for what had happened. As for himself, Rabbe, once he had got over the first impact of that terrible news he had recovered his uniform from his luggage and gone as quickly as possible to Garrison Command to get confirmation of what he had been told. There he had had the joy of learning from Doucet and Laborde – thought after a stern reprimand – that the news of the Emperor's death was, thank Heaven, not true, and that it was a case of a conspiracy already nipped in the bud. As for the participation, however involuntary, of the Paris Guard in the events, they should take that up with his officers who had carried out the presumed orders of the command without first making sure they were authentic, thus making party to the fraud himself, their commander, who had not received those orders but had merely had indirect cognizance of them. As far as he himself was concerned, Laborde could testify the trouble he had taken afterwards, riding throughout the city to restore order, clarify the situation, and send back the troops to barracks, in a word to repair the harm so carelessly done by his subordinates.

The interrogations of the subordinate officers, both of the 10th Cohort and of the Paris Guard, were merely monotonous variations on the same theme: they had acted in strict obedience to their superiors' orders, discipline forbidding the submission of such orders to check or control. As always throughout their army life, they had obeyed the orders received from the officer entitled to give them, in other words from their direct superior: Adjutant-Major Piquerel directly from the commander of the cohort, the company commanders from the Adjutant-Major, the platoon commanders from the company commander. Nothing that night had disturbed the normal hierarchical order: therefore each one believed he had done exactly what it was his formal duty to do. They were all old soldiers, these cohort officers, men who had not had brilliant careers but had got along on their pay without any particular ambitions: captains of forty-one years old like Piquerel, or forty-nine like Steenhower, and even lieutenants of forty-four or forty-five like Gomont Saint-Charles and Lefèvre.

In some cases, it was obvious, those orders had been carried out with especial zeal, dictated by frustrated ambition, rancour at failure to get promotion, and the pleasure of seeing the downfall of the regime's important personages, laden with wealth and honours.

The Commission concentrated its attention on Steenhower, who had stood passively by during Malet's attempt to kill Hulin. But in this case too the old officer entrenched himself firmly behind discipline and obedience. As a man, he declared, that brutal scene had turned his stomach, so much so that he had had to ask for a cordial to pull him together; but as a soldier, though he had not actually rebelled against the General, which discipline in any case forbade, he believed he had done as much as he could within the permitted limits of hierarchical respect in suggesting that General Hulin had the right to ask to see the written orders brought by General Malet. Moreover, when he learnt a few minutes later that the whole thing was an attempted outrage, he had at once put himself under the orders of Colonel Doucet and Adjutant Laborde and had seen to it that the troops returned to barracks without further incident.

The Commission was no more fortunate in securing information from the officers and N.C.O.s of the Paris Guard, who, too, were old soldiers who had not left the garrison for years. The orders had reached them in the usual way, brought by a courier. They seemed to be impeccably drafted: apart from the extraordinary fact of the Emperor's death and the establishment of a provisional government, all the rest appeared both in form and in substance to be a matter of perfectly ordinary administration. To be on guard at ministries or city gateways, to send out detachments of guards to public buildings, were tasks that the Paris Guard carried out every day: if the divisional commandant giving the orders was called Malet instead of Hulin, what difference did it make? What did they, the captains, lieutenants, or mere sergeants, know of important people like generals, superior beings who habitually gave orders while remaining invisible? In this case too, this new Commandant, this General Malet, they had never even seen him.

Neither the Commission nor Captain Delon could extract anything further; in particular, they could not succeed in establishing that there had been any prior understanding between the conspirators and some member, either officer or N.C.O., of the detachments that had so readily placed themselves under the orders of the conspiracy. The interrogations went on for four days, the most useless of all being that of the harmless Boccheciampe.

On the evening of the 27th, since both the Arch-Chancellor and the Minister of War were insisting that they should make haste, the Public Prosecutor, Captain Delon, declared the inquiry closed. The trial was to take place on the following morning at the Rue du Cherche-Midi.

Captain Delon was overwhelmed with the work he still had to do in the few hours before the trial began. He returned home laden with the records of the interrogations: from that mass of words, attempted justifications, excuses, and admissions, he had to draw up a lucid indictment of such overwhelming effect against the accused as to justify the sentence already decided upon in accordance with the orders of the Minister of War. Those orders were: the utmost severity for the chief accused, including the corps commanders and those subordinate officers whose particular zeal had been remarked, and some degree of indulgence for the rest.

Pierre Foucher found his friend and neighbour immersed in the wellnigh impossible task of transforming all that raw material into a formal indictment. Moved by friendship and professional comradeship, he felt, as he later confessed, sorry for him rather than for all those people condemned before being judged, and he offered to help him. He sat opposite him, and with his long experience as clerk to a war tribunal he put the records in order and summarized them, patiently reconstructing in the light of his official experience the events that made up the vast preamble to the indictment.

Delon, freed from this preliminary labour, began drawing up the actual list of charges, the indictment on which the trial was to be based. Neither Boutreux nor Cajamaño, though both under arrest, were included in the indictment: it was hoped, by means of prolonged interrogation and a separate trial, to learn from them something more about the origins and secret ramifications of the conspiracy. Nor did the person figure there who should have appeared as the chief accused after Malet – Abbé Lafon. The gendarmes were searching vainly for him throughout the country. But he had disappeared, vanished into thin air as if he had never existed.

They preferred not to judge him in absence but to continue the search for him. Referred for trial, together with the principal accused, were the two corps commanders and eighteen captains, subordinate officers, and N.C.O.s: twenty-four accused who on the following morning were to appear before the military Commission. The other arrested men would be sent back to their detachments.

Delon and Foucher worked side by side well into the night. It was two in the morning, only five hours before the trial was due to begin, when Pierre Foucher at last went home to bed. During those hours of work he had felt rejuvenated, as if he was back again at the war tribunal: who the accused were was of no importance, all that mattered for him was to finish the work he had taken on quickly and in a manner in keeping with the rules of procedure. Not for a minute did he think of Sophie Hugo and the human drama represented for her by that indictment on which he had worked so hard that he felt quite worn out.

Chapter 13

Rue du Cherche-Midi — 2

Night had fallen when the accused men learnt in prison that the trial was to begin next morning. The news spread panic among the lesser culprits, the officers who had been compromised in spite of themselves and who till then had retained the illusion that it would all pass off with a mere disciplinary punishment. They demanded lawyers and the time necessary to prepare their defence. But the only ones who succeeded in having someone to defend them during the trial were Captain Steenhower, who had a lawyer brother-in-law, and two sergeants of the Paris Guard. The others were denied any legal support. Lahorie was even refused a light, which he had asked for in order to study certain documents he considered necessary for his defence.

All along the corridor outside the cells at L'Abbaye the lamentations and plaints of Commandant Soulier could be heard, invoking the names of his wife and children, and the imprecations of Colonel Rabbe against the junior officers who had dragged him into this situation.

Malet, impassive as ever, walked up and down in his cell. He had only one anxiety : that they might stifle his voice at the trial and deny him the right to be regarded by history as the sole individual responsible for that decisive blow to the imperial regime. He was therefore concerned to establish the difference between himself and the insignificant people who would be with him on the bench of the accused : in the hall of the tribunal, before the servitors of Napoleon, there should be him alone, and however the trial ended –

and for him it could only end in death – the real victor in the judgement of history would be he, Malet.

* * *

The Chairman of the military Commission, General Count Dejean, entered the hall in the Cherche-Midi building at seven in the morning, followed by five judges, two generals, two colonels and a major, and by the public prosecutor Delon, whose eyes were red after his sleepless night.

By an unusual procedure, which demonstrated the haste with which this semblance of a trial was to be conducted and brought to its fore-ordained conclusion, the Public Prosecutor read out, in the absence of the accused, the documents connected with the trial, which included reports from Doucet and Laborde, all the alleged documents forged by Malet which formed the basis of the conspiracy, and the interrogations of the accused. The reading lasted for over an hour. The Public Prosecutor then asked that Malet, Lahorie, Guidal, and all the others should at once be brought before the Commission to answer accusations of conspiracy and attempt against the security of the State.

At a sign from the chairman the gendarmes brought into the hall the long line of twenty-four accused. At their head was Malet, who walked unhesitatingly to the highest of the three benches arranged in tiers for the accused, on the left of the platform where the members of the Commission were seated. Beside him on the same bench sat Lahorie, Guidal, Soulier, Rateau and Boccheciampe. The others took their places on the two lower benches.

* * *

It was a little after six and still dark in the rainy October morning when Sophie Hugo knocked at the door of the Fouchers' apartment in the same building in Rue du Cherche-Midi. She hoped to be able to catch a glimpse of Lahorie and make some sign to him when he arrived with the others from the prison, so that he might feel she had not abandoned him but was beside him, living with him through this drama into which she had unwisely drawn him through her love.

Pierre Foucher at once quenched her hopes, telling her that the prisoners would be brought in closed carriages into the entrance-way and from there the gendarmes would lead them by a separate staircase used on such occasions right into the antechamber of the tribunal hall.

Only a corridor and a few walls separated the hall from the Fouchers' apartment, but as the public was not admitted to trials of this kind Sophie could not hope even to put her head into the hall and give a long look at the man over whom, as she now could not but know, hung the penalty of death. In compensation Pierre promised her that if she would keep calm and wait patiently in his apartment he would let her know as soon as possible what was happening at the trial. He had arranged this, he said, with officers of the gendarmerie on duty in the hall, who would come round to his apartment every so often to report how things were going.

* * *

So far things were going badly for Lahorie. He had at once asked to be allowed to speak in order to request some documents which had been confiscated from him before his internment in La Force and which he considered necessary for his defence, since they demonstrated his complete innocence in relation to General Moreau's conspiracy for which he had been arrested two years before. But the Chairman cut him short, saying that those documents would be of no use since he was to be judged not on the basis of earlier accusations but only for his participation in General Malet's conspiracy.

Lahorie could only sit down again. Sophie would hardly

have recognized him, so changed was his countenance, hollow-eyed from lack of sleep and with a nervous tic, desperately aware that he had fallen into a fatal trap from which there was no way out.

Beside him and on the lower benches, the other soldiers involved despite themselves in this affair seemed only now to have realized the seriousness of their situation. Rabbe stared with incredulous eyes at the military magistrates' chairs where less than a year before he himself had sat as judge in the trial of the ex-Queen of Etruria's agents – which had ended in sentence of death for the accused. He found it impossible to believe that he, who had done nothing wrong and had never betrayed his loyalty to the Emperor, was now appearing himself in that same hall among the accused.

The Chairman began the interrogation of the principal accused, Claude-François Malet, ex-Brigadier General. This was the easiest and shortest of the interrogations. The accused admitted all the facts, in his first words took full responsibility for them, and recognized as his own the pistols of which Laborde had taken possession when arresting him.

At this point the Chairman asked him to give the names of his accomplices. Malet drew himself to his full height and in a calm voice, separating his words so that not one might be lost, replied: 'My accomplices? All France, and you too, M. le Président, if I had succeeded.'

The Chairman answered with a shrug of the shoulders and made a sign for Malet to sit down. Why go further with a defendant who so openly admitted his guilt?

Lahorie began his statement by repeating his protest that he had not been allowed the time or the opportunity to collect the necessary proofs to demonstrate his complete innocence and the absence of any understanding whatever with Malet. His defence, improvised but eloquent, followed the same line that he had adopted under interrogation: he was completely in the dark about the conspiracy, and his liberation from La Force Prison had come about in a perfectly regular way through the prison head-warder, who had told him he was being set free by order of the Senate. General Malet, whom he had not seen for eighteen years and to whom he was not bound by any ties of friendship, had declared himself the bearer of a Senate decree and stood before him at the head of an armed military detachment. Lahorie had therefore been certain that he was taking part, not in a conspiracy, but in a change of regime carried out by the authorities themselves.

'Shut up in prison as I was, how could I know it was untrue that the Senate had met to decide on the establishment of a provisional government following the Emperor's death? I believed I was reliving a day that I and all of you, gentlemen, had lived through once before – the 18th Brumaire. If the Emperor were here present in this hall, I am convinced that he would understand my explanation, just as he would understand that I would have feared to be taken for a coward if I had refused to carry out the orders of which General Malet was the bearer. While taking no initiative myself, I therefore confined myself to joining the troops that marched through the city in broad daylight and in perfect good order.'

As to his actions at the Ministry of Police and the arrest of the Duke of Rovigo, Lahorie declared emphatically that his sole aim had been to protect the Minister from possible violence. In acting thus, and in having recourse to the expedient of describing himself in writing as provisional Minister of Police in order to get the Duke into prison, he had, he maintained, in fact shown true generosity of spirit in concerning himself with the physical safety of one who for the past two years had subjected him to persecution.

His voice rang out so clear and sure, vibrating with such desperate sincerity, that the Chairman did not interrupt him. The nervous tic had gone and his eyes were once more sparkling and lively: he looked like a man who was fighting not so much for his life as for his good name and his honour as a soldier.

'If I have been mistaken, if the mistake I made is to cost me my life, I declare that from my tomb a terrible voice will arise to proclaim that I died to save the life of persons hostile to me. Though the position in which I found myself would have justified passion and violence, I listened only to the voice of humanity and generosity. And now, M. le rapporteur, I ask you to declare whether you have any proof of previous understanding between myself and General Malet.'

To this request, which showed Lahorie's complete confidence in his own affirmation of ignorance concerning the conspiracy, Captain Delon confined himself to replying curtly: 'I would remind the accused that he has no right to address the Public Prosecutor directly.'

Lahorie sank slowly back on his seat. He had tried to clarify his position to the judges in the only way permitted to him. Now he could do no more than keep silence and await his fate with dignity.

Dignity was shown also, and unexpectedly, by Guidal, who after complaining that he had no lawyer for his defence began by proclaiming his good faith and his ignorance of the conspiracy.

At this point the Chairman called on Lieutenants Lebis and Fessart to stand up and asked Guidal: 'Which was it of these two men who in your presence rushed with drawn sword into the study of the Minister of Police shouting "skewer 'em like frogs on a spit!"?'

Guidal knew perfectly well that it was Lebis. But he wished to be generous. He looked the two officers full in the face and answered the chairman: 'I know neither of these gentlemen.'

* * *

Commandant Soulier could barely stand when the Chairman asked him to rise. Even before the questioning began he appealed for pity for his wife and four children, and for himself who had been taken by surprise and deceived by an imposter as he lay ill in bed with fever. Nor could he find any other answer to give to the Chairman's questions: that night he had been too much overcome by fever and the news of the Emperor's death to make any attempt to check the alleged documents read out to him by the man he had taken to be General Lamotte. The only thing he had grasped was that this General, invested by the Senate with special powers, was ordering him to send his troops out from barracks. And when at this point the Chairman attempted to go into the question of the orders, asking who had given them and how they had been conveyed, Malet sprang to his feet and once again claimed the entire responsibility.

'Since I, a General, had given him the order for his cohort to march, the Commandant, my subordinate, had to carry out this order and obey me – it was his bounden duty as a soldier.'

The Chairman interruped: 'His duty would have been to have you arrested.'

The remainder of the interrogation concerned details of secondary importance as compared with the main fact that Commandant Soulier had believed it to be his duty to obey the orders of the Senate brought by General Lamotte. Subsequent actions and events were merely the consequence of this.

From the interrogation of Adjutant-Major Piquerel and the other officers all that emerged was that each of them had confined himself to carrying out his immediate superior's orders which he had never thought to question, and that they therefore considered themselves completely exempt from the conspiracy, about which they had known nothing whatever right up to the end.

Boccheciampe in his comical French declared himself entirely innocent. He had believed he was being let out of prison as the result of a general amnesty following the death of Napoleon. He knew nothing, he had done nothing, he didn't know anybody. He couldn't understand what they had against him or why they had dragged him there with all those unknown soldiers. He asked for a lawyer, or at least an interpreter to help him to make himself understood.

The Chairman told him to sit down.

Colonel Rabbe defended himself stoutly. He explained in detail his situation when the adjutant brought the news of the Emperor's death – how he was just setting out on a mission, with his uniform already packed. Overwhelmed at the news that Napoleon, whom he had served faithfully all his life, was dead, he had read the documents brought by the adjutant with only half his mind, certainly in no state to check their authenticity. His anguish and grief was such that he had had to lean against the chimney-piece for support as he said to his adjutant: 'We are lost – what will become of us?' 'The news of the Emperor's death,' he added, 'came as such a blow that it paralysed me completely, both physically and mentally.'

At this one of the judges interrupted him to observe severely: 'It is precisely when the safety of the State is at stake that soldiers must not lose their heads and remember that the Emperor is immortal. If the Emperor dies, they must say: "Long live the Emperor!" '

Malet sat with folded arms listening to this profession of faith in the regime which was really an indirect recognition of his victory. No one had, in fact, cried 'Long live the Emperor!' when he had announced the death of Napoleon I; no one had thought that there might be a Napoleon II ready to succeed him automatically, just outside Paris, at Saint-Cloud, in the arms of the Empress Regent. All those loyal soldiers had found it perfectly natural that the Senate should have proclaimed the Republic.

The interrogation of the officers of the Paris Guard also added nothing new except for a few details of a military nature about the orders received and carried out. They knew even less about the conspiracy than their colleagues of the 10th Cohort, for none of them had seen Malet, Lahorie or Guidal in the flesh or taken part in the liberation of prisoners or in arrests. All had confined themselves to obeying their immediate superiors, carrying out tasks just like those assigned to them every day such as standing guard at ministries or at the city gates.

Corporal Rateau was a good deal more explicit. Standing to attention with all the appearance of a zealous, eager young man he admitted all the facts while at the same time declaring he knew nothing of the conspiracy. He admitted having often met Malet at the Dubuisson clinic when he went to visit Abbé Lafon, and he also admitted having been in the Spanish priest's house ('quite by chance – Boutreux took me there when I went out with him to spend the evening in the town—') and having put on the aide-de-camp's uniform.

'Yes, sirs, I put it on for reasons of discipline and obedience. The General had ordered me to be his aide-de-camp, and like a good soldier I obeyed him.'

The Chairman cut him short and closed the interrogations. By now it was evening. More than twelve hours had gone by since the hearing opened, and the interrogations had lasted nearly eleven hours. But the Chairman did not wish to adjourn to the following day a trial which according to higher orders was to last only a day, and in which interrogation of witnesses was not allowed. The hearing was suspended until 11 p.m. The accused were taken into the antechamber of the hall to get some refreshment.

* * *

Throughout the day Sophie Hugo had followed the ups and downs of the hearing through the brief accounts of the gendarmerie officers, who according to promise called in at intervals at the Fouchers' apartment. When they reported that Malet had proclaimed all France would have been his accomplice had he succeeded, she glowed in agreement, 'Yes, indeed, the whole of France'. She was torn between remorse at having dragged Lahorie into the venture and regret at not having shared in it in person, bringing to that operation, so well conceived by Malet and so badly executed by his improvised accomplices, her own warlike spirit of the Vendée, accustomed from childhood to *coups de main* and rapid, resolute decisions. She did not weep when they told her of Lahorie's passionate and unavailing defence, for she could find no comfort in tears: she admired and loved him more than ever, imagining his 'diamond eyes' sending forth sparks against those marionettes sitting in the judges' seats in that sinister parody of a trial.

At eight o'clock, when they heard the hearing was to be suspended for three hours, she tried once more to persuade Pierre Foucher to secure her a brief meeting, even a mere exchange of looks, with Victor de Lahorie. Pierre, with his sharp nose like a ferret's and his gentle, implacable manner, categorically refused. It was quite impossible, he said: the accused were kept in complete isolation and according to military legal regulations no one might communicate with them or even see them through the crack of a door. She must wait in patience: the trial was not over yet, and Lahorie had put up an effective defence. At the same time he was thinking that when the hearing resumed his friend Delon would pronounce the indictment on which he had so zealously collaborated; he knew perfectly well that it concluded with a request for the death sentence for all the guilty, among them of course, next to Malet, Lahorie, regarded as his chief accomplice. And he knew that the request was only a formality to respect procedure, since the condemnations had already been decided on personally one by one by the Minister of War, the Duke of Feltre.

Sophie walked up and down in the drawing-room, refusing Madame Foucher's offers of food and drink. Little

Adèle had been put to bed and perhaps she was the only one who before going to sleep thought of Victor and his brothers who, left with the servant in the house in Passage des Feuillantines, had not seen their mother since morning.

* * *

It was a quarter before midnight when Delon finished reading the indictment and pronounced his requests: the death penalty for all the accused judged guilty by the Commission.

Soulier groaned and put his head between his hands. The others appeared impassive, some, like Malet, Lahorie and Guidal, already certain of their fate, other paralysed by the request that seemed to them a murderous negation of justice, a barefaced act of vengeance and the end of all hope.

At this point the Chairman called on the defence; and since there were only two defence lawyers present, in the majority of the cases the accused themselves made brief final statements in their own defence.

'Prisoner Malet, have you anything to add in your defence?'

Malet answered in a cold, precise voice as if calling on history to note his words: 'A man who has constituted himself the defender of his country has no need of defence: he either triumphs or dies.'

Lahorie repeated that he had believed he was living through another 18th Brumaire: 'I followed Malet in the same good faith with which I then followed Bonaparte.'

Guidal asked only that they should make an end of it as quickly as possible – he had given up his life long ago and had had enough of waiting.

Soulier could not resign himself. He tried once more to move the judges by speaking of his wife and children and his long military service, but his voice rose in indignation as he refuted the suspicion that he had let himself be tempted by Malet's offers of money and promotion.

'Less than a year ago, in February, in Spain, the enemy

surrounded Mount Jouy, which my troops were holding. I was offered half a million francs and the rank of general in the Spanish army if I would surrender. My answer was to counter-attack and put them to flight. Give me back my honour, gentlemen, give back their father to my children.'

Rabbe stood up. He strove to impress his former colleagues of the tribunal by his drum-major's stature and by the sonorous sentence: 'I commend myself to your justice.'

'In that case you're done for,' murmured Guidal in his ear.

Boccheciampe continued to repeat that he knew nothing about anything and wasn't even able to express himself in French.

Next the two lawyers spoke, Caubert as defence for his brother-in-law Steenhower, and the other lawyer defending the two sergeant-majors of the Paris Guard. Neither was exactly a leading light in his profession and they had, moreover, been called only at the last minute; so they could only repeat the familiar arguments about military obedience that obliged a subaltern to carry out orders without having to establish their legitimacy. Both concluded on an optimistic note, relying on the understanding and clemency of the tribunal.

The last of the accused with no lawyer to defend them, Rouff, Régnier, Borderieux, the lieutenants and the other sergeants, could only stammer that they had been deceived, that they had obeyed, and that they had cried, 'Long live the Emperor', as soon as they had realized it was all a trick and the Emperor, thank Heaven, was still alive.

Rateau put himself in his questioners' hands reminding them that he had always been considered an honest soldier belonging to an honest family. At this point Malet rose again to defend the young man, repeating that he had deliberately tricked him and that the corporal had acted in good faith knowing nothing whatever of the conspiracy.

When he sat down again, Rateau, slightly encouraged by this intervention, stood to attention before the judges and cried in a loud voice: 'Long live His Majesty the Emperor and King!'

'And his justice,' added Lahorie *sotto voce*.

Soulier got up again to invoke clemency for himself and the other unfortunate soldiers, all with long years of service, all with families, all loyal to the Emperor, as they had shown on the battlefield.

At this point, by which time it was nearly two in the morning, the Chairman, Dejean, closed the hearing and ordered the accused to be taken back to prison where the verdict would be read out to them when the tribunal had pronounced its judgement.

The twenty-four accused came down from the benches and filed out before the judges who were to decide their fate. Two of them, Borderieux and Rateau, still possessed the strength to cry: 'Long live the Emperor!'

'They salute Caesar like dying gladiators,' remarked Lahorie, ever mindful of his classics, to his neighbour.

They left the hall which, just ten years later, was to be the scene of the wedding reception of Victor Hugo, aged twenty, and Adèle Foucher, aged nineteen. Not even on that very different occasion would Sophie Hugo set foot in that tribunal hall transformed for a festive gathering: she had died, struck down by a sudden illness, more than a year before.

* * *

They waited for two hours in the cells at L'Abbaye. Then six of the accused were brought out, surrounded by gendarmes, into a large room. The six were Malet, Rabbe, Soulier, Piquerel, Borderieux and Lefèvre, all of whom possessed the decoration of the Legion of Honour.

Captain Delon had them drawn up before him, ordered the gendarmes to present arms, and announced: 'You have acted dishonourably and therefore I declare, in the name of the Legion of Honour, that you cease to belong to it.'

They looked at each other and turned pale: it was the preliminary to sentence of death. They were joined at once by the other accused and Delon, assembling his remaining strength, in a toneless voice read out the sentence.

Condemned to death and to confiscation of property were Malet, Lahorie, Guidal, Rabbe, Soulier, Steenhower, Piquerel, Borderieux, Fessart, Lefèvre, Régnier, Beaumont, Rateau, and Boccheciampe. Fourteen men to be shot.

Absolved were the other ten: Captains Rouff and Godard, Lieutenants Gomont, Lebis, and Prévost, and non-commissioned officers Valhavielle, Caron, Limozin, Julien, and Caumette.

The sentence ended with these words: '*—orders the public prosecutor to have the sentences carried out in full within twenty-four hours*'.

Within twenty-four hours: how many of those hours had they still left to live? With this thought uppermost in their minds, the fourteen condemned men were led back to their cells. The others, those who had been absolved, prepared to pass what they hoped would be their last night in prison.

* * *

One look from Pierre Foucher, from those sharp eyes of his that strove to seem gentle, sufficed to tell Sophie that the sentence was death. All through the night she had waited, now walking up and down, now leaning against the mantelpiece by the fire which Madame Foucher had lit because it was cold in the room.

She asked only: 'When?'

'Today at four, twelve hours from now. In Plaine de Grenelle.'

Sophie wrapped herself in her shawl and shedding no tears set out homewards in the dark beneath the rain to the Passage des Feuillantines.

Chapter 14

Plaine de Grenelle

How many hours of those twenty-four had they still to live?

Each of the fourteen condemned men asked himself that agonizing question in the short time left before dawn. Malet was perhaps the only one who contrived to rest: he considered his task done and had already left it to history to decide what importance his attempt would have for the future of France. To Soulier, who was weeping and tormenting himself at the thought of his family after hearing the sentence, he had said: 'What's happening to us is nothing: far graver events are preparing for the country in the next six months.'

He was conscious of having worked for the future, and that he had dealt the imperial regime a blow no less serious than those it was receiving amid the snows of Russia, news of which was already beginning to circulate in Paris with the first reports of the retreat from Moscow.

Lahorie asked for writing materials. We do not know if he sent a last letter to Sophie. Probably not: as a man of honour he would certainly have wished to avoid compromising her by a letter that would end in the hands of the military judges. He wrote to Savary, and the letter still exists as documentary proof of a noble mind. He wrote to the Police Minister to ask him to hand over to his relatives a sum of money sequestrated from him which in fact belonged to them, and which they had lent him for use on his arrival in America after deportation. But the real point of that letter to his former comrade was to stress the extraordinary challenge that had developed between the Minister, who wished to deport him, and Fate, which had decided to keep him there in France. He was dying the innocent victim of that challenge, knowing nothing of Malet's conspiratorial fantasies.

But one consoling thought accompanied him in those last hours, the knowledge that he had acted solely from motives of generosity, to save a man who had not been generous to him. He concluded:

> You can be in no doubt that I am dying because I accepted a mission in which my sole aim was to save your life, and in particular because of the order for your transfer to prison, which was the one and only means of saving you. I remind you of this not for my own sake but for the concern I bear for my family, which has already suffered so much on my account. I have given you the example of generosity. Farewell, Savary.
>
> V. F. LAHORIE

Whether this letter was also dictated by a last hope that Savary might intervene on his behalf we shall never know. Savary had already, as we have seen, spontaneously intervened for him with the Arch-Chancellor, and to no purpose. Equally useless had been another attempt of Savary's, made before the trial, on behalf of Soulier, whose case he had tried to get suspended in order to pursue further inquiries into the possible complicity of the Paris Garrison with the conspirators. The obvious aim of this step was not to save Soulier but to compromise the armed forces by involving them in the conspiracy or at least increasing suspicion of it, and so turning on them the accusations of ineptitude and mismanagement that the military were busy formulating against the police.

But in the now open conflict that had developed between the Minister of Police and the Minister of War, the War Minister was in any case in the stronger position, for the

Arch-Chancellor, and with him the other Ministers, desired more than anything else to be done with the whole business as quickly as possible, so that when the Emperor came to know of the conspiracy he should hear at the same time that the guilty persons had been punished with the utmost severity. With this end in view the Minister for War had even before the inquiry began given the necessary orders to General Fririon, Hulin's temporary replacement, to prepare for the execution, already decided, of Malet and his accomplices, whether real or presumed. The orders included surrounding the place of execution with a sufficiently large deployment of armed forces to impress public opinion and dissuade any possible accomplices of Malet's who might be still at liberty from making a further attempt at sedition, and above all to provide a spectacular and sanguinary warning for the Paris Garrison itself, which had so signally failed to demonstrate its devotion to the Napoleonic regime.

The execution was entrusted to the Imperial Guard, who were to appoint the requisite number of fusiliers known to be first-class shots. These instructions of the Minister of War were dated October 24th, the day after the conspiracy and four days before the trial.

At ten in the morning the condemned men were told that at three in the afternoon they would be brought from prison to the place of execution. They were shut up in the cells, some, including Malet, Lahorie and Guidal, alone, others two or three together. There was no sign of the ceremonial that normally precedes executions, inspired apparently by a pious wish to keep the condemned men's minds occupied. No chaplain offering consolation, no visitors or lawyers were to be seen; even the warders – some of whom had been in service in that prison since the days of the Terror – and the gendarmes seemed to avoid contact with the condemned men. All were eager for the business to be done with, for those soldiers, till yesterday their colleagues, whether innocent or not to disappear from their sight, to cease from lamentation or scornful aloofness and be borne away to their fate. All had some feelings of shame and guilt.

The condemned men had been refused a last meeting with their wives and children or other relatives: this unusual severity was also perhaps dictated by the wish to get it over quickly, to close the episode and say no more about it. None of them saw his wife and children before dying, none could utter farewell words, reiterate his innocence or tell of his despair at dying for no fault of his, for no betrayal.

Soulier, who suffered most of all from this departure without farewell, could not get out of his mind the picture of his wife leaning over the banister of the staircase at home to exhort him to make his mark with the new leaders, not to be too modest as he usually was but to profit by that stroke of fortune.

All of them asked to be allowed to write a last letter of greeting. All but Malet: Denise had no need of last words or exhortations for the future. She had fought with him, she was in prison for him, and she had planned to ensure a better future for their son in a world free from tyrants, the world that he had striven to bring about and for which he was to die.

* * *

From early morning the troops were on parade in all the Paris barracks, for the whole garrison was to take part in the day's orders and be present at the execution.

At Popincourt Barracks there were new officers, brought in from other cohorts, since the Commander, the Adjutant-Major and several other officers were in prison and the soldiers had already heard rumours that they had been condemned. But the real command was in the hands of gendarmerie officers who had been installed in the barracks ever since the day of the conspiracy and kept the men under strict control. For the past six days the entire cohort had been confined to barracks, kept in quarantine and cut off from all contact with the outer world.

It was a gendarmerie officer who gave the order that most disturbed the men and that would have driven them to protest had they not been feeling so lost and miserable: they were to wear their tunics inside-out with the lining uppermost so that the uniform would not show, to mark them out to the citizens of Paris as soldiers who had put themselves at the service of the conspirators.

Polyte – Flatfoot felt absurdly clumsy with the tunic inside out and the metal buttons bruising his skin. On the first day he had been very pleased with himself, showing off to everyone that he knew much more than they did. It was he who had carried the lantern and accompanied the General to Commandant Soulier's house, and afterwards he had taken the orders to the Paris Guard. He felt like an important person and kept on adding fresh details to his story. Then he became afraid that he might find himself arrested as an accomplice for having admitted the conspirators to the barracks, might be put in prison and even have to testify against his officers, and so he turned silent and tried to conceal himself among the rest of his companions. No one looked for him, and he suffered the same fate as all the other soldiers: confined to barracks, and now this humiliating business of wearing your tunic inside-out through the streets of Paris, almost like being in the pillory.

So with their sweat-stained linings uppermost full of holes and darns, with their cartridge-pouches buckled and their knapsacks on their shoulders, but without rifles, they were drawn up in rank and led out of barracks. They looked like a troop of lepers, a regiment of sweepers without brooms.

They set out to march through the city ('We're going to Plaine de Grenelle – they're taking us to see our officers shot': they knew it now and muttered the words from one to the other).

Along the Seine they came up with another large detachment and saw that they were in the same state themselves, their tunics inside-out and without rifles. From the lantern they carried in front they saw that they were the Paris Guards : gone were the white and green uniforms that could be seen from far off when they walked in the Luxembourg or the Palais-Royal. Their linings too were outside, they too were marked out for all to see as a detachment in disgrace.

The troops continued to march towards the western quarter of the city, towards the Ecole Militaire and the Plaine de Grenelle, trying to keep in step in spite of the shame and sadness they were feeling : they were going to see their officers shot, and they forgot all the resentments of the past, the punishments and fatigues, thinking only how unjust it was to treat men in that way who had done nothing but obey and behave as they themselves had been taught by them that a soldier should behave.

* * *

It was half past two, and seven cabs already stood waiting at the gateway of the prison where an imposing escort was drawn up, a hundred and thirty infantrymen and a hundred and eighty on horseback, all of the Imperial Guard.

A crowd was gathering in Place Sainte-Marguerite where the prison stood, and the gendarmes lined up the people on the pavements, stopped the traffic, and put pickets at the corner of every street. A bitter wind was blowing, and the soldiers and bystanders stamped their feet to keep warm.

Captain Delon and Adjutant Laborde appeared on horseback; they dismounted and went into the prison. There they asked the condemned men if they had any wishes to state or anything more to say. This was soon done, for although there were fourteen prisoners the two officers reappeared within half an hour and remounting their horses moved off in the direction of Grenelle.

It was not long after three when a knot of gendarmes emerged from the prison with the condemned men in their midst held firmly by the arm. They made them get into the cabs two by two, accompanied by gendarmes. The line of cabs moved off with its escort of infantrymen and cavalry. The coachmen drove at a walk so as not to outpace the infantry. The crowd raised no sound either of greeting or of imprecation.

The cortège had only just turned into the rue Sainte-Marguerite when a horseman came up at a gallop wearing the uniform of an orderly officer of the Emperor. He spoke to the commander of the escort and showed him a paper. The cortège was halted and the commander, followed by two gendarmes, made Colonel Rabbe and Corporal Rateau get out of the cabs. The paper that the officer had brought was an order for suspension of execution signed by the Chief Justice, the highest magistrate in France.

The two pardoned men were taken back to prison. Staggering side by side, the gigantic Colonel and the poor little corporal, brought back from death to life, they walked towards the prison which suddenly seemed the most splendid and desirable of resting places.

It was said afterwards that Rabbe owed his salvation to an intervention of Savary's, who had represented that it was impossible to eliminate in that way a man who had been one of the judges of the Duke of Enghien. But his pardon was really due to his old friend Laborde who, profiting by his newly-won renown as saviour of the Empire, had insisted that the Colonel should be spared and his death sentence commuted to imprisonment as a prisoner of the State.

As for Rateau, his pardon was perhaps conceded either as a reward for the information he had given or in the hope of obtaining further revelations from him against Boutreux and, above all, against the vanished Abbé Lafon.

The cabs resumed their slow progress, bearing with them the twelve destined for execution. From Rue Sainte-Marguerite they went towards the Invalides, along the Avenue La Motte-Piquet and across the Champ de Mars.

Malet was in the same cab as Boccheciampe, who was telling his beads, holding the rosary tight in his fingers. Chroniclers have attributed various comments to Malet during that journey. The only witnesses, the gendarmes with him in the cab, never reported anything, or perhaps only to their superiors. To Boccheciampe, Malet, to sustain him, is said to have repeated what he said to the others the night before: 'Our death will be avenged. Before six months have passed everything in France will change.'

But the poor Corsican, who thought only of his soul's salvation and was indifferent, particularly at that moment, to France's future fate, answered: 'I'm only guilty of having listened to you – otherwise I shouldn't be here.'

It is also said that, as they passed the Ecole Militaire, Malet leant out of the window and shouted to the bystanders watching the procession: 'Citizens, I am dying, but I am not the last of the Romans!'

Phrases which, in any case, would correspond to the General's mode of expression and the style of the times, and which writers at various times have subsequently reported.

They went through the Grenelle barrier and entered a large open ground which belonged to the territory of the Vaugirard commune. On this ground, the Plaine de Grenelle, were drawn up, on three of its sides, a thousand men belonging to all the corps of the Garrison of Paris. The fourth side of the quadrilateral was occupied by the wall of the Ecole Militaire in which was the opening of the Grenelle barrier. In command of the troops, riding back and forth on a nervous sweating horse, was General de La Briche. In the centre, their weapons loaded, waited the execution platoon.

Various problems had arisen owing to the unusual number of condemned men. The regulations prescribed that the condemned should be placed at a distance of ten metres from each other, each one facing a squad of twelve fusiliers. This would have meant a row 120 metres long and would have called for 144 riflemen. It was therefore decided not to adhere to the regulations but instead to put the condemned men into three groups lined up along the wall, each at six paces from the squad which was to fire: ten men of the Imperial Guard facing each group of four condemned. Malet was in the right-hand group, Lahorie in the centre, Guidal in the group on the left. Beyond the troops a crowd of curious spectators could be seen, and some had climbed the trees to miss nothing of the scene.

Steenhower, Piquerel, Borderieux and the other officers had let themselves be brought in by the gendarmes and divided up into three groups, moving in a trance as if even then they had not grasped the incredible fact that they, who had always been so disciplined and loyal and had spent their whole lives in unquestioning obedience, were about to be shot as rebels and traitors. And before them, beyond the squads with their rifles at the ready, were their own soldiers watching them: it was a nightmare, beyond comprehension. So they moved and obeyed the gendarmes without a word or sign of resistance. Boccheciampe, his rosary grasped tightly between his hands, walked with bowed head as if about to receive the sacrament.

The drums sounded and Captain Delon once more read the sentence, the last task of those days that had been so arduous for an official used to a quiet life. The drums sounded again and in the deep silence that followed Soulier could be heard sobbing out desperately: 'My poor, poor wife and children!'

Polyte seemed to hear again in those words the bewildered accents of his Commandant on that feverish night when he had arrived at Soulier's house with the General. His arms were behind his back in the standing-at-ease position, and he could not raise a hand to his face as he longed to do to dry his eyes and blot out the scene.

General de La Briche took up his stand near the group on the left, where Guidal was, to give the order to fire.

Malet said not a word, nor does he appear to have performed any of the actions or uttered any of the words attributed to him by some writers, according to whom he actually attempted himself to give the firing order. He bore himself with courage and dignity like a man who knows that he has inscribed his name in the annals of history, consistent to the end.

Lahorie appeared calm, concerned right to the last to be as he had always been, an officer and a gentleman.

Guidal seemed positively arrogant and anxious to get it over : he had taken off his head-covering while the sentence was being read and then with a derisive gesture threw it away.

General de La Briche lowered his sword and the three squads fired simultaneously. Most of the condemned men fell at the first volley. Malet and Lahorie were left standing. Malet shouted : 'But get on with it – shoot !'

And Lahorie chimed in : 'And me too !'

A second volley followed, and then the head doctor of the Paris dragoons certified that all were dead. Military hospital orderlies came forward with three carts into which straw had been thrown. The bodies were piled up in them, and at the same time the officers gave the command for the troops to withdraw. The three carts passed through the barrier and turned towards the Vaugirard cemetery.

Beyond the barrier, standing apart from the people coming away and the troops returning to barracks, a woman waited drawing her shawl around her to protect her from the cold and the fine rain that had begun to fall. When the carts reached her she moved after them, quickening her pace to keep up with the horses. So Sophie Hugo accompanied to the common grave in the cemetery the only man she had loved.

* * *

The execution at Plaine de Grenelle did not end the punishment of the soldiers involved in the conspiracy of October 23rd. The ten officers and N.C.O.s who had been absolved by the Commission were kept in prison for an indefinite period.

The authorities showed great severity towards the Paris Guard, and especially the I Battalion. In the middle of the Champ de Mars and before the entire garrison of Paris drawn up on parade, all the non-commissioned officers of the battalion, the whole company of grenadiers, and the fifteen most senior soldiers of the *voltigeurs* company were told to fall out from the ranks. The non-commissioned officers were degraded, and the other men were deprived of their epaulets, swords, and all the badges of their special corps. After which they were handed over to the gendarmerie and taken to Walcheren, in Holland, there to work as sappers.

All the other men of the Paris Guard were transferred to infantry regiments of the line and the Guard itself was abolished. The white and green uniforms vanished for ever from the streets of Paris.

The 10th Cohort of the National Guard was merely transferred to Bremen, in Germany, under new officers. Polyte, with his knapsack on his back, set out to march with his comrades towards the far-off Hanseatic town. Dragging his flat feet along the roads leading towards the east, where the fighting was, he cursed the night when he had let the conspirators into the barracks and the authorities who showed so little pity to unfortunate, innocent soldiers.

What happened after

The Grand Army had been in full retreat for the past two weeks under the first snows of the Russian winter, with the thermometer at eighteen degrees below zero. The Emperor and his General Staff were encamped at Mikhailewka, on the road to Smolensk, when on November 6th a messenger arrived from Paris. It had taken less than a fortnight for relays of couriers on horseback to bring the Emperor the first news of Malet's conspiracy. Standing in the snow Napoleon opened the dispatch and glanced rapidly at its contents while his companions gathered round waiting eagerly for news from their far-off homeland.

The Emperor showed nothing of his first reaction of amazement and indignation and went to shut himself up in the *isla* of tree-trunks where he was to pass the night. Count Daru, Commissary of the Army, and General Rapp were witnesses of his first words, uttered in anger bordering on despair: 'Is the crown on my head so insecure, then, that in my own capital a *coup* by three adventurers can cause it to totter? And the King of Rome? And the Empress Regent? Did no one think of them, of the legal succession, if I had really died?' No one realized more fully than Napoleon how serious was the blow struck by Malet to the stability of the Empire.

In the following days further couriers arrived bringing reports in which the Emperor read the opposing versions of Savary and Clarke. On one point alone the two rivals agreed: both emphasized the deplorable conduct of Frochot, who had shown no hesitation but had at once prepared a room for Malet's hypothetical provisional government to meet.

The Russians were close upon them and they were in danger of being surrounded. The march to Smolensk and the Beresina must be speeded up, while at the same time the snows of the Russian winter were thickening fast, overwhelming the army with its light summer uniforms and its ill-shod horses unable because of the ice to drag the artillery over the snow-covered hills. Abandoned cannon and frozen corpses marked the path of the retreat.

The Emperor was absorbed in all the multifarious duties that crowded in on him on this disastrous march, but his mind never ceased to meditate on the significance of the *coup* attempted against him in his absence by a man whom the reports took pains to describe as a madman, a crackpot.

A report had come in from Frochot himself, in which the Prefect of the Seine strove to clarify his position and diminish his own responsibility. By now they had passed Smolensk and were marching towards the Beresina, which seemed like the gateway to the west, the road to salvation. The danger of being surrounded increased. The order was given to burn all the field archives, and in the flames there finished all the reports on Malet's conspiracy and also a letter to Frochot which the Emperor had begun to dictate. Napoleon had had time, however, to send couriers to Paris with strict orders that the inquiry should be pursued with a view to discovering possible ramifications and accomplices. The Emperor, on learning of the execution of those judged guilty, had objected to the pardon granted to Rabbe, whom he blamed for his violent conduct, as he also blamed the disputes between the Minister of Police and the Minister of War, which he regarded as both absurd and dangerous. On the whole, however, he inclined towards the Minister of War, since it was not the police who had cut short the conspiracy but the army, the General Staff of the Paris Garrison.

The terrible experiences of the Beresina, where the remains of the Grand Army sustained heavy losses in crossing the river, absorbed Napoleon's thoughts completely during the following days. It was not until later, when the relics of his army had reached the borders of the Russian empire leaving behind them thousands of dead, wounded, and prisoners, that Napoleon began to feel the imperious need to return to Paris, not only to embark on the reorganization of his forces but also to galvanize by his presence the capital where the fervid fantasies of a conspirator had sufficed to endanger his very throne. He departed, as is well known, in strict incognito with only five companions, travelling by the swiftest means which enabled him to cross half Europe in only a few days.

During that headlong journey, so Caulaincourt, the Duke of Vicenza, who was with him, relates, he spoke frequently of Malet and of the consequences of his *coup,* which had failed only to outward appearances. He critized Savary for having exposed himself to ridicule by getting himself arrested in a nightshirt, and he also criticized Clarke, who saw conspirators everywhere and had apparently arrested half France.

The conclusion of these discourses in the darkness of the carriage as the horses galloped along the roads of Poland and Germany was bitter: 'If I were to die France would fall into chaos. . . . I am forced to admit that all I have built is fragile.'

* * *

He reached Paris unannounced on the night of December 18th-19th. The sentinel at the Tuileries hesitated to admit him. Everyone imagined he was still in Russia. The next morning, when they learnt of his unexpected arrival in Paris, ministers and dignitaries trembled and each one prepared to defend and justify himself.

He summoned the Council of Ministers to the Tuileries

and addressed them, lashing them with stern rebukes: 'Did you believe me to be dead? And the King of Rome and your oaths of loyalty? How can I count on you in the future?'

Savary felt the ground giving way beneath him: this was certainly the last council he would attend. His colleagues eyed him as a reprobate, a condemned man, hoping the imperial thunderbolts would all fall on him.

They continued to eye him thus as they stood apart from him in the antechamber waiting to be received by the Emperor one by one, in order of seniority, after that brief and stormy council.

'When it came to my turn,' Savary relates in his memoirs, 'the crowd thronging the room parted as if to let a funeral cortège pass through.'

They were closeted together for two hours, the Emperor and his old companion who had in the past shared in bold *coups* and thankless tasks. When the door opened everyone expected to see a Savary humbled and reduced to pulp; instead, he walked out calm and self-assured with a smile of triumph on his lips. What was said between them no one knows, though Savary later averred that the Emperor had approved his conduct and found his diagnosis of the conspiracy correct: 'If that was what happened, you were the one who saw through the affair.' He remained Minister of Police, and in court circles they gave up speaking of him with familiar indulgence as 'Savary', instead referring to him more respectfully as 'M. le Duc de Rovigo'.

Malet's other victim, Pasquier, the Prefect of Police, also got off lightly. No steps were taken against him for his scanty supervision of dangerous political prisoners like Malet, and he did not even suffer for having let himself be ignominiously arrested. On the contrary, according to his own account given in his memoirs many years later, when on the following Sunday the Emperor saw him at Mass he spoke to him jocularly: 'So, my dear Prefect, you too had a difficult day. . . . Well, days like that happen to us all.'

The one to pay up for them all was Frochot, upon whom everyone, ministers, courtiers, and dignitaries alike, strove to direct the imperial wrath. He was brought before the Council of State, after vainly seeking an audience with the Emperor to explain, as he had already tried to do with Cambacérès, how, finding himself with no armed forces at his disposal, in order to gain time he had pretended to accept Malet's orders to prepare a room for the imaginary government, meanwhile keeping quiet the troops that occupied the Hôtel de Ville. Of one particular charge against him he claimed complete ignorance, namely that Malet had included him in the list of his provisional government. The combined sections of the Council of State after considering his case decided he should be removed from office. Thus after many long years he had to leave the Prefecture of the Seine. He did not feel like remaining in Paris, and departed to the provinces.

For a less serious fault, men invested with infinitely lesser responsibilities, such as Commandant Soulier and the officers of the 10th Cohort and the Paris Guard, had been put up against the wall to be shot or, in Colonel Rabbe's case, condemned to prison for life. Rateau too was condemned for life, and he also had inflicted on him the brand of infamy for traitors, the three letters T S P (*Traître à sa Patrie*) burnt on to his shoulder with a hot iron.

* * *

A conspiracy psychosis had, indeed, cropped up everywhere alike among high officials and among the people – denunciations, frequently anonymous, flowed in, in some cases from people who had quarrelled with Malet ten years before in one of his provincial garrisons. But there were also more definite signs of intrigues, political manoeuvres, and rapprochements between monarchist right-wing and Jacobin left-wing opponents of the regime, especially in the south – in preparation for popular risings which were to have taken place simultaneously with Malet's *coup* in Paris but which had been postponed following its failure. If all had gone well with Malet even for a few days, a popular rising would have broken out in the south, possibly supported by the English fleet, which would have fostered the spread of anti-Bonapartist movements throughout the country and hampered the reaction of the Napoleonic forces.

Even now in various parts of France and in Paris opponents of the regime, whether or not they had been in contact with Malet, were meeting, reckoning their numbers, making plans, and preparing to act, for they had been shown that the Empire was not immortal. Present military disasters and the even more serious disasters nearer home in the foreseeable future linked the fate of Napoleon's regime more closely than ever to his own life, exposed as it was to all the risks of war. Malet had pointed the right way to bring down the Empire.

The gendarmes continued to search in vain for the vanished Abbé Lafon. Twice they believed they had recognized him, first in a man found hanged in a wood, then in a drowned corpse fished out of a river; but neither was he.

Where he was, he himself revealed eighteen months later, when all danger was past, with Louis XVIII installed in Paris and Napoleon on the island of Elba. While they were hunting for him up and down the country, he was teaching Latin grammar at Louhans, in a seminary of which he was later to become rector. His friends among the clergy and the right-wing opposition had managed to move him on from one hiding-place to another, from monastery to monastery and castle to castle, until at last the ideal safe retreat was found for him as teacher of Latin in a respectable provincial boarding-school.

Meanwhile poor Boutreux was still shut up in L'Abbaye, and with him that veteran of French prisons, Abbé Cajamaño. While awaiting trial André Boutreux sent petitions to Savary and wrote a good deal of poetry – idylls of a pastoral nature, arcadian poems full of tender sentiments, addressed to two very different muses of his inspiration who became strangely coupled together in the poor young man's poetic compositions: 'Eulalia', the girl of his dreams, and Savary, the all-powerful personage from whom he awaited not only pardon but also a job. The poet sighs and longs to fly free, now to the arms of his 'Eulalia', now to the arms of M. le Duc whom he exhorts to show clemency, to be kind, to regard him as a son, and to call him his André.

But in reality M. le Duc de Rovigo, miraculously still Minister of Police, paid little attention to these verses and supplications; while his colleague the Minister of War, still ruthless in pursuit of anyone who had taken part in the conspiracy, had already sent the Emperor a report in which he stressed the role played by Boutreux, who had personally assisted Malet in drawing up copies of his false documents and had installed himself at the Prefecture of Police after the arrest of Pasquier. He was therefore an obvious accomplice, to be condemned to execution like all the others who had taken a considerably less active part in the plot.

As for the Spanish priest, though he bore the responsibility of having received the conspirators in his house, the Minister depicted him as harmless and not really responsible.

On the basis of this report, which was approved by the Emperor, the same military commission that had tried Malet and the others met again at the Cherche-Midi on January 29th and swiftly transformed the Minister's conclusions into a sentence. Thus the unfortunate poet André Boutreux bachelor of law, devoted lover of 'Eulalia' and admirer of the Duke of Rovigo, ended up against the wall in the Plaine de Grenelle before a firing-squad of twelve fusiliers, and his body joined the others in the common grave in the Vaugirard cemetery.

Cajamaño remained in prison and continued his usual life as a detainee for the rest of the time that Napoleon was on the throne; then he was set free and returned to live in the bell-tower of Saint-Gervais which had housed him before. He was never heard of again.

* * *

Before returning to rejoin his army in Germany which was preparing to encounter the Allies, Napoleon found time to reward those who had distinguished themselves on October 23rd. Doucet was made a General (as Malet had promised him), Laborde a Colonel, Baron and Golden Eagle of the Legion of Honour, which merely served to increase the hatred felt for him by the whole garrison. Delon was promoted Major, and promotions and titles of nobility were distributed among the members of the military Commission.

General Hulin got no particular reward for having risked his life: as a reminder of that day he was left with a bullet in his jaw and the nickname, which became highly popular, of General Bouff'-la-balle.

* * *

There followed the defeats of Napoleon's army in the great battles in Germany, the campaign in France in which Napoleon's military genius of his early wars seemed to be born again, and then the final collapse and the Allies' entry into Paris.

The Senate, repeating almost word for word in an authentic document what Malet had made it affirm in his forged Senate decree, declared the reign of Napoleon and his successors at an end. The exile in Elba began.

Once Napoleon had vanished from the scene, Abbé Lafon

reappeared at once. His first care was to get into touch with Madame de Malet, who had just come out of the Madelonnettes prison, and to start writing a short history of the conspiracy. He was as good at writing as he had been at evading the gendarmes' searches, and in less than two months the little book was finished, set up and printed, and put in circulation. The conspiracy was presented in a new light, an interpretation which made not only Lafon but also Malet appear as convinced monarchists, champions of legitimacy, and victims of the personal rancour of the Corsican usurper who had never forgiven Malet for having reproved him for an error of strategy in one of his youthful battles. All trace of Malet the Jacobin and intransigent republican had vanished.

Malet the hero of monarchist opposition, the legitimist soldier and conspirator, proved very convenient for Denise, who had come out of prison in a state of great poverty and needed help from the new Bourbon Government. She thus became extremely active in addressing prayers and petitions to His Majesty King Louis XVIII and his ministers to secure a pension that would provide a livelihood for herself and her son. The widows of the other men who had been executed did the same (including Guidal's widow, who had been divorced from him for years), and naturally Abbé Lafon ceased to be satisfied with his provincial school and went to Paris to put to good use his merits as a conspirator in the service of throne and altar.

At this point, with the sudden violence of a summer storm, news broke that cast terror among all the anti-Bonapartists, causing them to rush for shelter: Napoleon had escaped from Elba, landed in Provence, was marching on Paris, was already at the Tuileries, once again Emperor, once again at the head of an army against which the Allies were assembling their forces to face him anew.

That outburst lasted longer than a summer storm. It went on for three months, a hundred days, and then at Waterloo the curtain fell for the last time on Napoleon. The island to which he was exiled this time was not Elba but one of those islands from which there is no return.

They all emerged once more from their places of refuge, Denise and the other widows, Abbé Lafon and the other heroes of clandestine anti-Bonapartism. During the Hundred Days the Abbé had fled to Switzerland to gather together, so he said, a regiment of French volunteers to fight Napoleon.

A young poet destined to become famous in succeeding decades, Alphonse de Lamartine, relates that, seeking to enrol in that regiment, he discovered that it consisted for the time being of only one man : Abbé Lafon himself, installed in a little inn in La Chaux-de-Fonds, at the head of a detachment no less imaginary than the provisional government invented by General Malet two-and-a-half years before. Denise de Malet secured a pension as a widow of a divisional general (the rank, that is to say, that her husband had attributed to himself in his forged decrees) and all the back payments due, while her son Aristide became a trooper in the King's Guard.

The Minister of War of His Majesty the King of France who signed the decree bore a name familiar to readers of this chronicle : General Clarke, Duke of Feltre – the same signature for the husband's sentence of death and the widow's pension in reparation.

Rabbe and Rateau were released from prison. While the Colonel regained his rank and resumed service in the army, the corporal, abandoning a military career, opened a confectioner's shop in rue Saint-Denis.

As for Abbé Lafon, he was made a Chevalier of the Legion of Honour and tutor to the court pages : a felicitous choice since no one was in a better position than he to teach future courtiers of the King the secret of success, which is to put reality to the service of one's own imagination.

A document discovered in the French National Archives

twenty years ago and cited in a penetrating study by a French authoress, Bernadine Melchior-Bonnet, opens a new door on the history of the conspiracy, suggesting some completely different aspects of the conspiracy and certain of its protagonists.

According to this document, in January 1816 a lady requested an interview with the chief of the General Staff of the Minister of War. The lady, Madame Sophie Hugo, née Trébuchet, separated wife of General Hugo, had presented herself in order to make certain statements which are reported in the document in question. Madame Hugo describing herself as a personal friend of General Victor Fanneau de Lahorie, executed with General Malet, declared that to her own knowledge General Lahorie, far from being in the dark about Malet's preparations as he had maintained at the trial, played a decisive role in them. He had in fact while in prison established close links with Prince Talleyrand, at that time in disgrace with Napoleon and opposed to the Russian campaign. Talleyrand knew of the conspiracy and planned, once the imperial regime should be overthrown by Malet's operation, to call to the throne, not the legitimate king, brother of the beheaded Louis XVI and a relative of that Duke of Enghien whom he, Talleyrand, had been instrumental in getting shot, but the Duc d'Orléans, of the younger branch of the royal house at that time exiled in Sicily, son of Philippe-Egalité who, after having supported the Revolution, later ended up on the guillotine.

These declarations of Sophie Hugo's seem to have been not merely inspired by her desire to transform her Lahorie from a noble and innocent victim into an active hero; for other sources also bear witness to Talleyrand's anti-Napoleonic activities during the Russian campaign, and to his desire to put an end to the megalomaniac founder of the French Empire who had now chosen to discard Talleyrand's political advice, once so decisive in the days of Napoleon's greatest fame. The part played by Talleyrand in the fall of

Napoleon, and his subsequent pro-Orléans attitude, the last volte-face of his tortuous political career, could lend support to Sophie Hugo's statements.

It has furthermore been proved that, doubtless through the instrumentality of Abbé Lafon, quite a number of people in France were well informed about the conspiracy and ready to intervene should it succeed. Such people included various groups of Catholics, religious congregations, associations like the Chevaliers de la Foi, and opponents of the regime among the aristocracy such as Mathieu de Montmorency and Jules de Polignac. Doucet's and Laborde's action had thrust back into the shadows all these potential allies of Malet's who would have been ready to support him had his attempt proved successful.

It is also suggested that not even Guidal's participation in the conspiracy was fortuitous, for that General served as a link with the opposition elements in the south of France who were preparing to rise if Malet's *coup* had succeeded.

* * *

If Malet's *coup* had succeeded. . . . We may well ask what would have happened then, and how the history of France and of Europe might have been changed. There might have been no sanguinary battles in Germany and Spain, no Leipzig and Vitoria, no campaign in France, no Hundred Days – and tens of thousands fewer dead among all the peoples of Europe. Sophie Hugo's son would never have sung: 'Waterloo morne plaine . . .', but in recompense, if Napoleon the Great had vanished thus summarily from the scene, with no martyrdom on St Helena and no apotheosis of the Return of the Ashes, there might probably never have appeared forty years later the lesser Napoleon, Napoleon III, to be driven on the wings of that myth into exile in England.

Perhaps the Allies would not have needed to occupy Paris

if France had already given herself a government, if Napoleon, as Malet dreamed, had been shot at Mainz by French troops. Perhaps, since there was the hand of Prince Talleyrand in the conspiracy, France would not have become a republic but a monarchy, a constitutional monarchy with an Orléans on the throne, preceding by eighteen years the reign of Louis Philippe without a revolution of 1830.

If Malet's *coup* had succeeded. . . The 'ifs' of history do not make history, but it is, all the same, made by the explosive force of men who strive to make reality of their own dreams.

Bibliographical Note

This book is not a work of historical research but a chronicle of events. It has therefore not been thought necessary to indicate in full all the bibliographical sources. The author nevertheless wishes to assure his readers that he has consulted such relevant personal memoirs, documents, texts and historical works as might enable him to produce a faithful reconstruction of the facts.

Among historical studies, those of Louis Garros and Bernardine Melchior-Bonnet have been especially useful; for Sophie Trébuchet Hugo, André Maurois' biography of Victor Hugo; and for Abbé Cajamaño, the penetrating short study of G. Lenôtre, a master in this genre of *petite histoire*. I wish to express my special gratitude to these authors.

G.A.

List of Persons

ANGLÈS, Jules, Count, Divisional Chief of the French General Police; Minister of Police in the Provisional Government on the fall of Napoleon; Prefect of Police under Louis XVIII.

AUGEREAU, Pierre, Marshal of France and Duke of Castiglione.

BARRAS, Paul, Viscount, member of the Convention and later of the Directory.

BAULT, head warder or *concierge* in La Force Prison.

BAZIN, Rigomer, Jacobin agitator, member of the Philadelphians' Society.

BAZONCOURT, Lieutenant, commanding the 2nd Company of the II Battalion of the regiment of the Paris Guards.

BEAUHARNAIS, Alexandre, Viscount, General of the Republican Army of the Rhine; husband of Joséphine, future Empress of France, and father of Eugène, future Viceroy of Italy; guillotined in 1794.

BEAUJEAN, Second-Lieutenant of the 5th Company of the 10th Cohort of the National Guard.

BEAUMONT, Lieutenant, commanding the 2nd Company of the I Battalion of the regiment of the Paris Guard.

BERNADOTTE, Jean, Marshal of France, later Crown Prince of Sweden; in 1818 became King of Sweden as Charles XIV.

BERTIER DE SAUVIGNY, son of a high official of Louis XVI's who was assassinated in 1789; imprisoned under the Empire for his persistent opposition to the Napoleonic regime.

BESSE, Captain, commanding the permanent guard of the Senate (veterans' battalion).

BIGONNET, member of the Legislative Assembly, opponent of the Napoleonic regime.

BOCCHECIAMPE, Corsican, State prisoner.

BONAPARTE, Napoleon, General of the French Republic, later First Consul and Consul for Life, finally Emperor of France.

BORDERIEUX, Captain, commanding grenadier company of the I Battalion of the regiment of the Paris Guard.

BORIES, DE, Mayor of Courcelles, in whose family André Boutreux was tutor.

BOUDIN, Hippolyte, soldier of the 10th Cohort of the National Guard.

BOUTREUX, André, bachelor of law, poet.

BRIAND, vintner with shop in rue Saint-Honoré.

BRUNE, General Guillaume, later Marshal of France.

CAJAMAÑO, Fernandez José de, Spanish priest, imprisoned in France on suspicion of espionage.

CAMBACÉRÈS, Jean-Jacques Régis, French politician and jurist, Second Consul, Arch-Chancellor under the Empire.

CARNOT, Lazare, French mathematician and statesman, organiser of the Republican Army.

CARON, non-commissioned officer of the Paris Guard, accused in Malet conspiracy trial.

CAUBERT, lawyer, brother-in-law of Captain Steenhower, defended him in Malet conspiracy trial.

CAULAINCOURT, Jean, Marquis de, later Duke of Vicenza, aide-de-camp of Bonaparte; later Ambassador in Russia, Minister of Foreign Affairs; author of memoirs.

CAUMETTE, non-commissioned officer of the Paris Guard, accused in Malet conspiracy trial.

CHAMPIONNET, Jean-Antoine, General of the French Republic, commanded French army in Italy, established the Parthenopean Republic in Naples.

CLARKE, Henri-Jacques, Duke of Feltre, General, later Marshal of France, Minister of War.

CLOUYS, DE, former officer in the Chausseurs; secretary of Savary.

CORNEILLE, landowner, member of the Philadelphians' Society.

DARU, Pierre-Bruno, General, Count, Commissary of the Grand Army.

DEJEAN, Jean-François, General, Count, chairman of the military Commission set up to try the accused in the Malet conspiracy, later Grand Chancellor of the Legion of Honour.

DELON, Captain, *rapporteur* to military tribunal, public prosecutor in Malet conspiracy trial.

DEMAILLOT, Arthur François Eve, French actor and playwright. Soldier and commissary of the Convention. His successful comedy *Madame Angot* (1797) was followed by two others on the same personage. Imprisoned for conspiring against Napoleon; wrote a book on prisons in France during the Empire (1814).

DESMAREST, head of Security division of the French police.

DESNOYERS, French General, put on retired list for anti-Bonapartism; arrested following Malet conspiracy.

DESTUTT-TRACY, Antoine-Louis de, Senator of the French Empire, Peer of France after the Restoration.

DOUCET, Colonel, Adjutant-Commandant, Chief of General Staff of the Paris Garrison command.

DUBOIS, Prefect of Police.

DUBUISSON, Dr, owner of clinic in which anti-Bonapartist political prisoners were kept in confinement.

ENGHIEN, Louis-Antoine, Duke of, last descendant of Condé, member of collateral branch of the Bourbon family; Napoleon had him captured in Germany, shot at Vincennes in 1804.

EVE, known as Demaillot (q.v.).
ent of the Napoleonic regime.

FESSART, Lieutenant, in 3rd Company of the 10th Cohort of the National Guard.

FLORENT-GUYOT, member of the Legislative Assembly, opponent of the Napoleonic régime.

FOUCHÉ, Joseph, French statesman, former Jacobin, Minister of Police and Duke of Otranto under Napoleon.

FOUCHER, Adèle, daughter of Pierre Foucher, childhood friend of Victor Hugo, later his wife.

FOUCHER, Pierre, former clerk to military tribunal, official in Ministry of War.

FRA DIAVOLO, nickname of Michele Pezza, bandit chief, fought against the French in Southern Italy, captured by General Hugo and hanged.

FRANCARD, stable-boy in Seine Prefecture.

FRIRION, François-Nicolas, Baron, Divisional General, replaced General Hulin in command of the First Division, later military Governor of Paris.

FROCHOT, Nicolas, Count, politician, member of the Legislative Corps, later Prefect of the Seine.

GARAT, Joseph, Count, Senator of the French Empire.

GARIOT, condemned for Philadelphians' conspiracy.

GAULLIER (or GAULLIÉ), warder at La Force Prison.

GEORGES, Nicolas, cabman.

GILLET, soldier in 6th Company of the 10th Cohort of the National Guard.

GINDRE, condemned for Philadelphians' conspiracy.

GODARD, Captain, commanding 1st Company of the I Battalion of the regiment of the Paris Guard.

GOMONT, known as Gomont Saint-Charles, Second-Lieutenant of the 1st Company of the 10th Cohort of the National Guard.

GRÉGOIRE, Henri, French politician, former priest, Senator, Secretary of the Senate.

GUIDAL, Maximilien-Joseph, French General, accused of espionage for the English in the south of France.

GUILLAUME, French General implicated in the Philadelphians' conspiracy.

HESSE, Prince Charles of, General in French Republican Army.

HUGO, Sophie, née Trébuchet, separated wife of General Joseph Hugo, mother of the poet Victor Hugo, mistress of General Victor Fanneau de Lahorie.

HUGO, Victor, son of General Joseph Hugo and Sophie Trébuchet, godson of General Victor Fanneau de Lahorie, poet.

HULIN, Countess, wife of General Hulin (see below).

HULIN, Pierre-Augustin, Count, General commanding the First Division of the Paris Garrison.

JACQUEMONT, member of the Legislative Assembly; opponent of the Napoleonic régime.

JOSÉPHINE (Marie-Josèphe Tascher de la Pagerie), former wife of General de Beauharnais (guillotined in 1794), mother of Eugène, Viceroy of Italy, and of Hortense, Queen of Holland; married General Napoleon Bonaparte 1796; Empress of France 1804; divorced by Napoleon 1809.

JULIEN, non-commissioned officer of the Paris Guard, accused in Malet conspiracy.

JUNOT, Jean-Andoche, Duke of Abrantès, French General, Governor of Paris.

LABINE, Captain, commanding 4th Company of the II Battalion of the regiment of the Paris Guard.

LABORDE, Colonel, Adjutant in the Paris Garrison command.

LA BRICHE, General de, in command of execution of the men condemned for the Malet conspiracy.

LADRÉ, General Malet's shoemaker.

LAFON, Jean-Baptiste, cleric and teacher, opponent of the Napoleonic regime.

LAHORIE, Victor Fanneau de, French General, arrested as accomplice of General Moreau.

LAMARE, ex-priest, Republican sympathiser in the Jura, member of the Philadelphians' Society.

LAMARTINE, Alphonse de, poet, Minister of Foreign Affairs in 1848.

LAMARTINE, Madier de, Colonel, suspected of opposition to the Napoleonic regime.

LAMBRECHT, Charles-Joseph, Senator of the French Empire, former Minister of Justice.

LAMETH, Alexandre de, revolutionary, fought with Republican Army, later favoured a constitutional monarchy.

LAMETH, Charles de, deputy in the Constituent Assembly, later fought in Rhine Army; eventually emigrated.

LAMOTTE, French General.

LANJUINAIS, Jean-Denis, French politician, Senator, secretary of the Senate.

LAVARDE, Captain, commanding *voltigeurs* company of the I Battalion of the regiment of the Paris Guard.

LEBIS, Lieutenant, commanding 2nd Company of the 10th Cohort of the National Guard.

LEFÈVRE, clerk at the Bourse, anti-Bonapartist, friend of Paban.

LEFÈVRE, Second-Lieutenant in the 2nd Company of the 10th Cohort of the National Guard.

LEMARRE, Captain, commanding the 3rd Company of the I Battalion of the regiment of the Paris Guard.

LEMONIER, Lieutenant, commanding *voltigeurs* company of the II Battalion of the regiment of the Paris Guard.

LIMOZIN, non-commissioned officer; orderly for the week of the I Battalion of the regiment of the Paris Guard.

LOUIS XVIII, brother of Louis XVI, Count of Provence, pretender to the French throne, later King of France (1814–1824).

LUCKNER, Nicolas, Marshal of France, in command of Republican Army in the North in 1792.

MADAME MÈRE, Letizia Ramolino, wife of Charles Bonaparte, mother of Napoleon.

MAILLARD, soldier of the 10th Cohort of the National Guard.

MALET, Claude-François de, French General.

MALET, Denise de, née de Balay, wife of General Claude-François de Malet.

MARIE-LOUISE of Austria, Empress of the French, Regent during the absence of her husband Napoleon I.

MARTIN, Captain, commanding 4th Company of the I Battalion of the regiment of the Paris Guard.

MASSÉNA, André, Marshal of France, Duke of Rivoli, later Prince of Essling.

MICHELET, Madame, portress at Popincourt Barracks, in charge of canteen there.

MOIZY, Lieutenant, commanding 3rd Company of the II Battalion of the Paris Guard.

MONTMORENCY, MATHIEU de, French politician, Deputy in the States General, Grand Master of the Chevaliers de la Foi, Foreign Minister after the Restoration.

MOREAU, Jean-Victor, French General, anti-Bonapartist, exiled to America, died in battle of Dresden (1813) fighting in the Russian army against Napoleon.

MULLER, friend of Boccheciampe, prisoner in La Force.

NAPOLEON, François Charles, King of Rome and later Duke of Reichstadt, son of Napoleon I and Marie-Louise of Austria.

NEUCHÂTEL, Louis-Alexandre Berthier, Prince of, Marshal of France, Chief of General Staff of the Grand Army. Adhered to Bourbon regime after the fall of Napoleon; committed suicide during the Hundred Days.

NOAILLES, Alexis de, former aide-de-camp of Bernadotte, deputy and minister after the Restoration.

PABAN, merchant of Marseilles, ex-Jacobin and anti-Bonapartist; friend of Guidal.

PÂQUES, Inspector-General of Police.

PASQUIER, Etienne-Denis, Baron, later Duke, French statesman, Prefect of Police under Napoleon, President of the Chamber of Peers and Chancellor under Louis-Philippe.

PELET DE LA LOZÈRE, Jean, Count, politician, deputy under the Convention, Councillor of State, in charge of superintendence of the police in Southern France.

PEZZA, Michele, *see* Fra Diavolo.

PILLON, soldier in 6th Company of the 10th Cohort of the National Guard.

PIQUEREL, Captain, Adjutant-Major in the 10th Cohort of the National Guard.

PIUS VII (Gregorio Luigi Chiaramonti), Pope.

POLIGNAC, Armand de, arrested and condemned to death, later to imprisonment for life, for the Cadoudal conspiracy, Duke and Peer of France after the Restoration.

POLIGNAC, Jules de, condemned to prison for the Cadoudal conspiracy. Aide-de-camp to the Count of Artois after the Restoration. Ambassador in London.

PRÉVOST, Lieutenant, in 1st Company of the 10th Cohort of the National Guard.

PUYVERT, Marquis de, monarchist sympathiser in southern France, anti-Bonapartist, confined in Dubuisson clinic.

RABBE, Colonel, in command of regiment of the Paris Guard.

RABUTEL, non-commissioned officer of the 10th Cohort of the National Guard, adjutant for the week of October 23, 1812.

RAPP, Jean, General, Count, Governor and defender of Danzig.

RATEAU, Jean-Auguste, corporal in the Paris Guard.

RÉAL, Pierre-François, ex-Jacobin, Count of the Empire, Councillor of State and high police official.

RÉGNIER, Lieutenant, in the 4th Company of the 10th Cohort of the National Guard.

RIS, Clément de, Senator, Chief Justice of the Senate.

ROUFF, Captain, commanding II Battalion of the regiment of the Paris Guard.

ROUGET DE LISLE, Claude, author of the 'Marseillaise', cousin of General Malet.

ROYCOURT, Sergeant, in 1st Reserve Company of the Seine department.

SAINT-FOND, Colonel Faujas de, suspected of opposition to the Napoleonic regime.

SAULNIER, Secretary-General of the Ministry of Police.

SAVARY, Anne, Duke of Rovigo, French General, Minister of Police.

SERVAN DE GERBEY, Joseph, French General, Minister of War in Girondin Cabinet.

SIEYÈS, Emmanuel-Joseph, French statesman, member of the Directory and the Consulate, President of the Senate.

SILLAN, chemist with shop near the Prefecture of Police.

SORBI, prisoner in La Force for espionage, police informer.

SOULIER, Gabriel, Colonel, commanding 10th Cohort of the National Guard.

STEENHOWER, Captain, in 10th Cohort of the National Guard.

TACHERAT, Nicolas, keeper of a wineshop in Rue de la Fondarie.

TALLEYRAND PÉRIGORD, Charles Maurice, Count, Bishop of Autun, Deputy in the Constituent Assembly, Ambassador, Foreign Minister under Napoleon, Prince of Benevento, Foreign Minister after the fall of Napoleon; head of Orleanist opposition under the Bourbons; Ambassador in London under Louis-Philippe.

TALLIEN, Jean-Lambert, politician; one of the main authors of the *coup d'état* of 9th Thermidor, anti-Bonapartist.

TRUGUET, Laurent, Admiral, Count of the Empire.

VALHAVIELLE, non-commissioned officer, adjutant for the week in II Battalion of the regiment of the Paris Guard.

VERDET, Captain, commanding 6th Company of the 10th Cohort of the National Guard.

VILLEMSENS, head of the First Division of the Prefecture of the Seine.

VIOTTY, Captain, commanding the grenadier company of the II Battalion of the regiment of the Paris Guard.

VOLNEY, Constantin-François de, Senator of the French Empire, Peer of France after the Restoration.

WELLINGTON, Arthur Wellesley, Duke of, English General, defeated the French at Vitoria (June 21, 1813) and Waterloo (June 18, 1815); later Prime Minister.